Tanzi's Heat

C.I. Dennis

TUESDAY

THE FLORIDA SUN IN LATE August can make you sizzle like a chicken-fried steak if you forget to close the blinds and accidentally doze off in your study chair. The phone woke me up before I was completely cooked, and I let the call go to the message machine.

"Vince Tanzi, leave a message," the machine said.

"Mr. Tanzi," the caller said, "this is Barbara Butler. I know this is short notice, but I need to meet with you as soon as possible. I need your help. You don't know me, but I knew your wife from the club."

I'm not working at the moment. I haven't taken a job since I got out. Chasing after deadbeats, runaways, and philanderers didn't appeal to me, and so I had just been pissing away the insurance money—the blood money. The sooner it was gone the sooner I might feel like a human being again and venture outside my house for something other than a thirty-pack. But she'd known Glory. I picked up the phone.

"This is Vince." My voice cracked like I hadn't used it, which I hadn't.

"Oh I'm so glad you're there. Can I see you today? It's important." I heard the voice of a woman who was trying her best to keep control but was on the verge of losing it.

"We can meet, but I may not take the job," I said.

"Treasure Coast Club at noon?"

"OK. I charge a thousand a day." At least, I used to. I wondered if I was still worth it.

"That's not a problem."

"All right. Do you know what I look like?"

"Yes," she said.

Dumb question. All of Indian River County knew what I looked like. I'd had plenty of free press coverage after Glory died.

It was eleven in the morning, and the club was only a few minutes away, so I had some time. I stripped off my T-shirt and shorts and headed for the shower, avoiding the mirror. Chicken-fried steak wasn't my best look.

*

The café at the Treasure Coast Club was separated by a glass wall from the workout room. I nursed a glass of ice water while I waited and watched the middle-aged clients in brightly-colored workout clothes sweating and grinding away on their machines, plugged into iPods or watching CNBC on the flat screen TV above. It was a somewhat unappetizing tableau, and so was the menu; avocado-and-watercress sandwiches, dainty little salads with seeds, and tofu-burgers. I'm more of a grouper-and-onion-rings type. Actually, I was in the mood for a Swamp Ape IPA in a chilled mug. Mrs. Butler was twenty minutes late. I called the waiter over to order one.

She came through the door the moment my beer arrived. Fortyish, salon-blonde, spray tan, fake boobs and real diamonds. Anywhere else it would be a bimbo alert, but in Florida it was just protective coloration.

"Sorry," she said, sitting down.

"No problem. I was watching the spandex flamingos next door."

"You get to a certain age, you have to work at it to look good."

"I won't have that problem," I said. "I didn't look that good in the first place." I'm on the tall side, with a full head of salt-and-pepper hair and a face that shows some mileage.

A young man in a polo shirt and apron came to the table and we ordered. There was a grouper sandwich special, not on the menu. Perfect. She had the avocado-watercress sandwich and a Perrier. She poured some in her glass and the bottle rattled against the rim.

"I don't know where to start." She put the bottle down and began shredding a napkin into tiny pieces. Something had scared the hell out of her.

"Start wherever you want to."

"A person took a shot at me. This morning. I was coming out of the bakery by the Publix. A car pulled up, and someone pointed a gun out the window and shot at me. It hit my purse and I fell over. The car took off. I guess they thought they hit me, but they didn't, it just knocked the purse out of my hand and it was all over the place. I got into my car, locked the doors and cried for ten minutes. Then I drove home and called you."

"By 'they', do you mean you saw more than one person?"

"I don't know. I couldn't really see. The windows were tinted, and it happened so fast."

"Did you call the police?"

"No, my husband would freak out."

"If someone is taking shots at you in a parking lot, you need to call the cops."

"We are very…private," she said.

"Meaning what?"

"Meaning my husband makes a lot of money, and I don't ask questions."

"So he's a crook?"

"He's a citrus broker. He buys and sells fruit. He's on the road half of the week."

"Did you get a look at the guy? The shooter?"

"No." She looked away. That sounded like the first lie.

The food came and neither of us ate.

"There's more, right?" I said.

"Yes. It happened before."

"Someone took a shot at you?"

"Yes. A week ago. I was in my car, and a bullet went through the windshield. I was turning into our road, off A-1-A by the Quail Valley Club. It scared the hell out of me. I drove home…and threw up. But I figured it was just somebody's stray bullet. I got the windshield fixed. I didn't tell my husband."

"Why not?"

"I don't know," she said. That sounded like lie number two.

"Where is your husband?"

"Today is his beach walk. He walks like, eight or ten miles, it takes all afternoon. He always does it before he goes on the road."

"So did you see the guy that time? The one who shot out the windshield?"

"Not really."

"If you keep bullshitting me, I won't help you." I took a big bite of the grouper sandwich, and waited.

"I really didn't see the guy, either time. But I did see the car, this morning at the Publix. It was my husband's other car. Not the one he drives around here. I'm not supposed to know about it, but I do. He keeps it somewhere else. It's a red Lexus sedan, the biggest one they make."

"There are a lot of those cars in Vero," I said.

"Not like this one," she said. "You'd know it if you saw it. It was his."

Back when I was a cop we didn't always assume it was the husband; statistically it's true for only about four percent of all murders. But today, it seemed like a good place to start.

*

We stopped briefly at her house to pack a bag and to leave a note for C.J., the beach-walking and possibly homicidal spouse. It was on a shady street in Riomar, an old-Florida community, not gated but still classy. I'm partial to the older neighborhoods in Vero Beach; they have mature trees and some personality. I live in a newer, cookie-cutter development where you don't dare go home drunk because you'd never be able to tell which house was yours. It was not my first choice, but Glory had liked it and it was affordable on a cop's salary.

I had decided to stash Barbara at the Spring Hill Suites on the mainland until I could get a read on what was going on. She was going to go underground for a few days while I snooped around. Her note to C.J. said she'd decided to take a break and would be at her sister's in Jacksonville. They had no kids, and she said she'd done this before and C.J. hadn't liked it, but he was away on business every Wednesday to Friday anyway, so she wouldn't be missed.

We left her SUV in the lot at the Treasure Coast Club; the place was open all night so nobody would notice it. I drove her to the Fresh Market on the way and pushed the cart while she shopped for food and supplies. Next, I got her a Tracfone at Radio Shack; there would be no using her regular cell, and she would need to stay off of the computer. She asked me to stop at the Vero Beach Book Center and came out with a load of paperbacks. On top of the pile was *Chronicle of a Death Foretold* by Garcia Marquez. So much for the bimbo alert; if she read books like that, then there was a light on upstairs, above the splendid front porch.

I helped her move her bags into the hotel room. It was modern and pleasant, had a kitchenette, and was completely anonymous. I told her to stay put, to call me from the Tracfone if she needed anything, but not to go out. She said she was looking forward to getting some reading done and not getting shot at.

Barbara unpacked her bag and stuffed panties, socks and bras into the hotel bureau drawers while we chatted. I hadn't been this close to a woman—an attractive one, complete with all the womanly under-things—since Glory. I realized I had stopped thinking about my dead wife for the last couple of hours. I felt guilty and stepped back into my emotional cold shower. It was time for me to go.

"When does your husband get home from his walk?" I asked.

"Five on the dot. He keeps to a strict schedule."

"I'll check in with you later," I said.

"You think it's C.J., don't you." It was a statement, not a question.

"Do you?"

"I don't want to think about it."

"Call me when you do," I said.

*

I left the hotel and drove to their house. If C.J. was on the beach until five, there would be time to spare. I thought about Barbara's refusal to speculate on whether her husband was trying to kill her, but she had a large helping of shock on her plate, with a side order of denial.

I let myself in with her house key and looked for their computer. The only one in the house was an old Compaq on a desk in the corner of a downstairs room alongside a row of exercise machines and free weights. I booted it up and began the forensic routine I'd learned from Roberto, my 14-year-old Cuban American neighbor who had taught me the basics of cyber-snooping. The Compaq revealed nothing: no business records, no secret email accounts, no hidden files, zero. From the look of it Barbara used it casually and C.J. not at all.

I tossed all the rooms, trying to be neat and again finding nothing of interest, not even a bedside gun, which was unusual in Florida, where breaking and entering was a sport and alarm salesmen got rich.

The place was as tidy and sterile as the Spring Hill Suites.

A nearly new white Chrysler Town & Country sat in the garage. The registration said "Charles J. Butler" and had just been renewed. I took a GPS unit from the back of my car and crawled under the minivan to wire it in. You can get one for $200 at Best Buy and keep track of anyone, just like James Bond; I didn't have the beeping display in my Aston Martin because I didn't have an Aston Martin. I had a '92 Ford Taurus SHO with a noisy muffler, and a MacBook Pro laptop with a software program that could connect to the unit. Roberto had kitted me out; he was my Latino version of "Q".

It took half an hour to wire in the tracker—the Chrysler's electronics were confusing even though I am handy at that sort of thing. C.J. would be back soon. I decided to go home and regroup and pick up a six-pack of Swamp Ape IPA on the way back. Or maybe not.

Maybe I'd just spend an evening without getting blotto for once. I had taken on a job, and I don't drink when I'm working; it's dangerous to get sloppy. Someone could get shot, including me.

*

I spent the evening in front of the computer with the windows of my study open to let in the night sounds. "C.J. Butler", "Charles Johnston Butler", "C.J. Butler, Florida", "C.J. Butler, Citrus Broker", not a damn thing in Google, not any way I tried. Barbara was in there, but just barely. I found a group photo from a half-marathon she had run three years ago, and she was smiling and pretty in her T-shirt and shorts. C.J. was absent—he was a cyber-cypher. Search engines had spoiled me in recent years; they did half of my job for me if I used them properly. People weren't supposed to exist outside of the web anymore, we had all been trapped in it, our identities and lives neatly wrapped in spider's silk, but C.J. was an outlier and it looked like I was going to have to do this the hard way, like a dime-novel gumshoe.

*

Barbara said C.J. had an office in Lake Wales, but she never went there because he was usually out in the groves. She had long since given up contact with him on his Wednesday-to-Friday trip; he seemed to want that and she acquiesced, for whatever reason. She had called me just before midnight on the Tracfone; she confessed she'd picked up a bottle of chardonnay at the Fresh Market and was about half way through it, but her nerves were still on edge. She began to spill about C.J. They'd been married twenty years, the same as Glory and I had. He was the most neat and tidy person she'd ever known, very respectful, and a model husband. He was built like an athlete: tall, broad-shouldered, and graceful. Money was never a problem. He wasn't exactly the passionate-type, but she'd accepted her life with him. She was content, if not "happy". She said happiness was just a form of temporary insanity.

"Amen," I muttered.

She had no clue why he'd shoot at her. She said she'd never cheated on him, although I took that with a grain of salt; Barbara was very attractive, and if her husband was a dud in bed that usually meant trouble. She said they seldom argued. She didn't pry. She had been curious once and followed him to Lake Wales and waited in her car outside his office. C.J. passed by her in the big red Lexus and looked directly at her, the tinted window down, not stopping. She would never forget the look. It cured her of any further curiosity and she drove straight home to Vero.

"So do you still love him?" I asked. "Or are you afraid of him?"

She was quiet on the other end of the phone. "Maybe both," she said.

Before we hung up she said he would leave the house the next morning at seven AM, sharp. I caught a few hours of sleep, packed some tools and an overnight bag, and was parked down the street from his house by six with my lights off, waiting.

WEDNESDAY

MY LAPTOP BEEPED AT ME and I knew I'd fallen asleep in the car. It was ten minutes after seven and C.J. was already gone. Fortunately, the computer pinned him to the map like a bug in a science exhibit. He was driving west on Highway 60, about halfway out to where it meets I-95. No problem, I could catch up; the early morning traffic was light, just a few golfers, early risers, and tradesmen. The Taurus SHO was old and modest-looking, but it was a wolf in sheep's clothing and would go like hell if I needed it to.

I caught up with him in Yeehaw Junction, thirty miles west of Vero where the road meets Florida's Turnpike. There's not much there except for a Stuckey's Pecan Shoppe and the Desert Inn, an ancient hotel that the old-timers used to frequent back when the Vero bars were closed on Sundays. C.J. was puttering along at the speed limit. I was still doing eighty and came up on him too fast—I almost had to hit the brakes to not rear-end him. I was annoyed at myself; I know how to tail somebody, and this was a bad start.

It was already hot, and very humid. The road was wet in places from overnight thundershowers, and I had to occasionally slalom around road kills, mostly skunks and armadillos. There was nothing on the radio except talk show nut-jobs and preachers. I contented myself with the rhythmic beeping of the GPS tracker as I followed C.J.'s progress with the laptop and stayed back, out of sight.

The road to Lake Wales is flanked by ranches, groves, and long stretches of open land. The town itself is at the epicenter of the orange juice business, and also happens to be the exact geographical center of the state. A big co-op is the largest employer, and there are several smaller juice producers from as far away as Brazil. It's a pretty, old-Florida town and would be a sleepy backwater except for the bustling citrus business. There isn't much for tourists there except the Bok Tower, a carillon outside the village set in a spectacular garden designed by Fredrick Law Olmstead. Mr. Bok was the publisher of the

Ladies Home Journal in the 1890s, and he erected the 200-foot-tall pink marble tribute to himself that some locals called the "Viagra Tower".

I caught up with C.J.'s minivan as he entered town. He turned down a slight hill toward the old section that had been restored in the 1990s in a burst of civic pride. It never really took hold since a Wal-Mart Supercenter went in on the main highway at about the same time and sucked the life out of the historic district. There were a few lingering banks, shops, and restaurants. C.J. turned onto East Stuart Avenue and slowed to park in front of a one story building. I fell back, looking for a shady spot for my gumshoe stake-out. All I needed was a *Racing Form*, a fedora and the stub of a cigar.

There wasn't a shade tree in sight, so I parked in a bank lot with a clear view of where he had parked, and prepared to fry. The air conditioning in the Taurus was on its last legs, but I'd rather lose some sweat than part with the car; we had too much history. C.J. got out of the van, holding a briefcase. He was tall and broad-shouldered as Barbara had described, but she'd left out that he was handsome. I could tell, even from across the street. Some people just carry themselves that way. He was in good shape, probably from all the beach walking. He wore a tan suit with an open white shirt and no tie; overdressed for the heat, but that fit with Barbara's neat-and-tidy description. He walked up to the squat, white stucco building and entered from a side door.

He was in there for a total of two hours and fifteen minutes while I microwaved in the Taurus. I played Scrabble on the laptop, checked my email, read Google News and the *Miami Herald* online and listened to an Emmylou Harris cassette. Finally, C.J. reappeared and walked over to the van. He started it and drove off. I decided I'd let him run free for a while because I wanted a look around—I could pin him down on the laptop later.

The only lock was an old Kwikset in the side door handle. I went back to the Taurus and got the small duffel bag that held my tools. I popped the door lock with a #2 short hook and a tension wrench; it only took a few seconds and no one was in the area watching. It was dark and blissfully cool inside with the shades drawn. The space was divided into two sections, with a mini-apartment at one end and an office at the other. I started with the office. No computer, just a phone and a vintage adding machine on a grey metal desk. Everything looked like it might have fifty years ago; there was even a rotating fan on a file cabinet. I opened a file drawer and flipped through it. Growers, groves, shippers—nothing stuck out, everything looked normal but oddly unused. The phone was too old to have a stored-numbers feature, so that was useless. There were no photographs, no artwork, just an orange blossom calendar that was several years out of date. It was like a set for a low-budget porn movie, and everything looked as fake as the orgasms.

I searched the apartment side next. I usually start with the fridge, which can sometimes tell a story. In my cop days we'd find money, dope, weapons, body parts—you name it, they refrigerated it. C.J.'s held a six-pack of bottled water and an open box of baking soda. A row of shirts hung in the closet, freshly laundered and still in plastic bags. Several summer-weight suits were neatly arranged on wooden hangers, and a bureau held some socks and underwear. There was no television, no radio, no books, not even a magazine. The bathroom had fewer toiletries than you'd find in a hotel. If C.J. was having a fling with somebody, he wasn't doing it here; this was like a monk's cell, minus the crucifix. I was coming up empty again. What had he done here for all that time, while I'd baked in my feeble air-conditioning? I needed to look harder; this guy had secrets and they were somewhere.

It took me fifteen minutes to find his stash. I'd noticed that the toilet looked new. It was also mounted slightly off-center and there were scratches on the bolts that held it down. Nobody but plumbers, dope dealers and cops knew it, but there was a space in there.

I shut off the water feed, drained the tank and unbolted the toilet from the floor. It had a big pedestal base and when I tilted it off the wax ring I could reach my hand into the opening underneath. There were two plastic bags. One had five bundles of wrapped hundreds—fifty grand. It also held a Canadian passport, issued to "Avery Bellar" with a picture of a man I assumed was C.J., although I'd only seen him from a distance. In the other bag was a vintage Colt Commander automatic with three clips of nine-millimeter Super Velo ammunition. That was not a gun you saw every day unless you were into nineteen-seventies-era firearms. It felt awkward and unpleasant in my hand—a long time had passed since I'd handled a weapon. I put the gun and the clips back in the bag and taped it back to the porcelain. My fingers found something else there, something I'd missed.

It was another ziplock bag, with a map inside. At the top it said "South Vietnam" in letters faded from age and use. There were red grid lines overlaying it and markings in black ball point ink. One of the village names was underlined, twice: *TAN TIENG*.

The SHO's leather seats scorched my legs right through my trousers as I slid back into the car. I checked the computer—C.J. hadn't gone far, his van was just up the road on Highway 60 barely east of Lake Wales. I followed the blinking dot until I saw him, backing into a self-storage unit next to Quinn's, a modest-looking eatery on the highway. I drove to the far end of the restaurant's lot and parked, out of sight of the storage units. It was almost lunchtime, and I guessed that once he stashed the van he would be walking over here to eat.

After ten minutes I wondered if I was wrong. The van was still at the storage unit according to the tracker, but no one had entered the restaurant except for two high school girls in a beat-up Plymouth Neon. I was missing something—and now my tracker was locked in a storage unit, useless to me.

A dark red Lexus crawled into the restaurant driveway and parked next to my car. It was an ES 600 sedan, the biggest one they sold. A man got out, dressed in a golf shirt and slacks, tall and broad-shouldered, with the same confident gait. It had to be C.J., although if it was, he'd changed clothes. In the storage unit? And where had the Lexus come from? I waited and watched as he entered the restaurant.

*

D.B. ordered the crab cakes. He always seemed to know what item on the menu would be the freshest and the best. I said I'd share; I wasn't that hungry, it was too hot, all I wanted was an iced coffee. The air conditioning was strong enough, but all you had to do was look out the window and see the heat radiating from the car hoods to know it was as hot as the jungle. The Ford Taurus was at the far end of the lot, the same one that had been across the street from the office. D.B. would never notice those small details, but they screamed at me. Noticing details was the only reason I was still alive, forty years later. D.B. was talking about golf. He had a new hustle, and he had taken in a lot of money so far, though it was getting harder to find a country club where no one knew him. He said he might have to start driving to St. Pete or even Naples, where the big money and the biggest pigeons were. I looked out the window and picked at the crab cakes on his plate. I wasn't paying attention; I was concerned about Barbara and why she'd taken off so suddenly. Barbara knew that I didn't like surprises. I insisted on that, and she usually complied although she could be impulsive.

D.B. finished his crab cakes and drained the rest of my iced coffee. I was tired—I hadn't slept well, and the heat was sapping my energy. Not D.B., his batteries were now fully charged. He said he needed to get going, there was a country club he'd heard about in Dunedin where he wasn't known. He paid the bill and left.

*

After about half an hour the broad-shouldered guy came out of Quinn's and got into the Lexus. The side windows on the SHO were heavily tinted, so he couldn't see that I was in the car. He backed out carefully, and I got a better look at him. It was the same person, but—different.

I could see why Barbara had said she knew the car; there were plenty of that model around, but Florida cars are invariably white, and this was a sensuous, wine-red color—I could almost taste the lingering Bordeaux in my mouth as he passed me in the dusty driveway and accelerated onto 60 West.

So there had been a hand-off of sorts, and people, identities, and cars had been exchanged. My quarry had arrived in his van, dressed in a suit, and then this guy leaves in a slick luxury car in his golf clothes. OK. But this created one small hitch I hadn't planned for. The GPS unit was on the van, not the Lexus. I could tail him, but he'd see me. I had the impression from the stash in his office that he was very careful, if not paranoid. No matter, there were other ways to find him.

I texted Roberto. *See what you can find on FL plate NL5-8PT. Big Lexus.*

He answered immediately. *In gym class. Will hv it by lunch.*

Little bugger was in school, I forgot. And he was wearing his phone while in gym shorts, no doubt. These kids. I decided I might as well get some food while I waited for Roberto to text back.

*

Quinn's was part tourist trap, part local hangout. You can't smoke indoors in Florida anymore, but that didn't mean that the nicotine odor didn't linger in the pine walls, the Gators pennants, or the stuffed game that made up what you might generously call the décor. There was a deer, an elk, a boar, a sailfish and even a heavily-shellacked giant lobster that was a long way from New England. The clientele was a mix of workmen in caps, some business people, the two girls from the Neon and a wary tourist family wondering if they were about to get salmonella. I ordered red snapper with hush puppies, and the fish was fresh and delicious. To make it even better, some patron had the good taste to invest a stack of quarters in the Seeburg jukebox and play Patsy Cline. The songs were older than I was, but they still made the hair stand up on my forearms.

A teenaged waitress refilled my coffee. I asked her if she knew the man who had just left in the red Lexus.

"Oh yeah. We call him "Big Tip". He leaves twenty percent, sometimes more than that. Super-generous. Not like his brother."

"His brother?"

"Yeah. That's the one we call "Little Tip". I guess they're twins, one's just as good-lookin' as the other. Big Tip is nice. Little Tip is kind of a jerk. Not really, but he never leaves more than a dollar. Doesn't talk, kind of a stiff, and nobody wants to wait on him for his lousy dollar. Somebody would say something but his brother is too nice."

My lunch came to twelve dollars. I left her a twenty on the table—that was cheap enough for some good information. C.J. either had a twin brother or he was a quick-change artist. Either way, I'd stumbled onto something odd, and I wondered how much Barbara Butler really knew about this. Wives are supposed to know these things.

*

My phone buzzed with a text from Roberto.

David Butler Johannsen, 1221 Hibiscus Pond Drive, Tampa.

Thanks, talk latr ok? I answered.

OK, "latr" lol. Roberto got a kick out of my attempts at abbreviating words in a text message. There were certain unwritten rules about texting, but no one over the drinking age knew them.

I tapped the address that Roberto had given me into my phone's GPS and swung the Taurus onto 60 West. It was only an hour drive, enough time for me to listen to the rest of the Emmylou tape and cogitate a little on the Butler/Johannsen twins. It was apparently David Butler Johannsen's car that Barbara had seen, not C.J.'s, when somebody took a shot at her purse at the Publix. She said she'd seen C.J. driving it that time she followed him to Lake Wales. The waitress said it was Big Tip, not Little Tip who was having lunch today, so maybe I had seen Johannsen? Or it was the same guy, playing some kind of game with the waitstaff? That seemed like a longshot. I called Barbara.

"How's the hostage?"

"I'm sorry if I got a little carried away last night on the phone. I have a slight headache. Where are you?"

"On the way to Tampa. Does C.J. ever go there?"

"Maybe, but I don't know. He goes wherever the groves are."

"Does he have a brother?"

"C.J. doesn't have any family anymore. Just me."

"What do you mean by anymore?"

"They are all dead. It was that way when we first met."

"So how did you two meet?" I said.

"In a bar."

"Where?"

"Is that important? What's going on?"

"Is he a veteran? Was he in Vietnam?"

"Yes. How do you know that?"

"This is what I do, remember?"

"Well, you're good at it then, because no one knows that except me. He won't talk about it. I guess the war was a horrible experience for him, like it was for most vets."

"You're sure about the family? He never talked about a brother, or a twin?"

"No. If we see family it's my sister, for holidays and so on, but she comes to see us. We mostly stay home."

She sounded like she was telling the truth. "So," I said, "are you plowing through all that great literature?"

"Nope. I'm nursing a hangover, eating rolled-up prosciutto and watching *Friends* reruns. "

"I might be back tonight. Need anything?"

"More prosciutto. I only bought a pound."

*

The sun was directly overhead and the old Ford was trying valiantly to keep me cool, but it was a losing battle, and I was feeling queasy. I had to pull over in Brandon at a Seven Eleven and get a big bottle of water and a roll of antacids. I'd eaten too much at lunch, but it wasn't the hush puppies, it was me—handling C.J.'s gun in his office had given me a shock and it was just now hitting home. The last time I'd held a gun was a year ago when I had put two shots into Glory's chest in the pitch dark living room of our house. The Glock had been returned to me by the Sheriff after I was released and it had been checked out of evidence. It still lay in a padded envelope, unopened, on top of my refrigerator. I wished I would never have to open it, but unless I was going to do something else for a living I eventually would.

The remainder of the drive to Tampa was easy; most people stayed indoors in the intense heat so traffic was light. Hibiscus Pond Drive was in Sunset Park out by MacDill Air Force Base and the houses I passed were modest but well-kept. Number 1221 was at the end of a cul-de-sac and was bigger than its neighbors. It looked like it had canal frontage out to Old Tampa Bay, which would up the value considerably. That kind of house could have been worth a million or more before the crash; it might get half of that now.

No cars were visible, although there was a three-bay garage attached to the house. An elderly neighbor was working on his shrubs across the street. I parked and walked across his lawn, getting a disapproving frown.

"Not selling anything," I said. "Just looking for the Johannsens' place."

"That's it across the street."

"Anybody home?"

"Nope." Good. That meant that he, like any nosy neighbor, kept track of their comings and goings. He had a deep tan and wore no shirt though he should have, as his abundant belly was something best kept covered, like a crash victim.

I decided I'd be Bank Security Guard guy.

"I tell you," I said, "I've been sent on some strange trips but this is the strangest. I'm a security cop and the bank I work for is looking for the family. Seems they left an envelope in a safe deposit box and the records got screwed up and the bank isn't sure who the envelope really belongs to, but the envelope had their name on it. I'm supposed to check them out before the bank decides how to handle it."

The guy nodded; I think I had his attention. I was making it up as I went along, like usual; it sounds more natural than when you rehearse something.

"So you know them pretty well?"

"Guess so," he said. "They're gone a lot. Le runs those coin machines, and D.B. plays a lot of golf."

"It's just the two of them?"

"And the boy, Philip, the hellcat."

"He's trouble?"

"He's only sixteen, but he's got a record. You ain't the first cop to stop out here." He tugged his shorts up until they stopped at the belly overhang. "So what did they find in the envelope?"

I leaned toward him and lowered my voice. "A hundred thousand dollars in cash. Don't repeat that or I'm in deep shit."

"Wow," he said. "I figured they have a lot of money. He drives a big Lexus and they got a nice boat out back. Tell the bank they probably got the right people. Unless they want to give it to me." He laughed.

"Off the record...are they good people? If you know what I mean?"

"I guess so," he said. "That Le works like a demon. I been here since before they moved in, must be seventeen years ago. She built up a hell of an enterprise with those vending machines, and that's a cash business. Him I don't know about. He's friendly, but he's away a lot and all I ever see is him getting the golf bags in and out of the car. The kid's spoiled rotten, but them Asians do that. If the father was around more maybe he'd straighten him out."

I had thought about tossing the place, but not with Hawkeye here watching. Maybe I could check out the business.

"You know where she works? I could go to her office, if that's the best place to find her."

"Over in Pinellas Park, by the Sheriff's office. I took the boy out there for them once. It's called Le's Vending, just a small office with a warehouse out back. I don't remember the address."

"Thanks." I left him to his gardening and Googled "Le's Vending" on the phone. There wasn't much information except for the address, which was all I needed.

*

I parked behind a pile of utility poles in a vacant lot adjacent to Le's building. The GPS had sent me in circles so I eventually found my Florida atlas, got out my reading glasses and located the office. It was in the middle of an area that was being renovated, though the work was probably stopped in '09 when everything in Florida ground to a halt. There was no equipment and there were no workers around, just half-demolished buildings, partially-built infrastructure, and evidence of lots of money gone down the rat hole. Florida was in the middle of a real estate bust, and it would be a long time until the next boom, but the cycle would happen again and the developers would swarm back like seventeen-year locusts.

The red Lexus was parked in a shady spot between the office and a warehouse building. Perfect. I thought about just barging in and making up a story, but I decided I'd rather be able to follow that car around, and I had a second GPS unit with me. I could get to the car without being seen unless someone came out, as there were no windows on that side of the building. I retrieved the extra tracker from the trunk of the SHO. This one was an older model, battery-powered, and would give me about a week's worth of service. With any luck that would be enough. I waited to see if there were any comings or goings, but it was quiet, and if I didn't want to lose the Lexus, I'd better get on with it. I walked across the hot tarmac and held the unit underneath the car, letting the magnets snap it firmly to the metal underbody.

Back in the Taurus I switched on the laptop for a trial run. The signal was clear.

D.B. Johannsen and a young man came out of the building, arguing. The kid was tall with choppy dark hair, Asian features, and a sour expression, and I assumed it was the son, Philip. I own a long-range microphone, but I'd left it at home—too bad, I would have liked to hear the conversation. People give up a lot of useful information when they're fighting. On the next trip I'd pack my whole arsenal. The two of them got into the Lexus. I gave them a couple of minutes' head start, then followed.

Johannsen stopped his car at their house in Sunset Park and then headed north toward the airport. I figured he had dropped the boy. I followed about a mile back, watching the display on the laptop. He turned onto 60 West and took the causeway across the bay to Clearwater. We turned north again on Highway 19 to Dunedin, where he took a series of turns and parked. I gave him a few more minutes and then parked a few spaces away from him, at the Riordan Oaks Golf Club. It was a private club, but in the doldrums of summer anyone could play the private clubs, member or not. They needed the money, and the regular members didn't care; most of them were snowbirds and were up North during the hot time of year.

The clubhouse smelled faintly of sweat. It was furnished in the Early Testosterone period with brass plaques, sports photos, leather chairs and spittoons. D.B. was at the bar drinking beer and chatting with some of the members.

I can hit a golf ball, but I'll never look like a golfer; more like an ex-cop impersonating a golfer. I thought I'd at least try. I went to the pro shop and bought some spiked shoes, a sixty-dollar size XL shirt, a glove, a dozen golf balls and a bag of tees. They agreed to let me demo a set of Callaways for another thirty dollars. I signed up for nine holes, which is my limit on a hot day like this or on any day really; if I play eighteen holes I get bored and end up detesting whoever I'm playing with. Four hours with anybody is too much unless it's in the bedroom, and I'm not even sure about that. I made my way back to the bar in my new duds.

D.B. was finishing a beer, and there were two empty bottles in front of him. That's fast drinking, I thought. He was talking about great shots he'd seen and so on, the usual golfer B.S. Then he said,

"We don't get the heat like this in Ohio, I don't understand how you guys play this time of year."

Ohio? He lived here in Tampa as far as I knew.

"So, is everybody too hot to play?" he said, to the room. "I guess that's OK, I got a couple grand in my wallet and maybe it'll stay there, for once."

I could see the facial expressions change. *We got ourselves a pigeon from Ohio, with real money in his pocket.*

"What the hell, I'll take your money," one of them said. "What's your handicap?"

"Budweiser," D.B. said, and the rest laughed. "Tell you what, since you ladies don't want to get your shirts all sweaty, let's just play three holes, Acey Deucy, a hundred a hole. Anybody else want to play?"

"I'm in," I said.

Another guy nodded, and we had a foursome.

*

The first hole was a long par four with a lake along the left side of the fairway. There was a deep stand of palmetto on the right and your tee shot would have to be very straight and damn long if you were hoping to get on the green in two shots. I hate this kind of hole. I went first and sliced one into the palmetto.

"You'll find it," one of the guys said. The other two in our foursome were members, Bill and Sal, and they both launched their tee shots safely into the fairway. It was D.B.'s turn.

D.B. teed his ball up high and brought out a driver, then put it back in the bag and took out his three wood. "After a few beers I can't hit my driver for shit," he said to the three of us. He hit his tee shot easily past where Bill's and Sal's balls were lying, and I watched their expressions. *Uh-oh.* Their earlier vision of scoring big off this guy was wilting in the heat of the afternoon.

I rode with D.B., or *Dave* as he'd introduced himself, and we drove the cart over to where my ball would likely be. I found it, beyond the palmetto, lying on a small patch of sandy grass, but in bounds and playable. I had a clean shot, though I'd have to clear some needle palms, and there wouldn't be much room for the ball to roll. I could at least see the green, and there was no bunker in the way. A truly great shot, and I'd be on. I hit it straight, but it was forty yards short, leaving a long chip shot. "Good save," *Dave* said.

"Thanks," I said. I'd noticed the Firestone Country Club tag on his bag, with "David Baker" written in where the member's name went. Firestone is one of the world's legendary golf clubs; you definitely have to be a *Somebody* to be a member, so naturally I was curious.

"So Dave, how long you been a member at Firestone?"

"Couple of years," he said. "You want a beer? I got a cooler."

"No thanks. What did you do around Akron?"

"Drug dealer," he said. I gave him a look, and he laughed and patted me on the back. "I'm a retired pharmaceutical rep. I had you there for a minute."

"Yes, you did," I said.

"How about you?"

"Interior decorator," I said. He laughed and slapped my back again. Whoever he was, he sure didn't match up with Barbara's description of a dour businessman who was no fun in bed.

He popped open a can of beer and took a swig. It looked good and I was tempted…but I was working. I sat in the shade of the cart while the other guys hit. All three of them easily made the green on their second shots. I was out of my league, but I'd told Barbara my fee was a thousand a day, so I wasn't going to worry about losing a couple hundred dollars.

I chipped onto the green, and the four of us stood back and measured our putts. In Acey Deucy the low scorer, if there is one, wins from the other three in the foursome. The high scorer also has to pay the same bet to the other three. So if you have one birdie, two pars, and a bogey, the bogey player is out $400, the birdie wins $400 and the pars break even. It can add up fast.

I had hit a pretty good chip shot, but I was the farthest away, with about thirty feet left to the cup. I putted, squinting in the sun, and made the shot for a lucky par. The other guys were impressed, but it was a fluke; I don't play often enough to putt like that consistently. Sal and Bill were next. They both missed, and had to settle for par. Dave was the closest to the hole but, incredibly, three-putted for bogey. A meltdown like that is not fun to watch, even if it means you just won a bet. He was out three hundred dollars, a hundred to each of us.

The second hole began like the first, with another long tee shot by Dave and respectable shots by the rest of us, bunched in the fairway about 230 yards out. He and I got into the cart.

"Hot out," he said.

"Must be in the nineties," I said. "Reminds me of Vietnam."

"You're too young to know about 'Nam," he said, frowning.

"Did you serve over there?"

He looked at me, and the backslapping bonhomie evaporated.

"No," he said.

I missed the green with my approach shot, lying a few feet short. Sal got on, ending up about twenty feet away from the pin. Bill hit a straight shot, but the ball rolled well past the flag. Dave chipped to within five feet. The three of them had potential birdies, and this hole might cost me $400.

The golf gods smiled on me, and I hit my wedge shot like a pro on TV; it even had some back spin and I had a tap-in for par. Sal two-putted for his par, and Bill hit a perfect downhill shot that rolled in ever so slowly for birdie. Dave missed his five-footer, and the ball rolled past the pin by another five feet. He missed again on the way back. It was excruciating. He kept his cool, but fell silent and just barely made his third putt, for a bogie and a $400 loss. This was twice he'd three-putted in two holes and he was down a total of $700. Bill and Sal were smiling furtively to each other. I was waiting for Dave's next move. I'm not much of a golfer, but I was a cop for a long time, and I know when I'm about to be hustled.

"Fuck it," Dave said. "You guys keep playing, I'm done." He took his bag off the back of the cart and walked toward the clubhouse while the three of us stood there. Maybe I was wrong—maybe there was no hustle.

At least, not yet.

*

We finished our third hole and returned to the bar, which was busy with drinkers. Dave was there, and he produced a roll of bills and paid his gambling debt in crisp new hundreds. He made sure that we all noticed that the bills came from a fat log. *There's the bait,* I thought.

Dave drank two more beers, which by my count made an even six, including the three he'd started with and one while we played. He had an obvious buzz. His voice got louder, and the bartender eyed our group, wondering if he was going to have to throw somebody out.

"Tell you what," he said, loud enough for the whole room to hear him. "That tractor shed out on the tenth hole, how far out is that?"

"About two hundred yards," somebody said. "It's about one-fifty, and then it's fifty yards out of bounds".

"Well then, I'll bet any of you guys that I can hit it. One shot. A thousand bucks."

"I ain't taking that wager," a guy said. "With my slice I hit that damn thing every day!" The golfers laughed.

"OK then, I'll tell you what," Dave said. "You can pick any club out of my bag and I'll hit with it. But you can't pick the wedges, or the eight or nine irons. Any other club—it's your choice. Show me your money, people."

Some of the men in the back of the bar began to mutter to each other, out of earshot. Somebody had an idea, and the rest were grinning as the word spread. Six of them took Dave up on the bet. There was a lot of fussing around and cash-raising, but eventually $12,000 was in the pot; $6,000 of it Dave's and $6,000 from his takers. The bartender took the money to a safe spot behind the bar and the crowd moved out toward the 10th tee.

"Dave, we hate to break it to you," one of the bettors said, laughing, "But you're fucked."

"What do you mean?"

"You said we couldn't make you hit the wedges, or the 8 or 9. Any other club in your bag, right?"

"That's right," Dave said.

"Then let's see you hit it with the putter."

Now, a putter is for just that: putting. It's for tapping the ball a few feet on the ultra-smooth surface of a manicured green; technically it's the shortest-hitting club in the bag. For a two-hundred-yard shot, you'd want some horsepower. A very good golfer might make it with a five iron. A pro might get two hundred yards of distance with a seven iron, but hitting a target would make it a lot harder. Most of us would just get out the driver or a three wood and hope for the best.

Dave teed the ball up about an inch above the grass. He positioned his feet and began his address, setting up with the ball in line with the inside of his left foot. The face of the putter is at a right angle to the ground like a driver, so you could get some distance if you hit it perfectly, but the shaft is short so you had to be strong and incredibly accurate. And lucky. The crowd hushed as he completed his setup and stood rock still with the club poised.

I watched the backswing as if it were in slow motion. A perfect arc, controlled, and then down hard on the ball, which flew off the tee like a bullet: straight, low, and directly at the corrugated metal roof of the tractor shed. It rang it like a gong in the smoldering sun.

*

We walked out to our cars together. Dave was treated like a hero in the clubhouse, but he'd never get a bet at the Riordan Oaks again.

"It went well, didn't it?" I said.

He gave me a look. "It doesn't always," he said, as he put his bag into the trunk of the Lexus.

"How often do you practice that shot?"

"I got it to about seventy percent accurate."

"Good odds."

"You're a cop, aren't you?"

I ignored the question. "Just curious, Dave. Do you have a twin brother? You look like a guy I know."

He took a long time to answer. "You don't want to know my brother. He's a hard ass. I'm the nice one."

He didn't wave as he passed me, getting into the Taurus. I could see him taking a good look at my car. Any cover I might have had was gone now, but that was all right; sometimes you have to get in someone's face and make things happen. It was time to go home and pick up some gear. I decided I would visit the Johannsen house again, and I needed my whole bag of tricks if I was going to do it quietly.

*

It was a long two hours on the road back to Vero. I thought about stopping at Quinn's for some food, but I still wasn't hungry after my red snapper lunch. I was wired from the encounter with D.B. Johannsen, and the adrenaline took away any interest in food. I reviewed the day as I drove and tried to lay mental odds about D.B. and C.J. One-in-two that they were the same guy. One-in-two that they were brothers. Three-to-one that I didn't have a frigging clue, yet.

If it was the same person, he had two marriages going and it was possible the wives didn't know about each other. How convenient. It was a little curious how C.J. was basically out of touch with Barbara from Wednesday through Friday, every week. He'd trained her to accept that, or perhaps she had trained herself to accept it, like people sometimes do in a marriage. It was like that with Glory; however much we loved each other, there were places where we didn't go.

I pulled the Taurus to the side of the road to text Roberto. I'm not the type to text while driving, I'd end up in a canal.

Want a research project?

Sure, he texted back.

Come ovr after homework. 8 PM?

Dnt hv any hmwrk.

BS, I texted. They load the homework onto the kids these days. But if anyone could breeze through it, it would be Roberto. I got back on the road and called Barbara. I can actually talk on the cell and drive; I'm not a total Luddite.

"So how many consecutive reruns of *Friends* have you watched?"

"I'm actually reading. I'm also bored and hungry and my skin is going to turn pasty white."

"I had an eventful day."

"Tell me."

"C.J. either has an identical twin brother or another wife."

There was silence on the other end.

"Sorry. I kind of hit you with that." I had been way too blunt. That was not the kind of thing you told a client over the phone.

"It's what I'm paying you for, isn't it?"

"Barbara," I said, "Get your big sunglasses and baseball hat. You know, the celebrity-in-public disguise, so nobody recognizes you. I'm going to take you out for some fresh air. I have a meeting at eight, but I can be at the hotel at nine. Do you like the Citrus Grillhouse?"

"I love the Citrus Grillhouse."

"I'll see you at the hotel."

*

I was home at seven, which would have been a great time for attacking a few beers after a long day, but I wanted to keep my mind clear. I showered and dressed in a black Rayon shirt, one that Glory had picked out. Roberto let himself in and went directly into the kitchen for a Coke. It was a forbidden pleasure that his parents knew about, but they liked me so they let it ride.

"I have some work for you." We sat next to each other at my computer table, and I filled him in on what I knew so far. He listened and surfed the web at the same time. Roberto never gets too far from a screen; it's an extension of his body, or maybe even his soul.

"There are two different Social Security numbers," he said. "One for Johannsen, one for Butler. There's nothing for Avery Bellar." Jesus Christ that was fast; we'd been talking for less than ten minutes.

"How hard is it to get a Social Security number?"

"It's doable. He got a Canadian passport, right?" He drained his Coke, and I went into the kitchen and got him a second one.

"What about Tan Tieng?" I asked.

"Fail," he said. "It's not on Google maps, but I'll keep looking."

"Roberto, I need the computer for a few minutes," I said. "I have to pay my credit card bill tonight, or I'll get hit with interest."

"You got any other computers? I'm not ready to go home. This is fun."

The laptop was in the car, set up for the GPS, and I didn't want to disturb it. But I did have another computer that I had forgotten about. It was a slim little MacBook Air that I had bought for Glory the year before she died. She loved it and used it for recipes or watching soaps while she worked in the kitchen. I remembered exactly where she kept it; it was in a lower cabinet that had a vertical rack for baking pans. The thin aluminum laptop was still there, perfectly camouflaged between cookie sheets. The power cord was stashed behind it. I remembered that when the police had gone through the house they hadn't found it. Frank Velutto had been in charge and he'd asked me about it, but I wasn't volunteering anything; I'd been a suspect, not a cop on that day.

"Try this," I said to Roberto as I handed it to him.

"These things are awesome!" He powered it up and began to type. I paid my credit card bill on the big computer, and then brushed my teeth while he surfed on the Mac.

"I have to go out. You can stay here for a while if you like."

"Where do I put the computer?"

"Why don't you just keep it?" His eyes widened. "It was Glory's. I don't have any use for it."

Roberto is a kid, but he's one of those kids who understands people. He could see the expression on my face. He muttered a quiet thank you and accepted the gift.

Barbara was wearing a short, form-hugging black dress when I met her at the door to her room. Some disguise—if anything, it would attract attention. She retreated to the bathroom and leaned toward the mirror, applying eyeliner. This was suddenly looking like a date, and I was beginning to have misgivings about inviting her out. On the other hand, she looked pretty damn good.

She insisted that we stop at her house, and I waited in the car while she dashed inside. She took longer than she should have and my anxiety increased. I wasn't sure why I was so uptight; partly because I had been hired to protect her, for sure, but also because it had been a long time since I'd done anything at night besides getting trashed in front of the TV. It felt good to be sober, although I would be tempted to break my alcohol fast and have some wine at the Citrus Grillhouse; they had a decent list.

She came back out with a pair of shoes in her hand. "Sorry. I dawdled," she said.

"You went in there for shoes?"

"I didn't have anything that matched."

"Barbara," I said, "You're not thinking. Somebody is trying to shoot you."

"I thought it would be all right because you were here," she said.

"You can't—" I began, but I was interrupted by headlights in the rearview mirror. It was probably a neighbor. Just to be sure, I started the car and drove down her road toward A-1-A. When we got onto the main road I hit the gas, and the SHO took off like a bottle rocket.

"Fast car," she said. "I'm impressed."

"Sorry," I said, "Didn't mean to show off."

"You must be really hungry," she said, smiling.

I was hungry, but I was also worried. The headlights had turned right behind us, and I'd had to hustle to lose them. It was foolish to stop at her house, and I needed to set some ground rules.

*

We took an outdoor table; it was cooler inside, but I don't live in Florida to be cold. The August heat is so oppressive during the day that it feels fine by comparison at night, even if it's still in the eighties. We had a breeze, a low moon over the Atlantic, and a view of the people walking on the beach below us. Barbara ordered a Viognier, light and perfect for a warm evening, and I stuck with water. I had the tuna au poivre with grilled zucchini, roasted peppers, and a sweet onion relish. Barbara had spinach tagliatelle with garlic, olive oil, and parmesan, which was my second choice, and so we decided to share our entrees. No one was watching us, as far as I could tell, though some of the male patrons were sneaking glances at Barbara. I didn't come here much with Glory; it was a little touristy and she didn't like fish, which was about the only flaw she had.

I ran down the events of the day for Barbara. She seemed to have come to terms with the possibility that C.J. had another wife. She had no opinion as to whether there was one C.J., or a C.J. and a D.B. It was too much information to process after twenty years of marriage.

"What's he like?" I asked.

"What do you mean?"

"Tell me more about C.J. What does he do besides walk the beach?"

"Not much," she said.

"Come on," I said.

She picked up her wine glass and held it out toward me. "Have some," she said.

"No thanks."

"You need to relax, Vince. You're grilling me."

"Sorry. I don't mean to get personal. I'm just confused about C.J.," I said.

"So am I," she said. She took a long sip from the wine, and I noticed her eyes were getting glassy. "When you said that about another wife—it hit me like a punch in the stomach. I've spent half my life living by his rules. He didn't want me to get a real job, so I didn't. We didn't have kids. I've been playing house, working out, behaving myself and basically doing nothing. And then you tell me he's got a whole other life on the side."

"I don't know that for sure, yet," I said. "Barbara…this is a process. It gets ugly sometimes."

"Damn right," she said. "I already wish he'd just shot me."

"That's not going to happen," I said. "I want to talk to you about that, too. You can't take any more risks. I shouldn't have brought you here. It was a misjudgment on my part. We're going straight back to the hotel afterward, and I want you to lay low, OK?"

"I guess so," she said. "I'm sorry. And I'm glad you took me out, I was going crazy in there."

Neither of us said anything for a while.

"Mind if I ask you the questions, for a change?" she said.

"Fire away."

"What was jail like?"

"It sucked. It was incredibly boring. I was in a very bad frame of mind then, so in a way it was a good place for me to be."

"How long were you there?"

"Nine months—until they threw the case out. The forensic lab work was a total fiasco, and they couldn't make a case, although it was clear that I shot her. You probably read about it."

"You thought it was an intruder?"

"I don't know what I thought."

"Why didn't you make bail? I read that you could have."

"I think…I was punishing myself."

"Have you forgiven yourself yet?"

"No," I said. Not yet, and not ever.

*

I took the Merrill Barber bridge over to the mainland and turned north up Indian River Drive toward the Spring Hill Suites. It was eleven o'clock—past my bedtime. I wanted to get an early start in the morning, gear up and get back across the state to Tampa. I'd check in with Roberto by text to see if he found anything. Barbara was tired too, and she leaned her head against the car window.

I dropped her at the porte-cochere at the entrance to the hotel, and she thanked me and went inside. I pulled the Taurus back onto the roadway, in time to see a white Chrysler minivan coming the other way. It went right by me and continued on, past the entrance to the Spring Hill Suites. I drove a few hundred yards farther until the taillights were out of sight.

That looked a hell of a lot like C.J.'s van. I retrieved the laptop from the back seat and opened it up. It was still programmed to find the Lexus, which was in the driveway at Hibiscus Pond Drive in Tampa. I re-entered the information on the tracker for the van.

It was in Vero. I zoomed in on the map.

The little blue dot was moving, and then it slowed and made a U-turn. It slowed again, turned into a drive and stopped—in the parking lot at the Spring Hill Suites.

I left the Taurus at the hotel entrance and went straight to Barbara's room. I hadn't seen the van when I pulled in, but I knew it was there, and if there was someone sitting in it with a gun, I was not going to take any chances. I knocked at Barbara's door and yelled. She opened it, still in the black dress. I told her to pack a bag of essentials, we were leaving immediately, and we could come back later for whatever she left. She heard the worry in my voice and quickly stuffed a few things into a large purse. I led her out to the car, told her to keep her head down, and we roared out of the lot. I got the Taurus up to over ninety on Indian River Drive—no one was going to follow us this time. After a few miles I stopped on a side road and parked. The laptop was still on, and the van was still at the Spring Hill Suites. I finally took a few breaths, and Barbara stopped looking terrified.

"Sorry about that," I said.

"So, you couldn't wait to see me again?" she said. There was a pause until I got the joke, and we both burst out laughing. I explained what I had seen, and we tried to figure it out, but it was late and I couldn't think straight.

"I think I'm going to take you to my place," I said, "if that's not too awkward. I have an alarm system. There's a separate bedroom. I have—"

"You don't have to sell me on it, Vince."

I drove her to my house, parked in the garage and led her inside. Glory and I had our own bedrooms because I snore like a Harley Davidson going uphill, and Glory's room was untouched. It was awkward—awkward as hell, but Barbara smiled, thanked me, entered her room and shut the door.

THURSDAY

I GOT UP BEFORE SUNRISE, showered, put on a fresh shirt and wrote out a note for Barbara. I told her to stay put, it was OK if she needed to use any of Glory's stuff, and we'd pick up the rest of her things when I was back from Tampa. I said if it was an absolute emergency she could use the other car in the garage, Glory's BMW convertible which had sat there, unused. I'd kept the battery charged and rolled the tires around every so often so they wouldn't get flat spots, but I never took it out past the driveway. I couldn't bear to drive it, and I wasn't ready to sell it.

I started up the SHO and got on the road. This time I had every snooping toy that I own. I had also opened the padded envelope on top of the refrigerator and packed my Glock 26. The "baby" Glock, as it's called, is the ideal concealed-carry weapon, and I have a permit because technically I'm a retired cop although that's a long story.

I booted up the laptop in the car; the van was now showing up back in Lake Wales, stationary. The Lexus was on the move in Tampa. I guessed that D.B. was going out to the driving range; serious golfers hit balls for hours and hours every day, like musicians play endless scales until their neighbors beg for mercy.

Roberto had left me an email—not his usual mode of communication, but he had a lot of info to pass on. He hadn't turned up anything new about C.J., D.B. or Le, and there was very little to be found on them on the web. He'd found Tan Tieng; it was a South Vietnamese hamlet that appeared on maps prior to 1973 but not afterward. He said he was going to check that out at the library. That seemed strangely anachronistic, but not everything is on the internet. Yet.

He had also discovered that young Philip Johannsen was indeed a hellcat as the neighbor had put it. The kid had half a dozen grand theft auto arrests. None of that was supposed to be public record because he was a juvenile, but that didn't hamper Roberto, though it worried me that he could so easily hack into a court file. So—the younger Johannsen liked to steal cars. We used to call it joyriding when I was that age, and it was no big deal as long as we brought the car back in one piece. It was a good thing the boy was still a juvie, GTA is a minimum one-year sentence in Florida.

Roberto asked if there was any way I could get to their computer. Then, all I would have to do was log on to my Gmail account and send him an email. He'd send back a program which I would install, and then he'd cover my tracks. That way he could hack his way back into their computer and look around. I doubted I could get into Le's office unseen; it was too open and I had noticed security cameras on the exterior, but I had an idea of how I might get in the house without alerting Hawkeye, the nosy neighbor, and a home alarm system wouldn't present much of a challenge.

I was beyond Lake Wales and halfway to Brandon when my cell rang—it was Frank Velutto at the Sheriff's office. I hadn't seen Frank since the night I went to jail. That was the way it had been with most of my cop friends—awkward. When I got out they all swore they never thought it was me, although the evidence wasn't so clear. Frank and I were the only two Italian Americans in the department, although Frank is about as Italian as a Stouffer's French Bread Pizza.

"Vinny, you fucking homo," he addressed me, like he always did.

"Frank, you fucking homophobe," I replied. He was the only person who I would allow to call me "Vinny" except for my mother.

"So Vin, did you do a hit-and-run in the Bono's Barbecue lot yesterday afternoon?"

"I have no fucking idea what you are talking about." When cops are talking to each other they are expected to employ the f-word at least five times per sentence, interchangeably as a noun, adjective, or verb. Frank could use it in the pluperfect subjunctive.

"Dispatch got a call last night asking for a plate ID. From a civilian, not an insurance company. The guy calls at midnight. He said you bumped him in the parking lot and took off, but he got the plate."

"You tell him he needs to go through the insurance company?"

"Yeah, he said he didn't want to report it, just find you and settle."

"Well it wasn't me."

"I figured. Fuckin' whack-jobs out there."

"Can you give me the phone number?" I asked.

"Sure but guess what? It was from a pay phone," he said. "So—you making some kind of trouble?"

"Not yet. But I guess I'm back on a case."

"Good for you."

We chatted for a while about nothing in particular. Frank and his wife Carole used to be close friends. Glory and Carole did everything together; neither of them had children and that created a sort of bond. Frank is a handsome dog, and it shocks people sometimes when they're expecting a bullet-headed deputy to roll out of the cruiser and they get this movie star. Like I said, I never had that problem. We said our f-you's and our goodbyes and hung up.

*

By the time I got into downtown Tampa the traffic was knotted up tighter than a wino's dreadlocks. I had to cross through the middle of the city to get to the peninsula where the Johannsen house was and the roads were clogged with old people going to one doctor or another. That accounts for approximately ninety-nine percent of the morning traffic in Florida.

I passed Sunset Park and continued down the east side of Old Tampa Bay. The shoreline is a mixture of attractive housing developments, mangrove swamp, and industrial wasteland. Alongside the Army Reserve Center was a tumbledown yacht club that I'd Googled on the ride over. It was the nearest place that would rent me a boat.

By nine thirty I was motoring north up the bay in a fourteen-foot Boston Whaler with an elderly outboard motor that was about as stealthy as my Taurus' bad muffler. I had rented fishing gear to complete my cover. I also had my snooping toys, my lock-picking kit, and the Glock. To the untrained observer I looked like a cop, in a boat, with a fishing pole.

It was already ungodly hot, even out on the water. There was no breeze, and I had forgotten my hat. I motored under the Gandy Boulevard causeway and continued past some sand flats and residential neighborhoods. There was a nice stretch of beach punctuated by docks and boathouses about three hundred feet apart, some with boats attached and some without. Quite a few fancy boats had been repo'ed in the last few years since the economy went under. The GPS application on my phone directed me into a canal that was lined with big houses. No repo's here; this is where the one percent lived, and nearly every house had a yacht out back. I slowed the Whaler as I approached a cul-de-sac in the canal that backed up to 1221 Hibiscus Pond Drive. I cut the engine, dropped a line and began to "fish". With my luck I would probably hook an actual fish, so I took the precaution of not using any bait.

I waited for a while to see if there was any activity at the house, figuring this would be a good time of day. The last time I checked the laptop the Lexus was going south toward Bradenton—D.B. probably had another golf hustle scheduled. Philip might be in school, although I wasn't sure if classes had started in Tampa as they had in Vero. Le, a workaholic according to Hawkeye, would be at work. I tied up to their dock, next to a big Riviera sport fisherman that didn't look like it had seen a lot of use. *Nickels and Dimes* was stenciled across the transom in shiny black letters. There must be a rule somewhere that if you own a half-million-dollar boat you have to give it a dumbass name.

I approached the house from the back and tugged on a pair of latex gloves as I walked. A swimming pool was surrounded by a wooden fence with eight-foot-high panels, but there was only a wrought-iron bolt securing the back gate and I was able to slide it open from the outside. I didn't see security cameras, but the doors and windows were wired. I removed a small black plastic box labeled "X10 Sniffer" from my bag and plugged it into an outdoor electrical outlet on the back patio, next to the pool filter unit. The machine confirmed that the house was protected by a security system that used the phone line. I couldn't cut the line; that would definitely be leaving tracks. I had a companion box in my duffel, an "X10 Blackout" that would complete the job. It could jam the alarm signal right from the outlet. These were not devices offered at Best Buy.

Once the alarm was disabled I was inside within five minutes. The deadbolt on the back door was a good quality Medeco and it resisted my lock-picking like a high school virgin, but I prevailed. That never happened in high school.

The house was one of the strangest homes I'd ever broken into. Everything was ludicrously neat, bordering on antiseptic, like the inside of a hospital but with furniture. Somebody had a serious case of obsessive-compulsive disorder. There was little decoration, and all the upholstered furniture was wrapped in clear plastic slipcovers, like people would use if they had an incontinent dog. I went room-to-room, looking for a computer. The only room that was not pin-neat was the kid's, it was the usual disaster, and the death-metal band posters on the walls completed the look. There was a computer on his desk, but I wanted to find D.B.'s; that was the one that was most likely to hold some usable info. I finally found his man-cave, in between the garage and the laundry room; it had a steel desk with a Dell computer, a gun cabinet, some files, a TV and four bags of golf clubs. Out of curiosity I picked the gun cabinet lock. It held quite an arsenal—at least a dozen handguns, boxes of ammo, and several rifles, including a Browning BAR Safari .30-06 hunting rifle with a scope. That was a serious weapon, and in the hands of a good marksman it could hit a beer can in a parallel universe.

*

It was awkward to type with the latex gloves on. I logged in to Gmail on D.B.'s computer and sent a message to Roberto.

I'm in.

He emailed me back, with an attachment. I downloaded it and ran the program. The whole thing took about three minutes. Roberto texted me on my phone.

All good. Don't shut it down, just log off Gmail and clr the history.

Done, I texted back.

I put everything back where it was and got my bag of tricks out. I planted bugs in the living room, kitchen, man-cave and the master bedroom. That ought to do it. I went outside and taped the control unit for the listening devices to the back of the swimming pool filter and plugged it in to the outdoor AC receptacle. It was not likely that they'd see it, and I'd clean it up on the next visit, I hoped. Everything was voice-activated and stored on a disk, and I could connect remotely with the laptop at my leisure and have an eavesdropping party.

I went back in to make sure I hadn't left anything out of place. Somebody knocked loudly at the front door. Christ. Luckily, I was done. I hustled out the back, pulled my X10 gadgets and left through the fence gate to the dock. In a few seconds I was back in the Whaler, breathing easier. I could see the street from the water. A FedEx truck was beep-beeping as it backed away from the Johannsen house. That was a relief. I pointed the little boat down the canal and motored back toward the yacht club.

*

I had the afternoon to kill while I waited for the Johannsen family to get home and start talking. I could have driven back to Vero Beach, but I was in no hurry. Between their conversations and Roberto's hacking I hoped to learn where to point next. I had a fresh concern for Barbara's safety; Frank Velutto's call about someone looking for my plate number might have a connection to the case. The car headlights that followed us out of her road could have belonged to the minivan. I thought I had outrun it, but maybe I hadn't, and they could have picked up the plate number while we were at the restaurant, and then followed us back to the hotel. I didn't like that at all—the hunter's worst fear is finding out he's the quarry.

I decided to drive over to Le's office. The morning traffic had thinned out, and I made it to Pinellas Park in half an hour. I parked in the same spot as the day before, behind a pile of stacked telephone poles but with a view of the door.

It must have been lunchtime for Le's business because in the space of fifteen minutes a dozen panel trucks came into the yard. The drivers parked and entered the office, each carrying a large bank bag. Coins—lots and lots of quarters, dimes, and nickels—in heavy bags. I guessed that they made a cash drop at noon so that if they were robbed it would only be for part of the day's take. After the drop they backed up to an adjacent warehouse and loaded up. Candy, sodas, potato chips—all that good old, all-American crap that was puffing people up to morbidly obese levels and killing us off at great expense to the economy. Don't get me started. At least there weren't any cigarette vending machines anymore, although this stuff was just as lethal. The drivers ate their sandwiches in their trucks; there was a picnic table, but it was just too damn hot. I noticed they were mostly big guys, and they looked strong. I guess you have to be pretty solid to lug all that soda around, unless you were in charge of the potato chips.

I thought about getting the long-range microphone out of my trunk, but I was feeling lazy and was enjoying sitting still. Watching the guys eat was making me hungry, and I was thinking I'd look for a deli. At that moment the office door opened and two women came out, a small, slender Asian and a taller Caucasian, nicely dressed, with blonde hair. I did a double take. It was Barbara Butler, my employer and temporary captive. I looked over to the line of cars parked next to the office and there it was, a nice shiny white BMW 325ci with a black cloth top, Glory's car. I was somewhere between amazed...and extremely pissed off.

The two of them chatted outside for a few minutes, and then Barbara walked to the BMW while the other woman went back inside. Either something funny was going on or my client was just asking to get shot, a third time. I could feel my face getting hot, just like my father's used to turn red right before we'd get a whipping with his belt. My father's version of anger management was to beat the hell out of our backsides until he felt better. I inherited some of his temper for sure, but I don't hit kids or women, just bad guys, sometimes.

Barbara spotted me as she was pulling back into the street. She swung in alongside the SHO, her motor running. "Hop in," she yelled through her open window. I got out of my car and leaned into her window.

"Perhaps you'd like to tell me exactly what the hell you're doing in Tampa? In my wife's car?"

"This was important. You said I could take the car."

I calmed down enough to speak in full sentences. "Barbara, somebody is trying to shoot you. Trying to kill you, OK? You don't want to give them the chance. You're not safe here, and if that woman is involved you could be at even more risk."

"Vince," she said, "Get in the car." Her eyes were shiny with tears. Shit. I never could give a ticket to a woman who was crying. I opened the door and took the passenger seat.

"I stewed over this all last night. If she and I are married to the same man, then I need to know right now. Not that you couldn't have found out, but I was in there for half an hour and I learned a lot. Let's get some food somewhere, and I'll fill you in."

I went quiet and she drove. Maybe I'd made a huge mistake taking this case. Barbara was too impulsive and that could get her killed. I adhere to a strict double standard whereby it's fine for me to stir things up and make things happen, but it's definitely not OK for my clients to do it. I simmered in the passenger seat, pissed off and at the same time curious to know what they'd talked about.

We went to Rosie's Clam Shack on 49th Street in Pinellas Park, where I'd eaten before. The place is a little rough around the edges, but one of the few things I miss about my childhood in New England is fried clams, and Rosie's rivaled anything on the Maine coast. I ordered a large side order, meaning it didn't come with fries, just a big, hot heap of battered clam bellies. To maintain a little Florida in the culinary mix I also ordered a sweet tea. Barbara had the wahoo burger, which the waitress had enthusiastically recommended. The crowd was mostly local business people except for a group of bikers and a group of nuns at adjacent tables, giving the place a slightly surreal vibe. I wondered if the bikers would offer to buy the nuns a beer—and if the nuns would then whack the bikers' knuckles with a ruler, like they used to do to me at parochial school.

Barbara knocked me out of my reverie. "Her name is Bao Quyen Le. "Le" for short. She's a year younger than me, born in 1968. She lived in a hamlet in South Vietnam, but there was an attack and her whole family got killed except for her and her grandmother, who was sort of the village matriarch."

"You mean in the war? Americans?"

"Yes. She said she was a little girl, like four years old. The village was wiped out, but the story her grandmother told her is that an American soldier saved them. He was in some kind of trouble for doing that; she didn't explain why. He deserted, and the grandmother smuggled him into Cambodia, which was neutral, and somehow he got out. Then he went back to Vietnam in 1991 as a tourist, when the country first opened up to Americans again. The guy goes to find the village and it's gone; there's nothing there except jungle. But his interpreters get the word out, and they locate her. The grandmother has died and Le is—"

"Is what?"

She avoided my glance. "A prostitute."

"She told you that?"

"She was completely straightforward. Remember, this is girl-to-girl. Sorry, but you wouldn't have found that out."

Our food arrived and I dipped a fried clam in tartar sauce and took a bite. My clam ratings are good, excellent, and hold me. This was a hold me.

"So let me guess. The kind-hearted American guy rescues the poor hooker and brings her to the USA."

"You say that like it's a bad thing." She gave me a cold stare.

"Sorry. I don't mean to judge."

"Don't," she said. "It took him three trips. It was a crazy process, and she has no idea how much he spent, but everybody had to be bribed."

"So," I said, mid-clam, "was it love? Or guilt?"

"Who knows," Barbara said. "But I'll ask him. C.J."

"So you think they're the same person? C.J. and D.B.?"

"We were married in 1990. Back then C.J.'s citrus business was really good, and his biggest buyers were the Japanese. They paid top prices for Indian River grapefruit. He flew back and forth to Japan every few months."

"With a side trip to Vietnam," I said.

"Several, apparently."

"Whoa."

"No kidding. I don't even know how to feel," she said. She took a bite from her sandwich and looked away from me. "I'm part angry, part shocked. And part…sympathetic. She and I have something in common."

"You told her who you are?"

"Yes. She didn't seem surprised. She's kind of tough to read."

"Did you say anything about getting shot at?"

"No. I didn't want to scare her."

"So you're sure it was C.J.? It's not two brothers?"

"I think so. One thing though. There was a picture of the three of them on her wall, in a big fishing boat. The guy certainly looked like C.J., but it was strange."

"What was strange?"

"He was smiling. Happy little family, big grins. C.J. doesn't really have a sense of humor. He's a brooder. I used to think that was what attracted me to him. I don't think I've ever seen him smile, not like that."

"Did that bother you? Make you jealous?"

"It's not that. I mean, these two men have got to be the same person. But when I saw that picture, it was like, that can't be C.J. He just doesn't do that."

We ate the rest of our lunch without talking. Barbara was processing what she had learned and so was I. I was also leaning toward the one-guy theory, but it was hard to reconcile her description of her husband and the beer-drinking golf hustler I'd met the day before. If it was the same person, he was either a good actor or he was messed up. There were more than a few people who had had their brains scrambled in Vietnam, and the VA hospitals were still dealing with the consequences almost two generations later.

*

Barbara drove me back to Le's office so that I could pick up my car. I'd made her promise to drive herself straight back to Vero, to my place, and hole up. I told her I'd be home tonight and to have dinner ready and she giggled. She had a laugh like a tipsy soprano; I liked it. I wasn't upset with her anymore, I was glad that she had learned what she did. It was quite a story, and the wheels were turning in my head, working it out, playing what-if.

She pulled the convertible into the lot next to Le's, and I did a double take. The Taurus was gone. I realized I had been so angry at Barbara when I saw her that I'd left the car wide open, and someone had apparently stolen it. I cursed myself. I never do that, but I did, and there went not only my favorite car ever but also my computer, my lock-picking kit, a whole bag of snooping equipment and—I patted my side pocket just to make sure—the Glock. I'd left it on the seat in a moment of sheer unprofessional idiocy.

I called Roberto. He let it go to voicemail, and texted back. *I'm in class.*

Gotta talk, emergency, I texted.

My phone rang in five minutes—five long minutes. "It's me," he said.

"Somebody stole my car. It's got my computer in it."

"Did you put it on sleep?" I heard a flushing noise. He must be in the boys' room.

"Probably not, I had the tracking software on."

"Let's try something," he said.

Roberto showed me how to get to an application he'd installed on my phone, called "Find My Mac". He patiently walked me through the process to log in. A Google map came up, with a pulsating blue dot that said "Vince's Mac". Slick.

"Got it," I said. "Go back to class. You're a god."

"I know."

Barbara drove while I gave directions. The blue dot was moving. My Taurus was going east on Gandy Boulevard, toward the causeway, and the dot was well ahead of us. I told Barbara to get a move on, and she obliged—the woman could drive. The Beemer had the sport package and Barbara was using the Steptronic transmission to manually shift. She leaned hard on the tires while we weaved through traffic, drifting through curves as I held on tight and tried to focus on the map. We got onto Gandy Boulevard and she drove as fast as she could, but the road was congested. We began to gain on the blue dot when it made a hard right turn onto Snug Harbor Road, just before the causeway crossed Old Tampa Bay. The dot slowed down, and for a moment I thought we'd catch up—but suddenly, the traffic around us came to a halt. There was an accident ahead, and the cars were stopped in both directions. We were stuck, with nothing to do but watch the blinking blue dot on the phone.

The dot stopped at the end of Snug Harbor Road where it met the water, the Masters Bayou, according to the map. Barbara and I watched the screen as it slowly began to move again. It was now located over the water, in the bayou, and then it stopped blinking.

*

The cops must have been snarled in the same mess on Gandy Boulevard as it took them half an hour to show up at the water's edge. We'd parked the BMW at the top of a concrete boat-launching ramp, where someone had decided to launch my venerable Taurus. It must have floated for a while because it was a good thirty yards out, stuck in the silt of the bayou, the green roof barely visible over the waterline. Barbara gave the cops the details, and they began filling out their report; I was on the phone with Frank Velutto at the Indian River County Sheriff's office. I had a hunch that I wanted to play out.

"Vinny?" he said, when they put the call through. His voice was flat—even a little tentative, and he'd forgotten to tell me to go fuck myself, which was strange.

"What's up, Frank?"

"You tell me," he said.

"Did I say something?"

"What do you want, Vin?"

"I need a favor. Can you look up a juvenile and get me some background? Philip Johannsen, in Tampa." I gave him the home address. I didn't tell him I already knew he had a record—that information might tip him to Roberto's hacking and that would be bad. I could have had Roberto dig deeper, but I wanted a cop's perspective. I may have been way off base, but I wondered if the hellcat kid with the auto thefts on his record had just baptized my car. Frank said he'd look into it.

"Hey," I said. "You OK?"

"Forget about it," he said.

*

The cops gave me the name of a guy who owned a tow truck and was also a diver. This is not an unusual combination of skills in Florida, and it is also quite lucrative. He quoted me five hundred dollars, and when I complained he said there was a guy in Bradenton who would do it for a thousand. We agreed to meet the next morning as he was booked for the rest of the afternoon. I decided that there was no rush; the electronic devices would already be dead, and the rest of the gear would just have to be dried out.

The cops and I shot the breeze for a few minutes while Barbara waited in the BMW. They gave me some shit about leaving the Taurus unlocked. I probably should have told them about the Glock, but I had endured enough humiliation for one afternoon.

I got back in the car and told Barbara I was going to stay the night in Tampa; I'd get a hotel and a rental car, and she should get back to Vero. She wouldn't have to cook me dinner after all. She just smiled.

I drove this time. I hadn't driven Glory's car in a long time and it was a beautiful ride, but it felt strange to be in it. It didn't have the pure balls that the SHO had, although it could motor right along. Barbara was on my phone, Googling something, with a look of concentration on her face. "Look for a car rental place, ok?" I said.

"You're going to need a new computer," she said. "There's an Apple store in the mall out by the airport."

"Oh," I said, surprised. "Aren't you the efficient one?"

"There's some good shopping at the mall," she said.

"Barbara, I don't shop, as you can probably tell from my wardrobe."

"I'll shop while you get your computer and a wireless card. Are you Verizon?"

"AT&T."

"There's one at the mall."

She continued surfing on the smartphone while I drove us across the Gandy Boulevard causeway. "If you can find me a hotel too, go for it," I said. "Nothing fancy."

"I just booked us at the Hyatt, downtown."

"Barbara—"

"Don't worry, we have a two-room suite."

"Barbara, you should go back. I have a feeling this is going to heat up. You'll be safe in my house."

"Vince, I haven't felt safe in two weeks. I can help you. And I think I need to be around you right now, so don't freak out, OK?"

Maybe she had a point. Someone was already trying to find me from my license plate, and perhaps she wasn't so safe in my house. It might be smart to keep her close. But I was in the work mode; I didn't need any distractions if I was going to get the job done, and having her around could be dangerous if things got nasty.

I put my foot down. "No. I'm sorry, but the answer is no."

"Then you're fired, and I'll do my own investigating."

"Fucking A," I said, under my breath but loud enough for her to hear. She was in non-negotiable mode, I could recognize it. Glory behaved exactly the same way.

"OK," I said. "But I need to find a gun shop or a pawn shop somewhere. I have to get another gun."

"This is Florida," she said. "We've already passed three of them."

*

It took about an hour to get the laptop up and running. Buying it at the Apple store was a cinch, but the salespeople at the AT&T store tried to sell me everything in the shop while they filled out my new contract and got me a replacement card. I didn't even ask how much it was all going to cost; they said not to worry, it would show up on my next bill, which filled me with dread as their statements were about as readable as the Dead Sea Scrolls.

I sat at a table outside a Starbucks in the lower level of the mall and sipped an iced coffee while I set up the Mac. It ran about twice as fast as my old one, which was only a couple years old. I called Roberto, who was now out of school and at home, and he began emailing me links to the software programs I needed. He said that when I got back to Vero he would finish the job; he'd backed up everything on my old computer to a portable hard drive. Whatever I was paying this kid, it wasn't enough. Giving him Glory's laptop was the least I could do, and I was glad to be rid of it.

Barbara had disappeared into the mall. She would come back periodically to check on me and drop off shopping bags at my table, and then she'd go out again, like a pearl diver coming up for air. Setting up the computer was taking all my attention, but when I took a break, I noticed that quite a few bags had accumulated in a short period of time. I was trying to get the tracking software restored so I could check on the whereabouts of the van and the Lexus. It finally booted up, and showed C.J.'s van right where it was supposed to be, in Lake Wales. The Lexus was parked at Hibiscus Pond Drive. All quiet, all good. For a guy who had just watched his car float off, I felt remarkably calm. Being an ex-cop, I wondered how long it would take until all hell broke loose, because feeling calm was usually a bad sign.

Barbara returned with several more bags. She had a smug look, as if she'd won a prize.

"Oh my God, everything was sixty percent off!" she said, as I powered down the laptop.

"Yes, but how much did you actually spend?"

"That's not the point," she said. "It was sixty percent off!"

I kept my mouth shut. I'd probably spend as much on a gun anyway. A good automatic wasn't cheap.

*

We wedged the shopping bags into the small trunk of the Beemer and drove to the hotel. Barbara took the wheel while I looked out the window. She was obviously enjoying the nimble little car, and I didn't mind being chauffeured. The Hyatt was one of those downtown business hotels that catered to conventions and meetings, and pretty much everyone who was coming out while we drove up had a *hello-my-name-is* badge on their lapel. I got the bags out for Barbara, who handed them to a bellman. I told her to go ahead and check in, I'd be back in a few minutes. I was going to drive out east of town to Shoot Straight, a shop I'd found while searching on the new Mac. I'm not a gun-nut, but I thought I might have to dawdle there for a while; gun shops are the fifty-year-old ex-cop's equivalent of being a five-year-old in F.A.O. Schwartz.

The Shoot Straight gang was very professional and knew their weapons. I took four guns to the range; a Sig Sauer P238, a Kimber Super Carry and two Glocks, a Baby 26 like the one I had, and a slightly larger .45 caliber, the Glock 30, which had a little more heft, but was still an adequate concealed-carry weapon. I'd always lusted after the Kimber, which was well over a thousand bucks, but I couldn't yet forgive myself for letting my Glock 26 go for a swim, or worse. My suspicion was that it would not be in the car, so I wasn't worried about ending up with two guns, and even if it was still there I wouldn't trust it after the salt water bath.

The shiny Kimber shot like a smooth, lethal dream, but I couldn't justify it; that's a lot of money to me. A few days ago I'd been blowing through the insurance from Glory's policy, but my attitude had changed since I was working again. The Sig and the Glocks are ugly, dark automatics, but this wasn't a beauty contest. The Baby Glock was familiar and comfortable, but I was all over the target and couldn't cluster my shots. The Sig Sauer had a lot more kick—too much—and I put it aside. I finally decided on the Glock 30; I was more accurate with it and it fit my hand nicely. The sales guys ran a background check, took my six hundred dollars, and I was back on the road, packing heat.

*

It was five thirty in the afternoon, and I was going against the traffic as I cruised back into the center of Tampa. It was still in the nineties and humid, and I had the top down, which no one except mad dogs and Englishmen would do in Florida at this time of year. I blasted the air conditioning and played a Suzanne Vega CD that Glory had left in the car. The music was dark and brooding, like Barbara had called her husband, but I was in a good frame of mind despite the loss of the SHO. Losing the Glock was worse; it was emasculating. I feel naked without a gun, like Glory used to say about going out without any makeup on. She called it her armor. Getting a new weapon, now loaded and ready, was definitely increasing my sperm count. I know, it sounds ridiculous. It's a cop thing.

And hanging out with Barbara was fun. But I'd been at this long enough to know that it's not a good idea to get close to a client. Too often you solve the case and they hate you. People think they want to know the truth, but they usually don't.

I self-parked the BMW in the Hyatt garage to the dismay of the valet guys. The entrance led into a huge atrium decorated in brass and leather rectangles—business-class Bauhaus. A polite, dark-haired woman at the reception desk gave me a key, calling me "Mr. Butler", which made me laugh. I looked about three rungs down the social ladder from everyone else there; this was a high-class joint. It was modern to the point of being sterile, but that was preferable to some of the hotels I stayed in where a little sterilization might be in order.

I rode up the elevator with two guys in suits and a drop-dead-gorgeous model-type woman. The two men were trying not to be obvious about checking her out, and they were failing. They got off first and it was just her and me. I gave her a smile and she ignored me. We rode the rest of the way to the top floor in silence except for the whoosh of the elevator. She stepped off before me and walked away down the hall with that tight, high-heeled trot that beautiful women do. Girls that pretty are like Fabergé eggs—you wouldn't want someone to hand you one, for fear that you'd drop it and be out a million bucks.

Barbara opened the door when she heard me struggling with the key card. She had changed her clothes and wore an athletic-cut top and pants, like sweats, but lighter and probably ten times as expensive. She looked great.

The room was the biggest I had ever seen in a hotel. You could have slept a Boy Scout troop in it, and made s'mores in the full-sized, completely equipped kitchen. There was a master bedroom, a second bedroom, a huge dining and living area, two bathrooms, a spa room, spacious closets everywhere, and a stunning view south toward Hillsborough Bay. The place had more square footage than my entire house.

"Where am I?" I was in shock.

"I asked for their nicest room," she said. "Do you like it?"

"Yeah, it's nice. What time does the Mormon Tabernacle Choir arrive?"

"I got an amazing deal."

"I know," I said, "Sixty percent off."

"More. Keep guessing."

"Barbara, you are out of control. But thank you, this is fantastic." I wandered around the suite. It kept going on and on. I poked my head into the second bedroom and there on my bed was a change of clothes: a crisp, white, button-down Oxford cloth shirt, lightweight dress trousers and a navy blazer hanging on a stand.

"Where did this come from?"

"I went a little crazy at the mall. I had to guess your sizes; I hope it's OK."

The jacket was a 44 long, just right. The shirt was a 17 neck and I'm an 18, but I never wear a tie so it would fit. The perfect preppie outfit—except I went to high school with the rest of the proletariat. It felt nice to be taken care of, if a little embarrassing.

"There's a rooftop pool."

"I don't have a bathing suit."

"Yes you do, it's in the top drawer of the bureau over there." She flashed a big grin.

"It better not be a Speedo," I said. It was a Tommy Bahama, royal blue, and it looked modest enough. Barbara got a plush bathrobe out of the closet and said let's go.

*

Barbara looked fabulous in her bathing suit. She was just as pretty, in a womanlier sort of way, as the uber-being on the elevator. People are just so much better-looking when they smile. She did a lot of smiling at the pool and we horsed around, played Marco Polo and generally made fools of ourselves, which was fine as we were the only people on the roof. There wasn't a bar there, which was also fine; add alcohol to the equation and things could get out of hand.

Back in the suite I powered up the new MacBook. The first thing I checked was the car trackers. Everyone was still in their place. Next, I opened the program that would play any recordings from the bugs I'd placed at the Johannsen house. It took a while for the data to download so I figured I had something. Barbara was busy in her bedroom, so I had time to do some listening. I wrapped a hotel towel around my wet suit, sat back on a leather sofa, and plugged in the earbuds.

The recordings were clocked, and the first one began right after six thirty PM according to the display. I could hear someone arrive home and turn on the television news. So far I had a nice tape of Brian Williams.

I skipped ahead on the time clock to just before seven, recorded only a few minutes ago. The sound came from the bug I'd put in the kitchen, and I apparently hadn't done a very good job of it because I couldn't hear clearly, although the tone of the conversation was obvious. It was a fight, and a bitter one. One voice was a woman's, and the heavy Asian accent made it all the harder to distinguish the words. The other was a young man's voice at that particularly awkward stage in puberty where boys speak partly in the lower register and partly in a shrill falsetto. It's excruciating to be a kid that age; I remember it well.

They were really going at it, and the boy, who had to be Philip, blasted his mother with some obscenities, slammed a door, and then it was back to Brian Williams' calm tones. When that sort of exchange took place in my youth, the conversation always ended with the same words. "Just wait 'til your father gets back."

Barbara came out of her room in a dress, holding up two pairs of earrings. "These?" she said, holding up one set, "Or these?"

"I'm not qualified to make that decision," I said. She told me to get dressed; we had a reservation downstairs at the restaurant in half an hour. I closed the laptop and went into my room to try on my new duds. The pants were too tight, and I couldn't fit the conceal holster. I decided I would leave the new Glock in the room safe and hope that nobody gunned us down in the middle of our foie gras.

The menu was unspectacular, but the wine list read like an erotic poem. Some bottles were in the many hundreds of dollars, the kind that a business person might order to impress a client and then wake up the next morning wondering how the hell he or she would expense it and not lose their job. The other diners in the restaurant were mostly men, dressed in blazers like me, with a scattering of women; they appeared to know each other and wore name badges. I asked the waiter who they were, and he leaned over and whispered, conspiratorially, "It's the National Cremation Society. They operate crematoriums all over the country."

Barbara laughed out loud, drawing glances. "In that case I'll have the fire-roasted half chicken," she said, "well done." The waiter actually laughed; he was a good sport and we had a friend.

I had the pappardelle, which was forgettable. Growing up Italian you get picky about your pasta, and this was decent, but my mother's was better. I paired it with a glass of Pellegrino and a lime slice while Barbara sipped a straight-up martini from a stemmed glass.

"This is our second date," she said.

"It's not a date." I wondered if the vodka was already getting to her.

"Vince, has it occurred to you that you haven't asked me a single question about me? All you want to know about is C.J."

"Sorry. I try to keep it…"

"Professional."

"Right."

"Well, screw that," she said. "Come on, you have to be curious."

We were going to be here for at least another hour, and we had to talk about something.

"OK. So what do you do, back in Vero?"

"I teach some classes at the club, keep the home fires burning, clean a lot, read a lot, work out. I know, pretty dull."

"What do you teach at the club?"

"Pilates."

"We had pie ladies where I grew up," I said. "White-haired gals, cooking in the church basement."

She was about to correct me when she realized I was pulling her leg. She relaxed a little and told me about her life: the details, the routine, the boredom. She said her escape hatch was a floppy hat, a beach chair, and a good book. Within a few pages she could be thousands of miles away, having tea at Thornfield with Jane Eyre.

"Did you study literature at college?"

"I never went," she said. "I guess I'm self-educated. School of hard knocks."

"Hard knocks?" I said. "Excuse me but you don't look—"

"I know," she said, cutting me off. "But remember, you don't know me."

"That's why I'm asking."

"Let's go back to talking about you."

"We weren't talking about me."

"Then let's start," she said. I'd touched on something, and she'd put up a wall.

"I'm not finished," I said. "Two more questions, your honor."

"I might not answer them." She stirred her martini.

"Why do you settle for being at home?"

"A lot of women would take offense at that," she said.

"I'm not talking about a lot of women, I'm asking you. You're smarter than hell, whether you went to college or not."

"I was going to try nursing."

"Why didn't you?"

Barbara looked sideways toward a table full of crematory owners, who were now laughing loudly.

"C.J. wouldn't want it."

"So what?"

"You don't understand," she said.

"You're right, I don't," I said. "OK. Second question. Why no kids?"

"God, you're rude."

"It's my job," I said.

She said she envied her friends who had children. She and C.J. had tried, but it hadn't happened, and he wouldn't go for fertility treatment. I knew all about that; Glory and I had tried for years and had even blown big money on fertilization, to no avail. Glory had become adept at rationalizing why it was better that we didn't have children, but it was a dark territory that we seldom visited.

"My turn to ask you the questions," she said. She took a long sip of her drink. "How come you're so damn handsome?"

"Down, girl."

"Sorry," she said. "But really. Spill. Who are you?"

"I don't really like to talk about me."

"Not fair," she said. "You had your way with me, now I get to do it."

I grumbled an acknowledgement.

"Where are you from? You don't talk southern."

"I'm a Yankee. I grew up in Vermont."

"They have Italians there?"

"We lived in Barre. My dad was a stone cutter—there are a whole bunch of them there, it's where Rock of Ages is, the company that makes gravestones. I mean, memorials. Barre was like Brooklyn back then, you could get amazing Italian food, groceries, pizza, and the men hung out on the street corners when there wasn't six feet of snow."

"So why did you leave?"

"Too cold. Same reason everybody else does. I went to college on a scholarship for one year, but I was bored. I loved the reading, but I hated the classes. I dropped out and became a cop, and after a year I decided if I was going to be a cop I should at least do it somewhere

where I wouldn't freeze to death, so I moved down here and joined the Indian River Sheriff's department. I worked there for twenty-five years and retired, five years ago."

"Why?"

"Well…you're eligible for the pension after twenty-five years."

"You're leaving something out."

"I had a disagreement with the boss. He won."

"Do you like what you're doing now better?"

"It's different. I miss some of the guys, and it was go-go-go at the Sheriff's, lots of action every day."

She finished her martini and waved the waiter over for a refill. I said no to another Perrier.

We talked about everything that had happened during the day. Barbara had a glow in her eyes, from more than just the vodka. This woman was a princess who had been kept in a castle, under wraps, and she was aroused by the day's action. What I do can be very addictive, although it's not all glamour; most of it is waiting and drudgery just like anything else. She didn't know that yet; so far to her my job was a lot of fast-paced chasing around, and the occasional car sinking into a bayou.

We ordered dessert, and she ordered a third vodka.

"Barbara, no," I said.

She gave me a frown. Apparently people didn't say no to her.

"I'm a big girl, Vince," she said.

"You're getting shitfaced," I said.

She got up and threw her napkin on the table. "I'll be in the room."

I finished both desserts—my key lime pie and her crème brulee. I left her martini untouched and took the elevator back up to the room. I still had work to do.

*

Barbara was in the spa room when I got back to the suite. I took off my blazer and sat on the couch with the computer. There was more data from the Johannsen house bugs. I'd listen to that, but first I checked my phone; I'd left it in the room while we were in the restaurant. There was a text message from Roberto which became visible as soon as I turned it on.

Need 2 talk 2 U.

I called him. It was ten o'clock, but he'd be awake. "You OK?"

"Yeah. Where are you?"

"Still in Tampa. Back tomorrow, maybe."

"Oh," he said, deflated.

"Roberto, what's up?"

There was a very long pause, and I wondered if the call had been dropped, but he started talking.

"I was hacking. I saw something I didn't want to see."

"Like what?"

"Some emails. Love stuff. You know."

"Someone you know?"

"Yeah…sort of. The emails were between a guy and a girl. But the girl has a boyfriend already."

"Are you the boyfriend?"

"Me? Heck no. It's, like, just a kid I know. A friend."

"So you don't know whether to tell your friend that his girl is cheating on him?"

"Kinda like that. I think he'll hate me."

I took a deep breath. I'm not a father, and mine wasn't exactly a role model, so when I have to give a kid some advice, I'm basically winging it.

"Roberto, you're good at keeping secrets. Very good, in fact, aren't you?"

"Yes."

"You could easily keep this a secret, but it's going to eat at you."

"I know," he said.

"I'd say you tell the guy. He's going to find out sooner or later anyway."

Roberto took a while to respond. "Maybe not. It's complicated."

"My guess is he'll thank you, eventually."

"I don't know."

"Use your own judgment," I said. "But getting the truth out is usually the best thing to do. It's what I do for a living."

"Yeah."

"It hurts people at first, but they come around."

"OK. I'll think about it. Thanks."

"Go to bed," I said.

"Is the new Mac working OK?"

"Yeah, perfect," I said. "I'll try to keep this one from going swimming."

*

I was back on the laptop, trying to dial in the audio from the bugs at the Johannsens' when Barbara appeared out of the spa room and came into the living area. She sat next to me on the leather couch. She wore a plush white terry cloth hotel robe and smelled of scented bath oil and warm skin.

"I made an ass out of myself, didn't I?"

"You feel better after a bath?"

"Yes," she said. "And I apologize. I can come on a little strong. I don't drink that much, usually."

"I tend to bring out the closet alcoholic in people," I said, and we laughed. She was forgiven.

I got the audio going and we listened. It wasn't a recording, it was in real time, happening now; the bug can do that, too. It was D.B. and Le, in their bedroom. They were talking in lowered voices.

I twisted it bad playing golf. His voice.

How'd you play?

Total fuck up. It happens.

You lose money?

I broke even. I was up fourteen grand and they stiffed me. One of the guys couldn't afford to lose that much, and he threatened to call the cops. It was ugly.

Sorry, honey. That's not fair.

Le, can you walk on my back if I lie on the floor? I'm stiff as hell.

There was a rustling sound, and it got quiet except for D.B.'s moaning and his occasional instruction to Le about where to walk on his back. Barbara was leaning over me, looking at the display on the computer. It showed a timeline, and little sound waves that moved up and down with the voices. She whispered in my ear. "Can they hear us?"

"No, it only works one way."

I caught a glimpse of her breasts down the partially-opened bathrobe. They were not fake. They had the feminine slope of a woman her age, a woman who took care of herself. I'll never understand the silicone boob-job thing: they look like twin ice cream scoops. Barbara's looked perfect. The devil on my right shoulder was telling me to just reach in there and go for it, but the angel on the other shoulder was ready to bitch slap me if I did.

"Ooh-la-la," Barbara, said, over D.B.'s moaning. Another voice had joined in, Le's, and the moaning grew louder. Barbara looked at me with a grin. "So this is what you do for a living?"

"Yes," I said.

"Pervert."

The moaning from the computer turned into groaning, then some rhythmic slapping, and they weren't making hamburger patties. I closed the laptop.

"Show's over. I have to get to bed," I said, and I walked into my bedroom and closed the door.

*

I needed to catch up on sleep from the last two nights, but nothing that I did helped me to drift off. I thought about getting up and using the spa, and decided not to—that might invite trouble. I was trapped in the incredibly plush king-size bed, just me, about twenty-seven pillows, and my insomnia. I thought about Barbara. And then I thought about Glory. And then I thought about Barbara.

She opened the door and stood silhouetted from behind. She wore something that she must have picked up while shopping. I couldn't tell what color it was, but the light passed through the sheer fabric and it didn't leave anything to the imagination.

"I can't sleep," she said. She crossed the room and sat on the other side of my bed. She was a safe distance away; the bed was so wide it was like I was in Florida and she was in Nebraska.

"I can't either."

"Vince, can I ask you something?"

I prepared myself. "OK."

"What happened to your wife?"

That was not the question I expected. Now I really wasn't going to get any sleep. I sat up in the bed and faced her.

"You mean did I really shoot her?"

"No, that's not what I mean. What I mean is what really happened?"

"I did shoot her. That's what they said. I don't remember much of it."

"Start from the beginning."

"I was out drinking with a friend. I didn't think I was drinking that much, but it really hit me. I barely made it home; I was probably way over the limit. I went right to my bed, and assumed Glory was already in her bedroom. Something woke me up, and I remember being at the top of the stairs, and then I passed out. I was all banged up; I must have slid down the staircase."

Barbara moved closer, somewhere around Missouri. I kept talking. It hurt like hell to say the words.

"A neighbor heard the shots and called 911. The cops found me on the floor with my gun in my hand. They found GSR on me…I mean, gun-shot residue. So I'd fired the gun. Glory had been hit twice, in her chest. She was across the room from me on the floor. I don't remember any of it. I guess I was drunk and thought I was trying to shoot an intruder. I've had a lot of time to think about it and I still don't know…what…"

I couldn't talk anymore.

"But they let you go."

"Yes. It was a forensics screw-up, or an evidence screw-up—I don't know which. Guns have a signature, and you can tell what bullet came out of what gun. They didn't match. I mean, one bullet did match, but the other one didn't. So either the cops on the scene blew it or the evidence was mishandled somewhere in the chain. They didn't have a case. And no motive. So they dropped it, after nine months."

"Oh my God."

I lay back down on the bed. I was going into my black hole, the one that had sucked in all my anger, my grief, and my joy over the last year. My little purgatory of numbness.

Barbara moved over to Alabama. I could smell the bath oil again.

"We could just cuddle," she said.

"I can't," I said.

She got up and walked to the door. "My husband has been married to somebody else for twenty years. Some people could spend the rest of their lives feeling sorry for themselves. I'm not one of them."

She closed the door and went back to her room.

*

I felt sorry for myself, all right. I could wallow in it. Life was rigged and I'd been shit on, and now Barbara was just making it worse. I got up and went into the kitchen, looking for a drink. There was a fully-stocked bar, and I poured four fingers of bourbon and held up the glass.

Maybe she didn't mean to, or maybe she did, but she'd pegged me. I was awash in self-pity, sunk deeper than my Taurus in the bayou. A couple of times in my life people had said something to me and their words had cut to the bone, and this was one of them. I felt like an idiot. The bourbon suddenly smelled sour, and I poured it down the sink. I opened the door to Barbara's room, and could tell she was still awake. I got in the bed with her and lay down behind her, fitting my body to the contour of her back and legs. Spoons, Glory had called it, but I needed to leave Glory behind right now.

"What are you doing?" she said.

"Cuddling," I said.

Some minutes passed and I enjoyed her quiet, rhythmic breathing and her soft warmth. It had been a hell of a long time. Finally, she spoke.

"Vince?" she said.

"Yes?"

"Would you mind if I fuck you while we cuddle?"

FRIDAY

I WAS SUPPOSED TO MEET the tow truck driver in an hour. I hustled through a quick shower, didn't bother to shave, and dressed in the guayabera shirt and pants I'd worn yesterday. They needed laundering, but I also needed to carry, and I couldn't do that in the Oxford cloth shirt and too-tight pants. Barbara was sound asleep so I left her a note. I grabbed the MacBook and my new gun. There was no time for coffee, which was a misdemeanor if not a felony in my book, but I was late. I retrieved the BMW from the parking garage and sped down the Crosstown Expressway toward the Gandy Boulevard causeway and the Masters Bayou.

The sun was cooking up another steamy August morning and I should have been feeling like hell as I was rushed, unshaven, already sweating in my two-day-old shirt and lacking both coffee and sleep. But I felt terrific. I stood by the boat-launching ramp at the end of Snug Harbor Road and watched my Ford Taurus SHO, friend of many years, slowly emerge from the deep as the tow truck winched it across the silty bottom of the bayou and up the concrete ramp. I loved that car, but my mind was elsewhere. I was thinking about a certain bossy, pain-in-the-ass, headstrong, gorgeous and surprisingly limber client. That pie-ladies stuff must be good for flexibility.

The Taurus was now on terra firma, spewing briny water onto the launch ramp from the door sills. The tow driver was peeling off his wetsuit. I got some cash from my wallet to settle up and asked him where there would be an honest salvage yard as I wanted to sell it. He said he owned a salvage yard and he'd pay me $500 for the car so we could just call it even. Deal, I said.

I took my things out of the trunk, starting with the electronics and tools that I kept in a ballistic nylon duffel. Anything with a battery in it was now useless. My lock-picking kit was soaked, but the tools just needed to be dried out since they were mostly metal or plastic. The portable high-speed drill was kaput, along with its rechargeable batteries. I retrieved my sawed-off shotgun from the spare tire well, where I kept it for absolute emergencies. It was no better for the salt bath, but it wasn't a precision instrument in the first place. I'd just give it some rehab and keep it—those old guns die hard.

The inside of the car was a mess. It had already silted up because the windows had been left open. My car thief friend probably hadn't been too thrilled that he'd chosen a car with minimal air conditioning. The computer was in the back on the floor, open and still shiny, but its soul was now in laptop heaven. I left the maps, spare change, pencils and crud for the new owner. I got down on my knees and searched the wet floors and puddles under the seats for the Glock, which had been on the passenger seat as I don't like to drive with it in the small of my back where the conceal holster fits to my belt. It's too easy to accidentally leave the safety off and shoot myself in the ass, and I'm pretty certain my insurance wouldn't cover that.

There was no Glock, just like I had figured. If there's anything a thief likes more than a free car it's a free gun; they are easy to fence. He'd get a hundred bucks, max. If I'd known any of the fences in Tampa, I would have put the word out and bought it back for three hundred, but I had other things to do.

Sunset Park was on the route back, and on a whim I drove the convertible to a cross street a few blocks from Hibiscus Pond Drive and opened the new laptop. I checked the cars first; the Lexus was a few miles away, on the move. The van was still stationary in Lake Wales. I ran the listening program. Nothing, no signal. Either somebody had disabled it or it wasn't working properly. It was finicky, and I'd had to reboot it before. I needed those bugs working if I was going to do my job—sooner or later someone would say something more informative than "a little lower, honey." Also, I had another item on my agenda: I wanted to see the kid up close, and maybe he'd be home. I'd use my Pool Repairman routine, that way I could get close to the bugging unit and give it a quick reboot.

There was a white Ford Transit van parked in the driveway of the Johannsen house with "Le's Vending" stenciled on the door. Somebody was home. I pulled in next to it and waved at Hawkeye, across the street tending his domain, and he waved back. I tried to look like a Pool Repair Guy, but I was driving the BMW, which was the wrong set of wheels for the job. I decided I'd better be Pool Replacement Estimator Guy instead. They were the pencil pushers who didn't drive trucks. I knocked on the Johannsens' front door and Philip answered.

He was bigger than he'd looked from a distance, or at least taller. He stood almost as tall as D.B., but he hadn't fleshed out yet—he was still a skinny kid. His hair was somewhere between Asian-black and chestnut, and he had the beginnings of a beard. He looked at me with the distaste that kids his age reserve for anyone over the age of forty, not counting the members of Metallica.

"What do you want?"

"David Johannsen?"

"No."

"Does David Johannsen live here?"

"Who wants to know?"

Wiseass. "I do."

"Fuck off."

If my doorstep interview was going to continue like this I would have to sucker punch the little bastard. I'd seen plenty of bad attitudes when I was on the force, but his had a real edge on it. I decided to be nice, and smiled.

"Your dad called me. I'm supposed to do the estimate for your pool."

"It's out back," he said. "Knock yourself out."

He closed the door in my face. Fuck you too, kid.

I went around to the back and opened the pool gate. The little black box was still attached, so at least they hadn't discovered it. I got to work rebooting it. The kid appeared at the back door.

"Hey bro," he shouted. "What are you doing back there?"

I was done with the reboot, it only needed unplugging and replugging and the display went back on. I closed the gate and walked up to Philip.

"I'm doing what your daddy asked me to." I looked him right in the eye, from a few feet away. "Is that going to be a problem?" There was no smile on my face now. This was my Clint Eastwood squint; all the cops know that one. A little intimidation can sometimes reveal a lot.

He went back into the house, leaving the door open, and reappeared a few moments later. He had a Glock 26 in his hand, *my* Glock 26, I could tell from the scratches. You get to know your own gun. He pointed it at my face.

"Get the fuck out of here."

I could have disarmed him, he was just a kid, but I turned and left. I knew I had my car thief—and maybe my shooter, too.

*

I drove back to the hotel with my trunk-full of soaking wet snooping equipment. This time I gave the BMW keys to the valet and told him to keep it out front, we'd be leaving soon, and not to take anything out of it or I'd be very unhappy. I must have looked like I meant it; he bowed solicitously and swore he'd guard it personally. They're used to beer wholesalers and stockbrokers here, not coffee-deprived ruffians who needed a shave.

*

Barbara had ordered room service and there was a tray in the room with croissants, Danish pastries, melon, granola, fresh-squeezed orange juice and a big carafe of hot coffee. I heard her in the bathroom, and, while I waited, I ate everything in sight and poured a belated but extremely welcome cup of coffee. Apparently I had worked up a pretty good appetite the night before.

She came out, dressed up, made up, and looking fantastic. She gave me a cat-that-ate-the-canary grin.

"I found out who boosted my car," I said. Barbara frowned. Oops. I probably should have said something about how awesome she was last night.

"How wonderful," she said. Yes, I definitely have a way with women. It's called the wrong way.

"Sorry, I'm a clod," I said, backpedalling. "Can we just roll the tape back, and I'll come in the door all over again?"

"Sure. But this time, leave me a croissant." She laughed, and I was off the hook, at least for now.

"I'm going to shave," I said.

"You can't wear that shirt," she said. "Change it."

"OK." It wasn't even eleven o'clock and people had been bossing me around all day. Sticking guns in my face, making me change clothes. I retreated to the comfort of the bathroom, which was the size of my garage at home. It was equipped with disposable razors and Truefitt & Hill shaving soap, the best on the planet. Some guys don't like to shave, but I love it. I need coffee and a good shave in the morning to feel human again.

Barbara came into the bathroom and put her arms around my waist while I watched her in the mirror, the soap on my face and razor in my hand.

"What time do we have to check out of the room?" she said, purring.

"Right now," I said. "They have to get it ready for the Green Bay Packers—they're staying here tonight."

"Maybe I should stick around," she said, purring again. "But I wouldn't want to mess up my makeup."

"We have places to go," I said. "Isn't today when C.J. drives back to Vero?"

"Yes. He usually gets home in the late afternoon."

"We'd better get moving. I'd like to beat him to Lake Wales. I'll check and see where the Lexus is as soon as I finish shaving."

She let go of my waist and began to assemble her things. I scraped away the last few soapy spots, rinsed, patted my face dry with a plush towel and put on the Oxford cloth shirt. If I wore the blazer it would hide the gun, even though I'd be hot and would look like somebody called Chip from the yacht club. I was glad my parents hadn't named me Chip.

*

We were halfway to Lake Wales on Highway 60 with the convertible top down, at Barbara's insistence. She'd stopped in a roadside shop and bought us hats, a pink visor for her and a New York Yankees cap for me, which I could have been prosecuted for wearing back in Red Sox Nation. The Lexus was still in Tampa, so for once we had a head start. The wind noise in the car made it hard to talk, so we rode with our thoughts. I was mulling over what I'd seen at the Johannsen house. I wondered if it could have been the kid who had taken the shots at Barbara. The time someone had shot at her in the Publix lot she'd seen the red Lexus, and that would have been Tuesday morning, right before she'd called me. That was when C.J. was still in Vero, on his beach walk. Theoretically, the Lexus would have been in the storage unit in Lake Wales that day. So, even though C.J. was in Vero, he had something of an alibi because his car wasn't. Then who was driving the car?

My thought was that it was the kid. I tried to back into a rationale, a motive. Le may have been OK with the don't-ask-don't-tell marriage she lived in, but maybe the son wasn't. Maybe the boy was pissed that his dad was gone all the time. Not that a kid that age would ever admit it, but those years are when young people, especially boys, need their fathers the most.

I bet Philip knew everything. He had a record, he had the balls to steal my car right from under my face, and he was just—the type. He was no innocent, no dummy; he probably knew more about D.B. than D.B. knew about himself. And, he was pissed. His mother was getting two nights of D.B. while the other woman, Barbara, had him all the rest of the week. I liked it, it fit. Unless D.B. and C.J. were two different guys.

I hadn't heard back from Frank Velutto, and that was yesterday. Barbara had me stop for a bathroom break in Mulberry, a hamlet south of Lakeland. I called Frank. I got Myra, the day dispatcher, who sometimes handled the phones if it was busy.

"He can't take your call, sorry Vince," she said.

"Hey Myra, what's up? What did I do? Too many parking tickets?"

"Um...when's the last time you saw Frank?"

"I don't know. He never came to see me in the lockup."

"You know Carole left him, right?" she said.

"No, I didn't," I said.

"Six months ago. He looks like shit."

"Frank never looks like shit."

"He does now," she said, "and it's gotten worse in the last couple of days."

"Tell him to get off his ass and call me. Sorry to hear about Carole, that's bad."

We hung up. Poor guy—Carole was a looker, and a sweetheart, too. I hoped Frank would call soon; I really wanted to know if Philip had any gun violations. The car boosts were kids' stuff, but any kind of record of a gun bust would tell me I was definitely on the right track.

*

Barbara came out of the store with a couple of flavored waters and handed me one. She also gave me a small, white plastic bag with something in it.

"Present," she said. "They had some unbelievable things in there."

I reached in the bag. It was a dried alligator hand, attached to a key chain. It must have been from a young alligator because it was small, and the claws were splayed in a hideously deformed position, neatly varnished for eternity.

"Gosh, I don't know what to say."

"Don't say anything, just enjoy the moment," she said.

"Do you give one of these to all your lovers?"

"Seeing how you're the only one, I'd have to say yes."

I found that strangely nice. I was glad I wasn't just another notch on her belt.

"So how about you?" she said. "Are you a Don Juan?"

"You're kidding, right?"

"You don't have to tell me," she said.

"I've got nothing to hide. And no, I was pure, before I met you. I never cheated on Glory."

"That's the first time you've actually said her name," she said.

"I'm working on it. The self-pity thing. You got that right, last night."

"Sorry, Vince, I didn't—"

"No apologies, you were right on."

"Lots of wild sex will help you get better." She gave me a bawdy wink.

"Barbara, I—"

"You feel guilty about it, right?" she said.

"Slightly," I said.

"Me, too."

"You do?"

"I kind of manipulated you into it. I can do that."

"It was nice," I said.

"I agree," she said. "But you're not ready. And I'm not, either."

"I guess you're right," I said, and I suddenly felt as old and crusty as an embalmed alligator hand.

*

I had forgotten all about tracking D.B. in the Lexus. Damn. I pulled the car over to the side of Highway 60 and the traffic sped past us as I switched on the Mac. D.B. was about a half an hour behind us in Valrico, just this side of Brandon. We'd be in Lake Wales in ten minutes and he would arrive thirty minutes after that. I tried to figure out how to play it; whether we should stake out his office, or the self-storage unit, or maybe wait at Quinn's. My stomach was voting for Quinn's, but somehow that seemed too confrontational. *Oh, hi there D.B., or whatever you name is, great to see you! I'm just having lunch with your wife, or…one of your wives, ha ha…and by the way, she's sensational in the sack!* Getting in someone's face is one thing, rubbing it in someone's face is another.

Barbara wanted to stop at yet another store, and since we had the thirty-minute cushion, I let her, on the condition that she could not buy anything kitschy—we had already bagged our limit. She went inside, and I popped open the laptop. The tracking program was on, but now the Lexus wasn't showing up. I looked for the van and it appeared, in the storage unit where it had been since Wednesday. I tried the Lexus one more time. Nothing.

It had to be the batteries, and mentally I kicked myself. I hadn't used the tracker in more than a year, and I should have changed them before I'd attached the unit to the Lexus, but I didn't, and now I'd lost him. I went into the store, bought an eight-pack of double A cells, and met Barbara at the counter while she paid for her water and gum. I told her about the Lexus and she frowned.

"So how are we going to do this then?"

"Who is we?"

"I'm your assistant," she said.

"No," I said, "You're not. You're my client. And his wife."

"Leave me at the restaurant and go downtown. Keep your phone handy and I'll call you if he shows up at Quinn's first, and vice versa."

Actually, that sounded like a good solution. "Just stay out of sight at the restaurant, ok?" I said.

"Don't worry. I'm going to hide behind a big pile of french fries. I'm starving."

I dropped her at Quinn's. Lake Wales is small enough so that I could get back to the restaurant quickly if I needed to. We were taking a chance, but if we lost him I was worried that we would miss an opportunity. I went downtown to my steam-bath stake out spot in the bank parking lot across from C.J.'s office. I had a half hour to play Scrabble and beat myself up about forgetting the batteries.

*

C.J. looked like hell. I took the seat across from him and asked him what the matter was. He said he was still worried about Barbara. He wondered if she was going to be there when he got home. He'd never had any reason to worry about her, but he was getting a strange vibe. She was in her forties; it's the time a lot of women her age wondered if there was more out there. Not that he was jealous, he wasn't that way. Just sad. I said how do you know this, and he said he didn't, it was just a feeling. I tried to cheer him up with my tale about the golf game in Dunedin, and the ass-kicking I got the next day. Win some, lose some. My tuna salad came, but he didn't even order, even though it was his turn to pay. I ate it fast, I had to go. I told him not to forget to leave a decent tip. He didn't hear me—he was looking behind me at somebody. It was Barbara…right here in the restaurant.

C.J. walked over toward her table, and I got up and left.

*

I hadn't seen anything of C.J., or D.B., or anyone for that matter. Historic Downtown Lakes Wales on a summer Friday afternoon was dead quiet, and the heat radiated off the sidewalks and buildings like someone had left the screen door to Hell wide open. I waited with the car running and thanked the engineers from Bavaria who had endowed the Beemer with superb air conditioning, unlike my recently-departed Taurus. But an hour had passed, and C.J. must have been in town for a while. I wondered why Barbara hadn't called.

It dawned on me that I could call her. I dialed her Tracfone. It rang several times and then announced to me that "the voicemail feature has not been activated." I decided I couldn't wait any longer. I put the BMW in reverse and backed out onto East Stuart Avenue. Something had gone wrong.

*

There was no Lexus at Quinn's parking lot, and no van either. I ran into the restaurant. The waitstaff was cleaning up after the lunch crowd, and the only patrons were two older guys lingering over their coffees. No Barbara and no C.J. I didn't see the waitress I'd met the other time, the one who'd told me about Big Tip and Little Tip. I panicked. The first thing I could think was—self-storage unit.

Both of the bays were locked. I got my still-soggy tools from the trunk of the BMW and popped them one at a time. Door number one held the Lexus, still warm from the drive. Door number two, where the van had been, was now empty.

I had the presence of mind to quickly pull the tracker from underneath the Lexus and replace the batteries, which took me thirty seconds. I work fast when I'm mad at myself. I put the spent ones in my pocket, shut the bay door, re-locked it, and got into the BMW. I opened the laptop and checked. Yes—it was the battery, the tracking software confirmed that the car was right where it sat.

I switched it over to track the van. It was heading east on Highway 60, just below Lake Kissimmee. Whoever was in the van was halfway to Vero. I could drive as fast as the Beemer would go, but I'd never catch up.

I tried Barbara's phone on and off for another half hour. I finally got through, and I didn't know whether to be relieved or furious.

"Hello?" she said.

"It's me. Are you OK? Can you talk? Where are you?"

"Yes, I'm OK. I should have called you. We were talking. Everything is OK. "

I heaved a sigh of relief. "Where are you?"

"We're going home. We have…a lot to talk about."

"Barbara—"

"It's OK, Vince. I want to thank you so much for all your help. You really helped a lot, but we're all done. I don't need you to work on this anymore; I'm all set."

What? "Barbara, can you talk? Are you in trouble?"

"I'm fine. Really. I can take it from here. Thank you again, so much—I have to go." She hung up.

I sat in the BMW, dumbfounded. Her voice was quivering at the end, like she was on the edge of tears. I didn't like that, not one bit. All I could guess was that they had seen each other at Quinn's and that they were talking. They were husband and wife; it was reasonable, you're supposed to be able to talk to each other and you don't have to explain to everyone else. I just didn't like being fired, especially not before I'd determined who was shooting at my client. I like to finish what I start.

I decided I had a new client.

Me.

*

I reached the city limits of Vero and, on a whim, I turned left onto 43rd Avenue toward the Indian River County Complex where the Sheriff's department was. It stood across from the Indian River County Jail and was in the center of a whole neighborhood of lawyers' offices and bail bondsmen—I'm sure the bad guys appreciated the convenient, one-stop shopping. I breezed into the Sheriff's department parking lot with the familiarity that came from having worked there for so many years, though it had been a while. Frank Velutto was in the lot walking toward his car, a tan Mercedes sedan that he kept as neat as his hairstyle. It was about the vintage of my Taurus SHO, but it looked new. I parked next to it and got out.

He looked like a faded black-and-white picture of himself. The movie-star good looks were masked behind a pale, dazed expression. I wondered if he was getting chemo…and if all that thick black hair would soon end up in his brush, or going down the shower drain.

"Hey," I said, approaching him. He recoiled as if I was going to hit him.

"Vinny," he said, recovering. "What the fuck. I didn't expect you."

"Frank, I heard about Carole. I'm sorry."

"Well, that's ancient history." He fidgeted with his car keys. He looked like a man who wanted to be anywhere but here, talking to me. "What do you want?"

"The kid in Tampa? You were going to see if he had any gun violations?"

"That's what you're here for?"

"Yes," I said. Had he forgotten? I didn't get it. He must be sick, and it must be messing with his head.

"Ask Myra to get you the name of the JPO. She's still inside; she's on dispatch. Tell her I said it was OK."

"Frank…are you all right?"

"Yeah, I'm fucking great," he said, without the usual smile. I was going to say something else, but I didn't.

Frank started his car and left, and I entered the county building. Myra was behind the smoked glass window in the front, and she lit up when she saw me. She had been one of my friends back when I was with the office, and she'd visited me every week in jail. She always brought me cookies, and one time she brought a layer cake into which she'd actually baked a metal file. The guards had a big laugh about that, and it was one of the few light moments during my nine months of imprisonment.

"Vince, lookin' good," she said.

"You too, babe." We always flirted, although we looked like people from two different planets. She was part Seminole and part African and weighed twice what I do, although she got around pretty well. "I just saw Frank in the parking lot."

"You see what I mean?"

"Yeah. Is he sick?"

"I don't think so," she said. She leaned closer to the slot in the smoked glass that let in conversation, but not bullets. "Drinking himself to death if you ask me. The man had a buzz today when he come back from his lunch."

"He told me I could ask you to get the name of a Juvenile Probation Officer in Tampa. Whoever's assigned to a kid named Philip Johannsen."

"You wait right there." She got on the phone while I sat in the lobby and thumbed through a year-old copy of *Law Officer Magazine.* I found several items that I didn't own yet in the "More Gear" section. I wasn't a cop anymore, but that didn't mean I couldn't have all the toys.

"Got it," Myra said, as she hung up the phone. She passed a slip of paper with a name and phone number through the slot. I winked and blew her a kiss as I left.

*

I sat in the BMW and got my phone out. It was the middle of the afternoon and the weekend would start in a couple hours so I decided I'd better call the JPO in Tampa before I did anything else. Her name was Shirley Magan, and she answered the call on the first ring.

"Ms. Magan, my name is Vince Tanzi. I'm a P.I. over in Vero Beach, and actually I'm a retired deputy." I say that to open doors; sometimes it helps and sometimes it doesn't.

"Go on," she said.

"You have a kid named Philip Johannsen, lives over in Sunset Park. I know he's got a record, mostly car theft, but I need to know if he has any gun violations."

"I can't tell you that. That's not public information." It appeared the cop-to-cop door opener was going to be shut on my foot.

"Then we have a problem. I have a client who's been shot at, twice. Your juvenile had motive, opportunity, and has a gun." I was stretching on motive—I didn't really know that yet.

"If he has a gun, then that's a violation right there. Are you reporting that?" This woman had all the warmth of Judge Judy with a tequila hangover.

"Ms. Magan," I said, keeping my cool, "I'm just investigating. If I need to report something, you'll be the first to know. I know what you can and can't say—I've been a cop all my life and I play straight, OK? I just need some background. If you tell me he's a thief and that's it, I'll leave it alone. But I don't want people to get killed, and I don't want your juvie to kill anybody. Fair enough?"

"He's clean. You wouldn't want to give him your car keys, though," she said.

That much I already knew. "Just the GTAs?"

"And some fights at school, that kind of thing. He thinks he's tougher than he is—you know the type."

"Yes," I said.

"He has a chip on his shoulder, but I don't think he's your shooter."

"Thank you."

"Call me if I'm wrong."

"I will," I said, and hung up.

I fidgeted in the seat of the BMW while I tried to figure out my next move. What I really wanted to do was find Barbara, to make sure she was OK. Like most men I have bad instincts about women, but I have excellent instincts about trouble, and I still had the feeling that she was in someone's crosshairs. But if I got too close, she might be upset.

I was distracted by a car that pulled in to the space next to me. It was a brand-new Ford Taurus SHO; they'd revived the model after many years and it was 365 turbo-charged horses of pure muscle. I'd read about them, and they were in the neighborhood of forty grand. A deputy got out, and I knew him—Buzzy Siebert, one of the nicest cops on the force. I rolled down the window.

"Hey officer, how'd you afford that on a cop's salary?"

"Hi Vince. I robbed a bank. Hope you didn't have any money in it."

"Nice whip, dude," I said, and he walked into the building. I was drooling. The Ford dealership wasn't on my way home, it was down U.S. Highway 1 several miles. But it happened to be located right next to a car wash, and I decided I needed a car wash.

*

Two hours later I was back in the BMW, driving home with a sales contract on the passenger seat. It had been the usual ordeal; back and forth between the salesman, the manager, the business manager and God knew who else, maybe they had a spiritual manager, or they had to ask their moms. It was the first car I had ever bought brand-new, and it was way out of my price range, but I had the insurance money, and this would just about finish it off. Glory would have approved. They had to prep it, and told me I could pick it up tomorrow. The salesman said they didn't usually take a personal check, but I just happened to leave the Glock visible on my belt during the negotiating process, and they agreed.

*

I opened the bay door and parked the BMW. I had decided not to trade it, I could always sell it privately, but for now it looked good in the garage. One of these days I would clean out all of Glory's things and make a trip to the Salvation Army, but I wasn't quite ready for that. I could clear the cobwebs from the house, but that wouldn't get rid of the ones in my head.

Barbara's clothes were still in Glory's bedroom, in the bag she'd hastily packed back at the Spring Hill Suites, which seemed like a long time ago. I'd decide what to do with them later—for now I was hungry, as I had skipped lunch, and I went downstairs to the kitchen to make a salad. I'd had enough fatty food for a while. That salty, fried stuff is one of the more socially acceptable forms of addiction, like shopping, except that getting fat can kill you, and people don't usually die from shopping unless it's around Thanksgiving. I'm not an economist, but to my thinking the global economy is more about our addictions than our actual needs. There is enough of everything to keep the planet clothed, warm, and fed, but it's our nature to want *more* until it's all gone. More sugar, more fat, more sex, more shoes, more gasoline, more money—more *stuff*, until it's gone, or we're dead. A true crackhead doesn't leave anything in the pipe. Of course I had just blown forty grand on a car, but that was different.

I thought about driving by Barbara's place. I could say I was in the neighborhood and drop off her bag. Somehow that sounded like what I might have done in high school, and I nixed the idea. I'd get some sleep and start fresh, working for my new client, me, who wouldn't dump me before I got to the bottom of what was going on.

*

I woke up in my dark bedroom with one of my three AM brilliant revelations. At that time of the night my brain is still mostly asleep, and is fertile ground for crackpot ideas, conspiracy schemes and paranoid anxieties, most of which turn out to be rubbish when I get out of bed several hours later. This time it was—*what if I'm being set up?* Maybe the Asian trips that C.J. had made were about something more than grapefruit, or importing a second wife. The real money in trade with Asia was from drugs, and Vietnam was in the Golden Triangle, which was second only to Afghanistan in heroin production. C.J.'s office looked like a front. He had a gun, a passport, and money stashed. How many citrus brokers would do that? Was Barbara part of this? Did she really hire me to find a shooter, or was that a setup? She had come on awfully strong at the hotel, though I certainly hadn't put up much resistance.

And Le had a cash-intensive business, with built-in distribution—perfect for money laundering, so maybe she was in on this, too. Shit. Now I'd be awake for the rest of the night, trying to make the jigsaw pieces fit.

SATURDAY

I FINALLY DOZED OFF AND slept soundly until nine. This made two mornings in a row I'd overslept, and I wondered if the adrenaline rush of the last few days was pushing me into a different cycle, or was it the lack of alcohol? Either way, I felt better than I had in weeks. I did twenty push-ups and fifty sit-ups; that was the first time I'd done that since jail, when I did hundreds of each every day to relieve the boredom. It felt great, though I knew I'd be sore tomorrow. I had a bowl of granola with cut-up fruit, a big glass of Natalie's unpasteurized orange juice and two mugs of Green Mountain Dark Magic, which made me jumpier than a Jack Russell in a jock strap.

I cleaned the kitchen, tidied the bathroom, made my bed, took out the recycling, paid a few bills, filled the bird feeders, read my emails, vacuumed the foyer, and was about to replace the salt in all the salt shakers when I realized I had morphed into an over-caffeinated, domestic hurricane of efficiency—and avoidance. I had more important things to do, and I wasn't doing them. I brushed my teeth, splashed some water on my face, clipped my holster to my belt and got in the car.

*

It felt a little creepy to be driving down her road. C.J.'s van was in the driveway, outside of the garage. I knocked on the front door, and he appeared behind the screen, not opening it.

"Is Barbara here?" I asked. He showed no recognition, not a trace—although I was ninety percent sure this was the guy I'd played golf with, the day before yesterday.

"No," he said. He didn't volunteer anything else. Between him and Philip, I realized I probably didn't have a future as a door-to-door salesman.

"Mr. Butler, I'm Vince Tanzi. I have some stuff I need to give your wife."

"You can leave it here," he said. I wondered if I'd made a mistake identifying myself. I was stunned at the complete lack of a reaction—he was a flat-liner compared to his alter ego. It was uncanny. Either he was one hell of an actor, or I was ninety percent wrong. Finally seeing him up close was turning the whole thing around in my head.

"Do you know where she went?"

"To her club."

"OK, thanks," I said. "I'll just drop it there. I'm headed that way." He shut the door without another word. I felt like I'd been talking to an exhibit at Madame Tussaud's. But sometimes the lack of a reaction is as telling as a reaction, and I'd swear that C.J. believed he'd never seen me before.

*

The parking lot at the Treasure Coast Club was packed with the Saturday morning workout crowd. I was going to go inside and find Barbara, but I hesitated. I stayed in the car where I had a clear view of the entrance, and waited. Maybe if my three AM paranoid delusions were correct, I'd witness her making a big drug deal with some Colombians out of the back of her Yukon.

But that didn't happen. She came out of the club dressed in a bright pink outfit with her hair up, glowing from a workout and…looking very pretty. She had a great walk—not the bitchy supermodel trot, more of an athletic lope—feminine, but strong. She didn't see me, and she tossed a gym bag into her car and left. I started the BMW, and followed.

There was no rendezvous with two Sicilian drug lords under a pier. Instead, she parked on Ocean Drive just before Humiston Park and walked back to Cravings, a street café with the best pastries on the beach. I passed her and turned into the Waldo's parking lot, across Ocean Drive on the beach side. Waldo's is part of the Driftwood, an iconic hotel, built by Waldo Sexton back in the 1930s, which every year comes closer to falling into the water as the Atlantic nibbles at the shoreline. It is a funky and fun hotel, and if it ever does wash away, it will be missed.

Barbara took a table outside and opened the *Press Journal*. She was sipping something from a cup and had a pastry. This stake-out thing was hell on someone who'd only had a super-healthy bowl of granola for breakfast and was trying to be good. I salivated while she ate, until I couldn't stand it any longer.

"I was wondering how long you were going to stay in that car," she said as I sat down across from her.

"Busted," I said.

"You're staring at my bran muffin. Go inside and get yourself some food."

I came back out with two almond croissants and an Odwalla, some kind of mango-pomegranate thing that would no doubt neutralize the effect of the croissants like a Hail Mary cancels out a sin.

"I have some things of yours in the car," I said.

"I have your Tracfone," she said. "I should probably give it back."

I munched on a croissant and fidgeted. I'm supposed to ask people questions and solve problems, and I had a dozen questions for Barbara, but I was tongue-tied.

"Sorry," I said. "I feel like a goddamn teenager."

"It's awkward," she said.

"Sex complicates things," I said.

She laughed. "I think I'm going to have that tattooed on me."

"I know just where to put it."

"Yes," she said, "like the warning label on a cigarette pack." We both laughed, and the glacier began to retreat.

"Seriously," I said. "You kind of threw me for a loop."

She took off her shades and looked at me. "I care a lot about you, Vince," she said. "I didn't mean to drop out of sight like that, with no explanation. But the truth is…I don't have an explanation, yet."

"What happened in the restaurant?"

"He saw me. He came over and sat down, and we talked. He was terribly concerned when he'd seen the note about me going to my sister's for a while, and he said he'd worried himself sick. So I told him everything. About getting shot at the first time, about my getting the windshield fixed and not telling him, about the second time I got shot at, about seeing the Lexus, about calling you. Pretty much the whole thing."

"What do you mean by pretty much?"

"Well," she said, "I didn't say anything about going over to Tampa and talking to Le. She and I agreed to keep that between ourselves. And I didn't say anything about…you know."

"I met him, this morning, at your house."

"Omigod," she said.

"Is that a bad thing?"

"No," she said. "It's just…there's a lot that I'm trying to decide about right now. C.J. talked me into going home and swore he could take care of everything and I wouldn't be in any danger. He didn't say how, but he said he'd do it, and he said I had to un-hire you, and not to call the cops."

"Do you believe him?"

"Sort of. I feel like I owe him the chance."

"I don't like it," I said.

"Well that's your problem, then." She put her sunglasses back on and looked away.

"Barbara—"

"Look Vince. There are some things about me that you are…just never going to know, OK? You have to let it go. I know that's not your nature. But you have to, if we're going to stay friends."

"I'm really uncomfortable with that," I said. "And it has nothing to do with you and me, I promise. Maybe you really should go to your sister's, and let things cool off while I look around."

"Vince," she said, "with all due respect, I don't think this is an investigating thing. That's not the way this is going to be resolved. It's a relationship problem. I need to fix my relationship with C.J. It's a wreck, and it's been a wreck for years and years. Meeting you has opened my eyes to that, and I'm very grateful to you. I think I can handle this—in a different way than you, but I think it's the right way. Give me some time."

She was in the non-negotiable mode again, and I reluctantly retreated. "Keep the phone, please. Keep it charged and on you."

"You're scaring me a little."

"A couple days ago I met this woman who had been shot at, and she was shaking like a leaf."

"I have to go," she said. "Beach walk with C.J."

I got her bag out of my car, and walked it over to where she was parked. She took it, gave me a peck on my cheek, and drove away while I watched, fuming. She could fire me, that was her prerogative, but I could also call Frank Velutto and tell him the whole story. I was thinking I should, and be done with it.

*

Roberto was waiting at the house when I got back. He was looking a little forlorn, sitting on the front step. "Why didn't you let yourself in?" I asked.

"The key's not there," he said. He was right. I'd given the key I usually stash behind a shutter to Barbara. That would be my next excuse to check on her.

"Come on in," I said, and we entered the house and went to the kitchen for a Coke. "Want to go with me to pick up my new car?"

"Seriously?"

"Yeah," I said. "Taurus SHO, brand new, three hundred sixty five horsepower with a turbo."

"Jeez," he said.

"We have some work to do first, if you're up for it. I have a load of soaking wet gear in the back of the BMW."

"OK," he said. We retrieved the nylon duffel and laid the contents out on the back patio to dry in the sun. I had low expectations for any of it, but Roberto worked it over, piece by piece, while I dried the sawed-off shotgun and oiled it as well as I could. It looked like it would be fine. My "Lupo", as they called it in the gangster movies.

"The Mac is shot, and so are your X10 boxes," he said.

"I can get new X10's through the mail," I said.

"I don't know about this distance microphone thing," he said.

"No problem, it's a piece of crap anyway," I said. "Hey…did you do anything about that thing you called me about? That guy and the emails?"

Roberto was inspecting my jeweler's drill. It was a non-electric model that you cranked by hand. "Yeah, I took care of it," he said. "This thing may work—the mechanism is sealed."

I laid out my lock-picking tools. I had used just a few at the self-storage unit, but now that I had them all out everything looked fine, as they were basically all metal with a few plastic wedges for persuading car windows to let me in with a hook. I would need to pick up another spray can of graphite—the one in the bag had survived, but it was almost empty. The shotgun shells were the old-school, paper-sleeved kind, and they were soaked. There was a wet box of ammo for the baby Glock, but it was 9mm anyway, the wrong caliber for my new Glock, which was a .45. The bullets themselves would still be usable, if I ever got the gun back.

We lingered over the gear for about an hour, and talked about how the new school year was going. Roberto said he was already bored. I told him boredom was the enemy, especially for someone his age, and he should lobby to get into advanced placement classes. Vero Beach High was all right, but it was huge, and kids got lost there. If I had the money, I'd send him to St. Edwards, on the island. I suddenly felt guilty about blowing forty grand on a new car, but it was too late now.

*

Roberto asked me to drive with the convertible top down, but the midday sun was too intense, and even with the breeze it was insufferable. I pulled over to put the top back up—just in time, as a mini-storm had us in its sights and blasted the car with a sudden torrent of rain. Intense, small downpours are common this time of year, and the rain line is so clearly defined you can be sitting on the beach in the bright sun while people fifty yards away are getting drenched. We waited by the side of the road until it passed, and then continued on to the Ford dealership which had been missed by the storm entirely.

The salesman cracked jokes while we processed the paperwork, which was miraculously without any last-minute surprises or add-ons. I was sporting my Glock again, just to keep it real. He threw in a set of floor mats, which I had thought were included anyway, and he took one last try at selling me a service contract, but I declined. He said someone from the dealership would drive the Beemer back to the house, so that would be taken care of, and Roberto and I could just enjoy my new ride. The guy was actually very nice and professional, although somebody needed to do a cologne intervention. I carefully wrote out a check, and he congratulated me and took us outside to where the car was parked.

The SHO was a fearsome beast under the hood, but was modest enough on the exterior to pass for a family car. I liked that combination—power when I wanted it, with the ability to blend in. Roberto got in the passenger's seat to check out the electronics while the salesman took my phone and sat in the driver's seat. He said he could pair the phone with the car, and I could call people just by saying I wanted to call them. The two of them busied themselves inside while I walked around the exterior and checked it out. I noticed a tiny spot of goo on the front grille. Like any new car owner, I got a tissue out of my pocket to make it perfect.

I leaned over, and a bee stung me on the top of my head. A huge plate glass window in the showroom building behind us exploded into a million tiny shards, showering fragments into the palmetto shrubs below.

"Get down!" I yelled to Roberto and the salesman. I ran over to the passenger side and pushed Roberto down to the floor. He let out a yelp of fear, and the salesman opened the driver's side door and sprinted across the lot, away from us, as fast as his legs would carry him. People inside the showroom were yelling, and I crouched down next to Roberto, out of the line of fire, I hoped. It wasn't a bee—it was a gunshot, and the slug had nicked my scalp as it flew by and vaporized the plate glass window. I took a cautious look over the hood of the SHO, being careful not to poke my head up too far like a squirrel in a shooting gallery. There was no one—just rows of new cars shimmering in the heat. The shot must have been taken from a considerable distance. A sniper rifle? I got back into my crouch. A long minute passed, and there was no second shot. Whoever had taken the first one had missed his chance, and was probably long gone.

People came out of the building and gathered around us and the car. They would be in sight of the shooter if he was still there, but my intuition said no. I got into the driver's seat, started the ignition, and lowered the window as the sales manager came over.

"What the hell was that all about?" he said.

"I don't know," I said. "Maybe a stray bullet."

"Well, if you were about an inch taller, it would have killed you. Look at your head."

I felt my scalp. The hair was warm and sticky. The bullet had grazed the skin, and scalp wounds usually bleed like crazy, so this one didn't seem bad as there was only a small trickle of blood.

"You want a towel?" he asked. I said no, and we drove out the entrance to Highway 1.

*

I took Roberto directly home from the dealership. He regained his color after a while and wanted to drive around and enjoy the new car, but I had other plans. Also, I needed to see his parents.

I dropped him off, and after he went inside his house I caught Gustavo, his dad, in the driveway. He was washing his car, but when he saw my expression, he put the hose down and turned the spigot off.

"Everything OK, Vince?"

"Not really." I told him what had happened, and explained that even though Roberto might think so, it hadn't been a stray bullet. I apologized profusely, and I didn't expect any forgiveness. If your son almost got shot because he was hanging around with some risk-taking, ex-jailbird you wouldn't feel so good about it either. Gustavo said he'd talk to Roberto about it, and I said that was a good idea as the more times kids could talk about a traumatic experience the quicker it faded into history. Roberto's mother was out shopping, which was fine with me because I didn't have the guts to apologize to her too—she had a habit of wildly gesturing with whatever she was holding while she talked, and if it was a kitchen knife, I could end up looking like steak tartare.

*

The guys from the dealership dropped off the BMW in my driveway, and I went right to it and got the MacBook. My head wound didn't hurt, but it had distracted me, and I had forgotten about the two active tracking bugs. It would have been smart to know if either of them was at the Ford dealership when I'd been shot at, but now it was too late. I opened the computer and started the tracking program. C.J.'s van was at his house, where I'd last seen it. The minivan could have easily been at the Ford place and returned by now to C.J.'s house. The Lexus was in Lake Wales, parked in the storage unit. More than an hour had passed so it was possible, just barely, that someone could have driven it back from Vero in that time. I couldn't rule out either one. I was leaning toward C.J. because he might have a motive, if Barbara had told him more than she'd let on about our night at the hotel. But that was probably my Catholic guilt talking.

I entered the house and checked myself out in the bathroom mirror; the wound was little more than a scratch. I washed it out, combed my hair, and decided it would take care of itself as the bleeding had stopped. I gathered up the gear that Roberto and I had set out to dry, and restocked the duffel, including some fresh shells for the Lupo. With any luck I wouldn't have to use them, but I had decided to drive back to Tampa, and this time I'd be prepared, especially if someone was shooting at me. I packed juices and snacks in a cooler, put several days' worth of clothes in a gym bag, peeled off a few hundreds from my stash, set the house alarm and took off in the new SHO. The tires squealed on the way out of my driveway like in the movies. I could hardly believe I owned the car. It was beefier than the BMW, and the contoured seat fit my frame perfectly. I was already smitten with it, and even on the boring Florida roads I got a semi-erotic jolt from the precision and power.

Highway 60 is a straight shot west until you get to Twenty Mile Curve, a thirty-degree bend to the northwest that was a familiar spot to EMTs, until they widened the road a few years back. Drivers lulled by the monotony would miss the one-and-only curve, and go flying into the saw grass. The bend was several miles ahead, so I decided it was time to see how fast my new toy would go.

The cruisers at the Sheriff's department were Crown Vics, and could do an easy one-twenty, but above that they would rattle. In most cases that was plenty of speed as the bad guys didn't own anything faster—drivers who could afford Ferraris were more likely to be radiologists than crooks. The new SHO breezed past one-twenty like it was just getting warmed up. It had the performance package, which meant that the tires would cost twice as much as normal tires when I replaced them, but the car stuck to the road like gum under a desk. One-thirty, one-thirty-five, still not stressing and the engine seemed to love the high RPMs. The groves and ranches along the highway became a green blur. At one-forty the revs topped out. I took my foot off the accelerator, and eased back to the speed limit—I didn't need a four hundred dollar speeding ticket.

The adrenaline rush from speeding was preferable to the adrenaline rush from getting shot at. I reviewed my enemy list as I took in the roadside scenery. C.J. Butler, aside from my night with Barbara, had no motive I could think of, and my guilt had subsided. Barbara couldn't have said anything to him, or there would have been *some* reaction when we'd met at his door. Le didn't know I existed. Barbara? I wasn't sure where Barbara fit in to everything, but she'd have to be a real praying mantis to kill me off after the night we'd had, so I took her off the list. There was a long list of people I'd busted over the years, and maybe one of them had just been paroled. Philip was a possibility, but my intuition on Philip was that he was more likely to be thinking about removing Barbara and getting his father back than killing some tough guy, even if I'd given him the Clint Squint at his house.

But if I didn't have a motive for Philip, I did have something else—opportunity. It was Saturday, and Philip could be anywhere. He could have boosted a car and driven to Vero. It was possible he had access to the Lexus, or that he just took it whether his parents knew or not. And, he had access to a long-range rifle—D.B.'s, the Browning with the scope that I'd seen in his gun cabinet. If Philip could hotwire my Taurus then he could also pick a simple cabinet lock—I could do both at his age. My brother and I used to pick the lock on our father's liquor cabinet every week and water down his booze so that he wouldn't get hammered and smack my mother around. It worked for a while, but eventually he just drank more.

I decided I would stop in Lake Wales and check out the Lexus to see if the engine was warm, which might still be noticeable even if it had an hour to cool off. I breezed through town, and stopped at the self-storage unit. The Lexus was warm, but so was everything else; anything that was stored in a corrugated metal bay would be slow-cooking like a pot roast. I opened the hood and felt the engine, but I couldn't tell any difference.

I made it to Sunset Park in less than an hour. I stopped the car at a convenience store and checked the listening bugs. According to the program, nothing had been recorded for over two hours, so the family was not in the house unless they were sleeping. I snapped the computer shut. Now was my chance to get into the house before anyone returned.

Hibiscus Pond Drive was dead quiet, and hotter than hell. The temperature was well into the nineties, and tall thunderhead clouds were forming from the evaporation over the bay. A good rain shower would provide some cover, but though it looked like it would rain soon, it was still sunny. I parked the SHO on the street next to the Johannsens' driveway and looked around. No Hawkeye, for once. Some of those older guys in Florida spent more time outside tending their grass then they did inside, whatever the weather. Growing up in Vermont we used to judge a man by his woodpile—down here we check out his lawn.

I took out my lock tools and walked over to the back of the house. My X10 Blocker was dead, so there was no way I could disable the alarm system except for the old-fashioned method. I found the junction box where the phone line met the building, and snipped it with shielded wire cutters. None of the neighboring houses could see me, which was good, because I had just committed a crime and was about to commit a second one by breaking and entering. That sort of activity is something you generally leave off the application when you renew your P.I. license.

The Medeco lock on the back door was easier this time; I got lucky on our second date. I entered the house without sounding the alarm and went directly to the man-cave. The gun cabinet lock popped open in a few seconds. The hunting rifle was inside, right where it should be.

I tried to work out the timeline, and as far as I could figure, Philip would have had to replace the hunting rifle in the cabinet no longer than an hour ago. But the last recorded sound in the house had been over two hours ago. There was no way he could have entered the house and replaced it without making any sound; I had a microphone right above the cabinet in the man-cave, and it would have picked something up—Philip had no reason to worry about making noise. I still couldn't quite take him off my list.

I left as unnoticed as I'd come; nobody was around the neighborhood, anywhere. However, this time I'd left a hell of a trail at the house; the first time they picked up the phone or tried the Internet, they'd realize that the line was dead. It might take a while—for all I knew they might only use the phone line for DSL service and the alarm, and use cell phones for everything else. But either way, they'd soon realize they had been burgled.

*

There was a Best Western not far from the Johannsen house on Dale Mabry Avenue, and I turned the Taurus into the driveway. It wasn't the Hyatt, but the lobby was clean and nice, and I had nobody to impress. A slender blonde woman checked me in—and checked me out at the same time, or so it seemed. I asked her if there was any decent food in the area, and she suggested the Bonefish Grill, right down the road. "It's a chain, but they have good oysters," she said. She had a nice Southern accent, which you don't always hear in Florida. "Ahm very picky about mah oysters. And mah men." She gave me a wink that would have made Hugh Hefner blush. Maybe getting shot in the head was good for the sex appeal.

I checked into my room and got a quick shower. My plan was to monitor the MacBook, wait for Le and Philip to get home, and then take it from there. I'd eavesdrop on them if they talked, and I also thought I might do a little peeking in the windows after dark, although that might be futile as they probably closed their blinds like most people. I could be surprised though—I've seen some amazing displays in my police and P.I. career. Some people either really don't care or just like to strut their stuff, which a lot of the time ain't worth strutting.

The Bonefish Grill was noisy with patrons, but the host found me a relatively quiet corner table and I was able to listen to the audio track on my laptop with earbuds. The waitress brought a dozen Apalachicola oysters from the Florida Panhandle, which is one of the few places in the country where they still harvest oysters from small boats. They were briny and sweet, and I dipped them alternately in cocktail sauce and a shallot-and-vinegar mignonette. I tried to pace myself and make them last, but they were gone in a few minutes even though I felt like I'd exercised tremendous restraint. The waitress caught my eye, and I gave her the thumbs up for another dozen.

I was wishing that Barbara was across the table. I had a suspicion that she'd like oysters. I thought about calling her, but that was crazy.

She had a lot on her agenda, and I needed to respect her wish to be left alone. If C.J. had promised to keep her safe then he goddamn well better do that, but I felt helpless, and that wasn't my natural state. The whole situation made me highly anxious, and the sooner I figured out where the bullets were coming from, the better.

My earbuds suddenly crackled with conversation from the Johannsen house—originating from the kitchen, according to the computer. It was in real time, so someone must have just arrived home. Le's and Philip's voices were coming in clearly, and I could hear every word. Unfortunately, every word was in Vietnamese.

Philip spoke fluidly and quickly. He must have been speaking Vietnamese with his mother from a young age. Some immigrants avoided their native language, some cherished it, and Le was no doubt of the latter type. Their voices became louder, and Philip's cracked once or twice. This must be their pattern when D.B. was away, because I had only heard English spoken when he was there. The conversation turned into an argument, and in the heat of it Philip switched to English.

No way, I'm not going! I went last week. You can drive yourself.

It will be dark when we come home. I cannot drive in the dark. Her voice, accented and calm.

Mom, come on. It's Saturday, that shoots the whole night. This is crazy.

You must respect our customs, Philip. Go change your shirt. We leave in twenty minutes, she said. Bingo.

I called the waitress over and told her I had an emergency and to get me the check. She returned in minutes with the bill and the second dozen Apalachicolas in a Styrofoam box. I told her she was a goddess and gave her cash, with a generous tip.

*

Ten minutes later I was parked at the other end of Hibiscus Pond Drive from the Johannsen house. I'd found a sandy pull-off, out of sight, where anyone who left would have to pass by. I had the Styrofoam box open and was savoring the last of my slippery little bivalves. Someone really ought to invent a drive-through oyster bar. I had the laptop on, and I heard the front door shut as they left. I didn't have a tracker on their vehicle, so I'd have to just stay back and do my best—the early evening traffic should be about right. When you're tailing someone you hope for enough traffic to provide cover, but not so much that it gets in your way.

They passed me in the white Ford Transit van, with "Le's Vending" on it. That should be easy to spot. I pulled out after they had taken a turn and stayed about half a block back as we took a series of turns and finally turned north on South Westshore Boulevard, a leafy residential street with no stop lights, which was good. So far this was easy. Philip was driving, traveling just above the speed limit. I kept him in sight as we traversed the city center, and Philip picked up speed as we passed along the west side of Tampa International Airport. He took an exit, and we ended up going west on the Memorial Highway. I decided to let him get ahead some as the road was mostly clear and straight, and I'd be able to see if he took a turn. The navigation map in the SHO gave me advance notice of any stoplights, but I wasn't very adept at reading the display and still keeping my eyes on the road. It was no wonder that these distractions caused accidents, although with a navigation system you'd at least know exactly *where* you crashed, assuming you were still alive.

A white Buick sedan nosed part way into the highway. It paused to let Philip pass, and then lumbered out in front of the traffic, and I had to slow down. The road ahead curved to the right, and I temporarily lost sight of the Transit van. The Buick driver was now taking up both lanes. I could see the outline of two gray-blue heads just barely above the headrests—Grampy and Grammy, out for a spin. They were going twenty, and so was everyone behind them, while Philip lost us. I finally roared past the old couple, and the driver flipped me the bird. I would have flipped one right back, but I was too busy looking for the Transit, which was nowhere in sight.

I could see well down the road ahead—nothing. There were two other choices; Town 'N Country Boulevard on the right, and Bay Pointe Drive on the left. I made a quick decision and swung left onto Bay Pointe, making the tires squeal as I crossed the highway. I immediately realized it was the wrong choice; there was no sign of the van. I made a fast U-turn, and sped back to the highway. I turned hard onto Town 'N Country, cutting off a Camaro and earning another digital salute. I punched the SHO, and sped north through a neighborhood of double-wides, pickups, and barking dogs. I followed the road for a half mile until it met West Hillsborough Avenue, a main thoroughfare. No Transit van. Once again it could have gone in three possible directions. Goddamn it. I had become so dependent on my trackers and tech gear I couldn't even tail someone properly. I pulled the SHO into the parking lot of a dry cleaner to regroup.

When in doubt, Google. I opened the laptop, got Google Maps running and typed in everything I could think of; "Asian", "restaurant", "Vietnamese", and came up with several restaurants, but they were in the wrong direction. Maybe they were going to see friends in the area. Or maybe Philip had spotted me and lost me, on purpose. I tried to think back to what I'd heard on the bug, when they'd spoken in English at the house.

No way. I went last week. You can drive yourself. Respect our Customs.

Went to what? Church? Or a temple, or whatever the Vietnamese called it? Perhaps that was what I was looking for.

It took me one try to find it on Google. "Phap Vien Minh Dang Quang", a Buddhist temple, was all of three hundred yards north on Town 'N Country Boulevard, right across Hillsborough Avenue. I started the ignition and drove up the road to a stretch where there was a long parking lot on the right, adjacent to a yellow stucco archway with Spanish tiles on the roof. The name of the temple was written in red letters across the front of the arch, and beyond was a park-like grove of pines, palms, and fruit trees. There were several structures, one of which appeared to be a worship building. I drove slowly past Philip's van, now parked and vacant, and found a spot at the far end of the row of spaces. Other cars were arriving, and neatly-dressed Asian people got out and entered the temple. Some of them strolled around the grounds, and some entered the building to get out of the late-day heat. I waited with the motor off and my windows down; the heat was breaking and the evening breeze felt good.

The soft ringing of a gong resonated through the park. People who were strolling in the gardens now turned for the largest building, a stucco-and-tile job that looked like a cross between a pagoda and a Taco Bell. I decided to do some strolling myself.

The gardens were a mix of hard sand and patches of Bermuda grass, bordered by concrete walkways. Three enormous sculptures of Buddhas stood outside: one seated behind a fountain, one on a pink shell, and a third that lay on a concrete dais, under a canopy. Pots of colorful flowers were everywhere, and strings of yellow and red flags ran between the pines and palms. I was admiring the big supine Buddha when a short man in a neat white jacket appeared at my side.

"Would you like to join us?" he asked.

"Thanks," I said, "Maybe later…just enjoying the scenery."

"You Buddhist?"

"Catholic," I said. I'd studied a little about Buddhism in school, and it sounded like a lot of sitting around. Not like Catholicism where we were too busy either sinning or atoning for our sins to sit around much.

"Please feel free to join us."

"Thanks," I said. The man entered the building.

There wasn't much else to see outside besides the three Buddhas. I hadn't been in a church since Glory tried to drag me there a few times right after we were married, and finally gave up. I decided I'd go in, and hoped I could just stay in the back, unnoticed, which was probably not possible as I was about a foot taller than anyone I'd seen except Philip.

It was cool inside, and although the grounds were humble, some real money had been spent on the building. The entry hall was wood-paneled, with flowers in vases and several smaller statues of the Buddha. Two big doors led to an area where worshippers sat on square cushions, with a few rows of folding chairs in the back for the older ones. Three men in robes sat cross-legged on an altar that was covered in a yellow and red carpet with no other decor except for two pots of flowers. The only sound came from the trickling of water over smooth rocks in an artificial waterfall, behind the worshippers. I took a chair in the rearmost row, and watched. One of the priests was chanting, and the congregation chanted in response, all in Vietnamese. Philip and his mother sat on cushions in the front. The kid looked as bored as I was when my mother took me to Mass.

One of the priests said something, and then stood up and pointed directly at me. I froze. The entire congregation turned around, bowed, and greeted me in unison; it sounded like "Ciao, mung bean!" I smiled, and bowed in return. Jeez. I couldn't have been more conspicuous if I'd been playing the accordion. I briefly caught Philip's eye, and thought I saw a flicker of recognition. It was only a day before that he'd sighted me down the end of a gun barrel. If he did recognize me, I was fine with that. I wanted him off-balance; maybe I'd learn something.

Those Buddhists sure were a low-key bunch—no swinging chalices, no communion, no organ, no choir, no tabernacles, no albs, no vestments, no chasubles, no holy water, no rosaries, no crucifixes—just three laid-back guys and some chanting and bowing. I was enjoying the simple beauty of it, but I decided I'd best slip out the back before they decided to baptize me or something.

I got into my car and tried to think about what to do next. I'd learned that Le and Philip went to church—big deal. If I'd had another tracker, I could have attached it to the Transit van, but I didn't have one, and I was tired of following people around the old-fashioned way, it was too much work. I backed onto Town 'N Country and shifted into drive.

There was a loud noise as something hit the car, and I watched in the mirror as the rear window shattered. The glass held together, but there was a walnut-sized impact hole surrounded by jagged fissures that extended outward. A smooth, round stone sat on the trunk lid. It looked exactly like one of the rocks in the artificial waterfall I'd seen in the temple.

I stepped on the parking brake and got out. Someone was running back through the yellow entry arch toward the main building. It was Philip, and the little fucker had just thrown a rock at my brand-new car. My first instinct was to go inside and kick his ass, but that would solve nothing and the window would still be broken. I was starting to *really* not like that kid.

I decided instead to drive back to their house and see if I could get to the mother—alone. Maybe she would talk to me and maybe not, but I was thinking I would just lay out a few cards and see what happened. And if Philip answered the door instead of his mother, he'd better have dental insurance because I'd be sorely tempted to rearrange his bicuspids.

*

I was back in my pull-off spot on Hibiscus Pond Drive when my phone rang. It was Roberto.

"Vince…" he started.

"Hey," I said.

"I can't get in to the computer at the Johannsens' house. I was in looking around for a while after you left, but it went dead."

"No problem," I said. "I had to cut the line, so there won't be any way to get in until they fix it."

"Oh," he said.

"Did you find anything?"

"Yeah," he said. "A lot of money."

"What do you mean?"

"They have a lot of money. I got into a program that was hidden. It links to an external server, maybe in the woman's office. From there I got into a bunch of bank accounts. They have money all over the world."

"Is it in their name?"

"Some of it. There was a little under David Butler Johannsen, like a hundred thousand, and over a million in his name and Le Quyen Johannsen's joint name. There's about two hundred thousand under "Le's Vending". Then I found a lot more under "Empex Import/Export LLC", in the Cayman Islands and a bunch of banks in Europe. I totaled it all up."

"How much?"

"Like, thirty million dollars," he said.

"That's a lot of quarters," I said. We were quiet for a while.

"I'm not supposed to be talking to you," he said.

"Uh-oh," I said. "Your mom must be pissed."

"It's not your fault," he said. "You said it was a stray bullet."

"It might have been."

"Oh," he said, and went silent.

"Roberto…don't worry too much. I screwed up and I'm sorry. These things blow over, and it'll be OK."

"I don't know. She's, you know, she's crazy sometimes. She says I can't come over anymore, and she wants me to give your wife's computer back."

OK, now I felt like shit. I had some fences to mend with Roberto's parents. I knew I would feel the same way in their shoes, and they were right, I should be extra cautious if I was going to spend time with him, and if I could worm my way back into the family's good graces, I would be more careful. I really liked the kid, and I believed that hanging out with me was good for him. It was good for us both.

"Keep the computer; I'll talk with your mom."

"Vince?"

"Yeah?"

"There's some weird stuff on it."

"Like a virus?" I said.

"No, different."

"Like what?"

"Some stuff I found. I don't understand it all. I guess I'll show it to you when we can talk again."

"You relax, Roberto. I'll talk to your folks again. I'll run up a big bill at the florist. Watch out, I'm going to totally spoil your mom."

"She likes flowers."

"Roberto, see what you can find on Empex Import/Export, OK?"

"OK."

"'Night," I said, and we hung up.

*

Less than a minute later the Transit van turned into Hibiscus Pond Drive and passed by me. I opened the laptop and turned on the audio. I heard their front door open and shut, but no voices. There was some bustling around in the kitchen. I hadn't seen their faces when they'd passed me, and I wondered if both or just one of them had returned home. That would explain the lack of conversation—or—perhaps they weren't speaking to each other on purpose.

There was one way to find out. I drove the SHO to the end of the road and parked next to Hawkeye's driveway. It was around ten in the evening, and only a few of the houses in the neighborhood showed any light—if there was any, it was the blue flicker of television screens. I walked up to the front door of the Johannsen house and knocked, rather than ringing the bell. She answered the door.

"Mrs. Johannsen—I'm sorry to trouble you at this time of night, but I need to ask you some questions."

"You police?"

"I'm not police, but this is about Philip. Is he home?"

"He is in his room being unhappy." She gave me a shrug, like a mother would when she'd had a long day. Le was short with rounded features and a pretty face, but her eyes were hard, like polished stone. "We can talk outside," she said, and she stepped out into the evening.

"You met Barbara Butler," I said.

"Barbara Butler," she said, without acknowledging.

"I worked for her. Someone drove to Vero Beach and tried to shoot her, two times. I am concerned that it could be your son."

She showed no reaction. "Philip does not drive."

"Yes, he does," I said. "He just drove you home."

"He does not drive to Vero Beach."

"Does he know how to shoot?"

"No." Her eye flinched, just the tiniest bit.

"You have guns," I said.

"His father has guns. His father is not here."

"I know," I said. "Does that bother Philip?"

"Barbara Butler," she said. "You know my husband is married to Barbara Butler?"

"Yes. Did you know that before?" I said. "That he was married to both of you?"

Until now she hadn't betrayed much, but her body language suddenly changed. She was pissed. "My husband is two people," she said, "but he can only have one wife."

I began to say something, but decided not to.

"You followed us to the temple?" she said.

"Yes," I said.

"You leave us alone. You go away now," she said, and went back into the house.

*

I started the SHO and drove back to where Hibiscus Pond Drive met a cross street. It was still hot out and I had the windows down, enjoying the sultry air. The radio was playing the Allman Brothers' version of "Trouble No More," and I turned up the volume while I sat at the intersection, processing what I'd learned. Le had dodged and weaved like a welterweight in the one minute of conversation we'd had.

She had let one thing slip, which was that she was not pleased with D.B.'s dual marital arrangements. There was resentment there, and I wondered if it extended to Barbara. But Le was so diminutive I could hardly imagine her handling a hunting rifle with a heavy scope—those things had a kick that would have broken her shoulder. This time I had a potential motive, but not the means.

I was deep in thought at the intersection when a vehicle roared up behind me and slammed on the brakes, nearly rear-ending my car. It was the white Transit van. The driver honked loudly, and I pulled out into the cross street. It followed, right on my tail. Philip? Fuck you, kid. I accelerated.

I turned onto Bay-To-Bay Boulevard in the direction of Dale Mabry Highway where the Best Western was, but I didn't want him following me to the hotel so I kept going, past the turn. At fifty miles an hour the Transit van still right behind. He accelerated and swung wildly into the left lane and passed me. *Good riddance*, I thought, and I almost turned around, but my eye caught the shimmer of a streetlight in my fractured rear window, and I changed my mind. Someone needed to teach the punk a lesson. I punched the accelerator of the SHO and got it up to sixty-five—too fast for the quiet residential neighborhood.

I saw his taillights a few blocks ahead, in the direction of Hillsborough Bay. Fat, intermittent raindrops began to smack against my windshield, and the wipers automatically turned on and swept them away. The taillights were closer as I sped under the overpass of the Crosstown Expressway and swung a hard left onto Bayshore Boulevard, north toward the city. The boulevard was flanked by expensive homes on the left and the bay on the right, and the pavement was now becoming slick with rain.

The traffic opened and I accelerated. I began to close the gap. Up ahead heavier rain was sweeping in, but I wanted to catch him—I hit the accelerator again, hard, and was finally right behind him when his taillights disappeared into a wall of water. The rain hit my car with such force that the windshield went liquid and I was suddenly driving blind, at almost ninety miles an hour. I stomped on the brakes—too hard, and too late. The car lost traction on the flooded highway, and hydroplaned in a dizzying pirouette. I was no longer driving, I was watching. A slideshow of destruction began to play as the SHO caromed off a light pole, sideswiped a row of portable toilets, skidded across an intersection into a low wall, flipped onto its roof and finally came to rest. I was still strapped in, hanging upside down in the seat while the Allman Brothers blasted out guitar riffs to the beat of the raindrops on the undercarriage. Around me were the front and side airbags, now deflated and flaccid. I couldn't draw a breath, and the last thing I remember before I passed out was the sweet, sickening taste of blood in my mouth.

SUNDAY

"YOU'RE AWAKE." A nurse was adjusting an IV bag on a stainless steel pole.

"Yes," I said. "What's in the bag?" It hurt to talk. Everything hurt.

"Saline, a splash of oxycodone and a twist of lemon." He held up a pen about a foot from my face. "Can you see this?" He was a burly African American guy in light green scrubs with a name tag that said "Marcus". He looked like he could pick me up and carry me around like a bag of groceries if he wanted to.

"I can see it," I said. Fragments of the night before were trickling back into my consciousness, and the pain in my body was joined by the painful knowledge that I had just royally fucked up.

"Is it in focus?"

"Yeah."

"That's good," he said. "You remember anything?"

"Sort of. I don't remember how I got here, wherever here is."

"You're in Tampa General. You could have walked from where you crashed, it's right down the road."

"Shit," I said. I was thinking about the SHO. I wondered if it had survived. Meanwhile I was taking inventory of what hurt. So far, breathing, talking and thinking. "So I'm not dead."

"You have a few cracked ribs and a concussion."

"I thought the airbags would take care of that," I said.

"Airbags work for the first thing you hit, then they deflate and you're the airbag," he said. "According to the cops you took out about a quarter mile of Bayshore Boulevard. I'm supposed to call them as soon as you're awake."

"Give me some time to freshen up first, OK?"

He laughed. "If you can make jokes then I think you'll live."

"When can I get out of here?"

"They want to do an MRI, but Radiology is closed on Sunday. You were bleeding when you came in, so they want to check your innards. Tomorrow, at the earliest."

"Shit."

"Relax. You're in the highest-priced hotel in Tampa, and you have a nice view of the bay. The cops will be here soon."

I was going to say something, but I fell back to sleep instead.

*

When I awoke again there was a plainclothes cop in my room, sitting in the visitor's chair. At his feet was my black nylon duffel.

"Doc Edwards, Tampa Police."

"Vince Tanzi," I said.

"Yeah, we looked you up, but I remember you from the papers. I have family over in Vero." He had a crew cut and deep blue eyes—soft, for a cop, although he didn't look too sympathetic. "Your stuff is in the bag. The car is in the impound lot."

"Is it drivable?"

"Ha," he said, "We couldn't measure the skid marks; there weren't any because it was too wet. But our best guess was you were going between eighty and a hundred. I hope you have collision insurance. I saw the receipt. You really just bought the car?"

"Yeah."

"So how come you were going so fast?" he said.

"I was looking for a bathroom," I said. "I had to pee."

He frowned. "You wiped out a bunch of city property along with your car. I was going to let that go because you used to be a cop, but I won't if you start bullshitting me. What're you doing in Tampa?"

"I have a client in Vero who got shot at. There's a connection over here."

"People getting shot at is something for us, not for a P.I. You know that."

"I said the same thing, and the client refused," I said. "Give me your card. I'll call you if I find anything on your turf."

"I don't like it," he said. "By the way, the sawed-off is at the station. They're illegal, you know."

"It has an eighteen-inch barrel," I said. "It's legal."

He shrugged. "You don't look so good."

"I don't feel so good," I said. "Do me a favor. Pass me my laptop, OK?"

"Laptop?"

"You don't have it?"

"It's not in the bag," he said. "There wasn't any laptop in the car. There were a bunch of kids hanging around when we got there. Your laptop is probably history."

"Goddamn it," I said. I'd had the computer only a little longer than I'd had the SHO.

"Try Craigslist," he said. "The fences know better, but the kids use it all the time."

"I will," I said. "But now I think I have to go back to sleep." He left, and I drifted off to my room at the Oxycodone Hotel.

*

I was Googling on the phone when Marcus came into the room and scanned the various machines I was hooked up to. "You're getting some of your color back," he said.

"I feel a little better."

"I've got you pretty juiced up on the oxycodone. When you leave here they'll give you a prescription for that in pill form. Same stuff except the brand name is OxyContin. You got to watch out for that shit, you can get strung out on it."

"Marcus, I was a deputy for twenty five years. I know what it does."

"Rib fractures hurt for a long time, sometimes six weeks," he said. "You can ice it, but it doesn't help a lot."

I was navigating with the phone on Craigslist, under "Computers for Sale". There it was, right at the top of the list. The same model, same specs—an "almost new" MacBook Pro for a price of about three quarters of what I'd just paid for it. I called the guy, taking longer to dial than I should have as the phone's small keyboard and the IV drugs were a challenging mix. It rang four times.

"'Lo," he said.

"Still got the MacBook?"

"Yah."

"I'll take it," I said.

"Cash," he said. A tough guy. He sounded about twelve.

"No problem. Where and when?"

"There's a Seven Eleven on East Davis Boulevard," he said. "I can be there in five minutes."

"Where's East Davis Boulevard?" I said to Marcus, covering the phone.

"We're pretty much on it," he said.

"Give me a half hour," I said to the kid. "I have to go to the ATM."

"OK," he said. I hung up.

"I have to go," I said to Marcus.

"No you don't," he said.

"Some kid stole my laptop, right out of my car. I just bought it two days ago. The little shit put it on Craigslist, and I found it. Sorry, but I'm leaving."

Marcus smiled. "Not without your clothes you ain't. They're locked up in the closet." He pointed to a wardrobe. "You had a gun on your belt, so they locked everything up. Security is supposed to pick up the gun, but they haven't shown up yet."

"OK Marcus, you win," I said. He finished his rounds and left the room.

I unhooked the various sensors they'd taped to my skin and peeled off the tape that held the IV needle to my hand. I took it out slowly, feeling nothing, thanks to the painkiller. Sitting up was a shock; I was dizzy and unsteady. I swung my legs out to meet the floor and did a wobbly cha-cha over to the duffel bag. I opened my lock-picking kit and took out a tension wrench and a Peterson P-knife-C. I continued my drunken tango over to the wardrobe. Fortunately, it was a cheap foreign lock, and even in my drugged condition I popped it easily.

I called a cab company while I dressed, and they said they'd have one at the main entrance in ten minutes. I splashed some water in my face and looked in the mirror. That was a mistake. But on the plus side, there would be no problem scaring the shit out of the kid.

Marcus caught me in the hallway as I tried to make my way out of the hospital without passing out.

"You sneaky son of a bitch," he said.

"It's been nice knowing you, Marcus," I said. "Gotta run."

"Where are you going?"

"To get my computer. Then…home I guess."

"You are going to hurt like hell in a couple hours," he said. "Wait here." He went down the hall and came back in a few moments. He handed me a small white envelope. "There's two Vicodins in there just to keep you alive until you get a prescription. Don't tell anyone or I get fired."

"Thanks." I wobbled down the hall and found an elevator. Ten minutes later I was out in front of the hospital looking like I'd fallen down a coal shaft. My shirt was filthy, and there were drops of dried blood across the front of it. The cab was waiting, and the driver tossed his cigarette butt into a banana shrub when he saw me.

"Dude, you sure you're OK to leave this place?" he asked.

"You know where there's a Seven Eleven on East Davis?"

"Yeah. Five minutes from here, max. You need help getting in?"

"I'll manage," I said, and I got into the back seat as he put the flag down on the meter.

*

There were a couple of cars at the Seven Eleven, but it was Sunday and it was hot, so people were either at the beach or in their houses in front of the air conditioning. We parked next to a dumpster and waited for a few minutes until a kid wearing a backpack rode into the lot on his bike. I waved him over. He looked about Roberto's age, and was skinny, with spiked, reddish hair and a pasty complexion. Even though I wasn't feeling any pain, I was madder than hell when I thought of him and his friends swiping the laptop out of my wrecked car while I hung upside down in the seat belt. He propped his bike on a kickstand and walked over as I lowered the window. My driver must have sensed something was up, and he excused himself and got out of the car for a smoke.

"Let's see it," I said. The kid handed me the laptop through the window. I opened it up and turned it on. There were my programs, including the trackers and the listening bugs. It was mine all right.

"Where's the money, mister?" he said. "You said you had cash."

"You're out of luck, kid," I answered. "This is my computer. So fuck off."

He pulled an automatic out of his backpack and aimed it at me, through the rolled-down window. It was a Raven .25, a cheap piece of crap that would just as likely blow up in your hand as kill somebody. But it was still a gun.

"Hold on there," I said. "I have the money." I got out of the car, slowly. He backed away, but still held the gun close—too close—and I snatched it and twisted his arm behind his back. The boy screamed, and two guys who were at the pumps getting gas turned to look at us. I picked the kid up off his feet and held him over my head, then tossed him into an empty dumpster. He screamed again as he hit the metal floor. I got his bike and threw it in on top of him, and then I lobbed the gun up onto the high canopy over the gas pumps. The two guys who were filling up their cars stared at me, open-mouthed.

"New sheriff in town," I said to them.

My driver stubbed out his cigarette as I walked back to the cab.

"How much to drive me to Vero Beach?" I said.

He thought about it. "Two hundred plus the gas?" he asked.

"You got it," I said. "I have to stop at my hotel first."

"You ain't gonna stiff me, too, are you?"

"No. They allow you to do a long trip like that?"

"My shift ends in an hour. I keep the cab at my house on Sundays, and I got a way to roll the odometer back. So we're cool," he said.

"Christ," I said. "I think I'm in the middle of a crime wave." I settled in the back of the cab and we turned toward the Best Western. Old Smoky began to chatter about the Bucs, the weather and so on, but I was sleepy and not paying attention. I knew I would be paying for my punk-tossing episode when the drugs wore off.

*

I gathered my stuff from the hotel room and checked out. The blonde woman who'd flirted with me was behind the front desk again. She did a double take at my appearance.

"You all right?"

"Yeah," I said.

"Y'all didn't stay in your room last night, did you?"

"No ma'am," I said.

"I bet you're wishin' you did now." She batted her heavily mascaraed eyelashes. "I wouldn't have left no marks on you, neither."

She blew me a kiss on the way out. Too bad I felt like I'd been crushed under a rock, or I might have reciprocated.

*

We stopped at the Tampa P.D. building downtown, and I negotiated with the desk sergeant to get my shotgun back. I showed him on the web where the Florida gun regs were, and he got a tape measure and measured the barrel. He finally handed it over with no apologies, just a dirty look like I was going to do bad things with it and he would regret this. I was just glad to have it back; it's kind of a talisman, and is my weapon of last resort.

I wanted to sleep, but my driver wanted to talk. It was nice being chauffeured, although Old Smoky didn't exactly look like the chauffeur-type. He wore a grey ponytail and mirrored aviator glasses, and the interior of the car was decorated with POW-MIA stickers with green, yellow, and red stripes. The cab stank of smoke. I asked him a rhetorical question.

"You serve in Vietnam?"

"One-Oh-One Airborne, 1969."

"That rings a bell," I said.

"Hill 937. They called it "Hamburger Hill." The North Vietnamese had a whole regiment up there. I watched our guys die for ten days."

"We won that battle though, right?"

"Yeah, if you call it winning," he said.

"You know anything about PTSD?" I asked.

"I'm living it, mister," he said. "I don't sleep. That's why I drive a cab. They'll let me drive eighteen hours when they're short-handed, and that suits me fine."

"Do you get any treatment?"

"Yeah, I go to the VA, there's a big one in Tampa," he said. "But I been so many times they pretty much gave up. They just want to give you drugs. I'd rather wake up with the cold sweats now and then than live my whole life fucked up on downers."

"Have you ever heard of a kind of PTSD where a guy thinks he's two people? He even sets up two houses, two wives, everything?"

"Yeah, I heard of that, I think I read about it one time. I don't know if it's PTSD though. I used to go to a group where we sat around and told each other how fucked up we all were, as if that was supposed to help. There were some guys there who were pretty psycho, and there were some guys who acted completely normal, but who knows what was in their head. Personally I think you are who you are, and being in a war is only going to make it worse."

I looked out the window at the steamy central Florida landscape. We were getting close to Lake Wales, and I'd be home in a little over an hour. My chest was starting to hurt a lot, and I had the driver pull over at a store so I could get some water to wash down the two Vicodins that Marcus had given me. I slumped in the back seat and waited while he finished his unfiltered Camel. I had a lot on my mind and there were many things I could be doing, but my primary ambition was to get into my own bed.

*

Smoky woke me up when we got to Vero, and I directed him to my house. The Vicodins weren't doing the job; every breath was painful. I paid him off and sent him on his way, then took my gear into the house, stripped, and got into the shower. There were bruises on my left arm that would soon start turning colors, and a band of bruises across my chest where the seatbelt had been. I couldn't raise the soap any higher than my stomach without feeling like someone was knifing me in the chest. I toweled off and made a mental list of what I absolutely had to do before I could go to bed. I decided I really only needed two things; some food, and more drugs. If I didn't have some more of the Vicodin on hand soon, I wouldn't be getting any sleep. I had plenty of drugstore pain medicine in the house, but I needed something that was industrial strength.

I called Tampa General and got nowhere. Marcus was off his shift, and his replacement convinced me that there was no way I could get a prescription until Monday. She said that even then it was dubious, since I'd checked myself out. She recommended I try a twenty-four-hour clinic in Vero, or the emergency room at the hospital.

I dressed in a clean shirt and trousers and eased myself carefully into Glory's BMW. It's a low-slung car, and I wondered, once I got in, if I'd be able to get back out. There was an all-night clinic on the Miracle Mile, and I made it there despite a little Vicodin-induced weaving. If I was still a cop, I would have pulled myself over and administered a breathalyzer.

After two hours in the waiting room filling out my life story in my wobbly handwriting, I realized why they called it a twenty-four-hour clinic; because it takes twenty-four hours to actually see somebody besides the receptionist. I was pretty sure you could wander in there with an amputated leg and they would tell you to hop over to one of the orange plastic chairs and please not bleed on it while you wrote down your insurance information. The room was full of sick and injured people, and according to the receptionist I was in the middle of the queue, and she couldn't tell me for sure when I could see someone. I didn't know if I was going to live that long. I walked back outside into the heat and dialed a number on my phone.

"Sonny, it's Vince Tanzi."

"Dude," he said, "It wasn't me, man, I got an alibi." Sonny was Myra the dispatcher's half-brother and had been one of Vero's biggest cocaine dealers when I had been a cop. He'd done time twice, and as far as I knew he'd retired, because the third time you get busted for coke in Florida they tend to put you away for keeps. He lived on 28th Avenue in Gifford, which a generation ago they called the "colored" section of Vero Beach, and back in the day there had been of steady stream of white kids in their parents' Volvos visiting his place. Cocaine was a white drug; they had the money. Most of the African American and Latino kids had to settle for crack, which was cheaper and far more lethal, although there were plenty of white kids who had overdosed on crack too. It was an equal opportunity killer.

"You're off the hook, Sonny," I said. "But I want your help."

"What?" he said.

"I need some pain meds. I got banged up, and nobody will give me a prescription."

"Whoa," he said. "You got a wire on you or something?"

"No," I said. "I'm serious, and this is personal. A favor."

He laughed. "Come on over, man. I'll fix you up."

I re-inserted myself slowly into the Beemer and drove north on Highway 1, then turned west onto 45th Street and crossed Old Dixie Highway and the railroad tracks. Gifford didn't have much industry left; there was a citrus trucking depot, a middle school, several hundred modest homes, a few stores, some bars and some churches; the neighborhood was slowly being squeezed out of existence by higher-priced housing developments. I would miss it when it was gone; I'd spent a lot of time there when I was with the Sheriff's office, and I knew most of the residents. It had all the problems that come with poverty, but the people looked out for each other, which was something you didn't always see in the gated enclaves over on the barrier island where many Gifford residents worked as the help.

A kid on a motorcycle was leaving Sonny's driveway as I pulled in—part of the supply chain, I figured. Sonny had two pit bulls who greeted me as I walked to the door. They seemed to remember who I was from before, when I'd occasionally visited their owner for professional rather than personal reasons. I didn't have any dog treats, and once they realized I was empty-handed they trotted off to the shade. Sonny answered the door and showed me in. He was watching the Bucs play a team up North, and he had a beer open.

"You look like shit, man," he said.

"Gee, thanks," I said.

"I got you some goods. Fifty OxyContins. These are the forty-milligram ones, so you can take two at a time. Don't take more than six a day, and don't chew them. Just swallow them whole, or they will fuck you up good."

"You should have been a pharmacist, Sonny."

"A pharmacist would stop you at two a day. And he'd only give you ten of them, and when you ran out you'd have to get on your knees and beg for more. This shit is more addictive than any of the stuff I used to deal."

"Trust the big pharma companies to perfect the dope business."

"You got that right," he said. I took out my wallet. "Vince, no way, man. Put it away. Now you owe me," he said, smiling. "I like that."

*

I popped two of the pills, hoping that they would mix OK with the Vicodins I'd taken in the taxi. It was only a few miles to my house, and I figured I had plenty of time to get there before the effect of the drug kicked in. I passed through the middle of town and decided to stop at the Publix for some groceries as I was starting to feel a hell of a lot better. In fact, I felt great.

I was in the store for almost an hour, and I filled my cart with gourmet cheeses, several kinds of crackers, potato chips, beer nuts, salsa, French onion dip, Easy Cheese, kettle corn, a giant bag of Cheetos, and a frozen lasagna. I decided against getting any beer or wine; my off-the-books prescription was mellowing me out just fine. I smiled at the very pretty girl at the register, and she scowled back. I picked out a bouquet of Alstroemeria flowers near the checkout, thinking it would be a great idea to drop them off for Lilian, Roberto's mother.

I loaded the groceries into the trunk of the BMW and drove out of town to Roberto's with no problem at all. The car and I were one. I was a young buck again, and life was as fresh and sweet as sorghum syrup. I pulled into Roberto's driveway and almost bounded out of the car, flowers in hand.

Gustavo greeted me at the door, looking puzzled.

"Is Lilian home?" I asked. My tongue felt funny, like it had been coated in wax.

"Come in. I'll get her," he said. I waited in their entry hall with the flowers, wearing my most charming smile. I hadn't realized what a spectacular house they had. Everything was so nice and neat, and I wished I had a woman like Lilian to take care of me. Or Glory. Or Barbara. It was a little confusing. I was having some trouble focusing my eyes.

Lilian came around the corner with a rolled up newspaper in her hand, and for a moment I wondered if she was going to swat me like a bad dog. I held out the bouquet and leaned over to kiss her. She recoiled as if she'd been tasered.

"Anybody want a drink?" I said, my words echoing in the hall. Lilian, Gustavo, and now Roberto watched as I began to teeter like a Loblolly pine, just before the second chainsaw cut meets the first one.

I reeled sideways into a brass urn full of umbrellas, and knocked a bowl of potpourri off a side table before I hit the floor, chest first, crushing the flowers.

MONDAY

MY BEDROOM FACES THE EAST, and whoever had gotten me onto my bed had left the blinds open. The heat woke me up. The pain followed, and as I turned my head to look at the clock I felt the three Roman senators plunging their daggers into my chest. Eight AM. It was twelve hours since I'd trashed Roberto's foyer and they'd driven me home. I dimly remembered a lot of protesting, shouting and the three of them half-carrying me from their car into my house. Roberto knew the alarm code, so at least we didn't alert the whole neighborhood. I was fully clothed, on top of the covers, which had been at my insistence. If I was in deep shit with Lilian before, I was snorkeling at the waste treatment plant now.

I found the pills in the pocket of my trousers and swallowed two of them. I lay quietly on the bed to let the drug kick in, and then I made my way carefully down the stairs and got some OJ from the fridge. My groceries from the day before were stocked and put away, and I noticed the BMW was in the driveway; Gustavo and Lilian must have driven it back.

The message light on the phone was blinking, and I pressed the playback button.

"Vinny, it's me." It was Frank Velutto. "Hey, we got a call from Tampa P.D., they were checking you out. I told them you were legit. Listen...I need to come over. I want to ask you something. Call me when you get in."

Frank could wait. The drug was already working its magic and I could breathe again, although I didn't feel as invulnerable as I had when I'd been at the Publix. I fetched two days' worth of the *Press Journal* from the driveway and caught up on the local news while sipping coffee and eating some granola with fruit. The OxyContin was so effective I forgot all about going back to bed, and I made another mental list. For starters, I wanted to know more about the money. Thirty million was a lot more than any orange broker or vending company owner could stash away. If I could get in touch with Roberto, I'd see if he had found anything on Empex Import/Export LLC. Money leaves a trail; some of the biggest busts I'd made as a cop were courtesy of a tip-off by a friendly banker or a CPA. Sometimes it was in banks and sometimes in bills—I'd dug up more money in back yards than most people had in their 401Ks.

I also wanted to call Dr. Doug. Doug Leyburn was a psychiatrist I'd met when he'd given courtroom testimony in a case I worked on. I knew that there were veterans among his clientele, and I wanted to try out my PTSD theory. He had an office over by the Indian River Medical Center, and I would have to call first and hope to get lucky—he was a busy man, but we'd hit it off when he had been in court. He had also treated Glory when she'd had a rough patch a couple years back. She'd never explained what was bothering her, it was one of those things that was off limits and I'd let it go because she seemed better after a few sessions and stopped going.

I had to call the auto insurance company and take my lumps. I wondered how much I'd lose on that deal. I was thinking I should just pick one of the two remaining white SHOs on the lot and pretend like I'd never totaled the first one, but that sounded like the OxyContin talking. I'd stick with the BMW for the time being.

There was one other thing on my list; I wanted to see Barbara again. I wanted to know exactly what she knew about the family finances. She also had my house key. So I had two excellent reasons why I needed to go see her, neither of which was the real reason—I wanted to see her again, even though she'd dumped me.

Dr. Doug Leyburn freed up space in his schedule, so I drove to his office. His receptionist gave me a clipboard with a form to fill out. I explained that I was not there for treatment and handed it back, and she eyed me suspiciously. She had a point; most of us are teetering on the edge of some form of insanity. A periodic consultation was probably a smart idea, like changing the oil every five thousand miles. They could have you in and out in fifteen minutes—a Jiffy Lube for neurotics.

Carole Velutto came into the waiting room and saw me. I'd forgotten how attractive she was. She gave a little gasp of surprise and then we both grinned sheepishly. Meeting someone you know in the waiting room of a psychiatrist's office is a little like getting caught with a Playboy when you're fourteen.

"Are you OK, Vince? You look…"

"Slipped in the bathtub," I said. "I saw Frank the other day. He doesn't look so good either."

"I wouldn't know," she said. She brushed her black bangs off her forehead, revealing her beautiful dark eyes and an unfriendly expression. "Everyone has their demons. Even you, right?"

"Me?" I didn't get her drift.

"Vince. I'm not stupid," she said, "And I'm glad you're getting treatment."

"I'm just here on a case," I said. "As far as I know I'm not crazy."

The moment I said that I wished I hadn't. After all, she was there, dealing with something. I began to apologize, but she ignored me and sat down and opened a magazine. Dr. Doug opened the door just in time. I removed the foot from my mouth and beat a hasty retreat to his office.

*

The doctor's quarters were furnished with a desk, a leather-and-wood Eames recliner, which he sat on, several upholstered wing chairs and a loveseat with a blanket draped over it. It all looked cozy and worn—the kind of furniture you'd find in an old hotel that was due for a renovation. But it was comfortable, which was the desired effect: people needed to feel at ease if they were going to spill their innermost secrets. I took one of the wing chairs by the solitary window.

I gave him the details on C.J. and D.B., as much as I knew. I said although it was possible that it was two different men, I had sidelined that notion when Le had said "my husband is two people." To me that was her way of saying he was two different people in one body.

"That's where I wondered if PTSD would come in," I said. "It sounds like he went through a lot in Vietnam, especially if he deserted, as the wife number two told the wife number one. I'm wondering if that's what started it."

Dr. Leyburn was leaning all the way back in the Eames recliner, completely motionless, with his eyes closed. I was starting to think he'd nodded off—or perhaps he was communicating with the spirit world. Finally, he spoke, with his eyes still shut. "Have you met both of the men?" he asked, "That is to say, both the personalities?"

"I played two holes of golf with D.B.," I said. "He's the gregarious, hard-drinking, hustler-type. I've only met C.J. once, though I've observed him more times than that. He's a very serious guy. I can't imagine him acting like D.B.; it must be a hell of an effort."

"Have you heard either of them talk about the other?"

"Yes," I said. I told him about talking with D.B. in the parking lot after his golf hustle and how he'd referred to his brother as a hard-ass. He was right about that, I said—C.J. was as unemotional a person as I'd ever seen.

I thought I'd lost him again—his eyes were closed and I could barely hear his breathing. "That fits," he said, finally.

"You mean the PTSD?"

"No," he said. "The correct acronym would be "DID." Dissociative Identity Disorder. It's quite different from PTSD and somewhat more severe. Both originate from traumatic experiences, but DID is usually caused by events that take place at a younger age than someone would be during military service."

"C.J. was probably around twenty when he was in Vietnam," I said.

"That's old for DID," he said. "Someone with multiple personalities as distinct as your friend's is a severe case. It probably began in his youth. Parental abuse is a common trigger. The victim develops one or more separate identities to escape from the reality of the bad things that are happening. Sexual abuse can do it, or severe beatings. The patient becomes another person, outside of the person who is being abused, so they don't have to experience it. It's a survival mechanism."

"Understood," I said. I'd been beaten a few times, and remember wishing I was somewhere, anywhere else.

"I've treated patients with DID, and the stories can come out during hypnosis. One of them told me she remembered peeking around a door when she was a young girl, watching her sister being raped by her father, when in fact there was no sister, just her. It was the only way she could escape."

"Whoa," I said.

"People do awful things to each other, as you well know."

"Yeah," I said, "I know."

"His Vietnam experience may have exacerbated it," he said. "And then going back and finding wife number two as you described her, was likely the beginning of actually being two people, with two lives and two spouses, even a son."

"So the disorder came first, and the two-wives thing followed?"

"Probably," he said. "Two different households and identities would be a perfect environment for DID."

"Do you think this guy is dangerous?"

"He could be. Some are, and they're especially dangerous to themselves. There are cases where one of the personalities actually hates the other, and there are even suicides because of the inner conflict. As if one personality had to kill the other one off. How old is he?"

"About sixty."

"That's remarkable in itself. They don't tend to live long lives."

"This is a big help," I said. I groaned as I rose from the chair.

"Are you in pain?" he said, leaning forward and opening his eyes.

"Yeah. I crashed my car, the night before last."

"Do you need a prescription?"

"No thanks," I said, "I'm all set."

*

The next item on my agenda was to figure out what to do about Barbara. I was at a loss as to how to go about it. I didn't want to knock on her door; C.J. might be there and it would definitely look like I was interfering. I could call her, but I didn't know exactly what I was going to say. I could follow her around until we met up, but I'd already done that two days before, and it would look like I was stalking her. Roberto would have texted her; texting walked the line between casual and intimate conversation, it was non-committal. I could text back and forth with Roberto no problem, but somehow the thought of texting Barbara made me feel old.

I drove back to my house and made a salad out of some remnants in the fridge. I couldn't believe all the crap I had bought during my shopping binge at the Publix; I'd probably toss half of it out. I washed the salad down with a cold Pellegrino and retreated to my recliner, closed my eyes and leaned back, Dr. Leyburn-style, in an attempt to clear out my mind and wait for inspiration. None came. Clearing my mind was futile—the moment I hauled everything away it just accumulated all over again, like an enchanted recycling bucket. They used to offer a meditation class at the Sheriff's, but whenever the instructor encouraged us to "be in the moment," I'd be trying to remember what it was that Glory wanted me to pick up on the way home.

My cell phone buzzed, yanking me out of my reverie. It was Barbara, solving my dilemma by calling me—I recognized the Tracfone on the caller ID.

"Hey," I said.

"Hey yourself," she said. There was a long silence. "Is this the party to whom I'm speaking?"

I laughed. "No, he can't come to the phone right now."

"Well, please tell him to call me," she said. "I want to take him to the beach. I miss him."

I missed her too, but I was starting to feel like a ping pong ball, and she was holding both of the paddles.

"What beach would you be taking him to?"

"I'm partial to the Tracking Station. It's quiet, and we'll have it to ourselves because the kids are back in school and there aren't any tourists in August."

"Good," I said. "I can't stand autograph seekers."

"Half an hour?"

"I'll be there," I said. "Barbara…"

"Yes?"

"I got a little banged up. I'm probably not good for the whole afternoon."

"Are you talking about our night in the hotel?"

"That was the good kind of banged up," I said. "This is the bad kind. I don't look so great."

"What happened? Do you want me to come get you?"

"No, I'll just see you there," I said, and we hung up. I collected a beach hat and a folding chair, and changed into my trunks. It was as nice as it gets outside; mid-eighties with a slight breeze that would be more noticeable on the beach. Maybe some time in the sun would help me heal.

*

Tracking Station Beach is the site of an old NASA installation from the earliest days of the space program. Cape Canaveral is seventy miles north of Vero and when there is a launch you get a perfect view from the shore. A few concrete foundations are still scattered among the palms and sea grape—leftovers from the big radar dishes that followed the astronauts' progress into space.

I parked in the lot and carried my gear across a wood-planked walkway and down a few steps to the sand. There was no one on the beach except for Barbara, already settled in a low, brightly-striped beach chair with a big straw hat and a cooler by her side. I looked back at the lifeguard station, which was shuttered, with a "Swim At Your Own Risk" sign hung across the front. Glory and I used to go to the beach a couple times a month to sit and read. We were partial to South Beach, currently Vero's widest as in recent years it was the beneficiary of the constantly shifting sand. Tracking Station was much narrower, but the warm, blue Atlantic was the same. I dropped my chair next to Barbara's and unfolded it.

"Oh my god, Vince, what happened?"

"Do I look that bad?" I had a loose Hawaiian shirt on, and I'd thought that the shirt and my sunglasses would cover the worst of the damage.

"What did you do to yourself?"

"I bought a new car," I said. "But it's gone now."

"You crashed it?"

"Unfortunately."

"You can hardly move," she said. "Why didn't you tell me?"

"I sort of told you," I said.

"Take your shirt off," she said.

"I can't," I said. She unbuttoned it and peeled it back. My bruises were starting to color in nicely, and the ones across my chest looked like an archipelago of volcanic islands, seen from a satellite.

"How did this happen?" she said.

"I was going too fast, and it was raining."

"You're not telling me everything."

"No."

She opened the top of her cooler. "You want a beer?"

"I'd better not," I said. "A friend already fixed me up. I'm full of painkillers."

"Vince," she said, "Are you still looking into, you know…"

"Yes. I don't expect you to pay me. I just want to know."

"So do I. That's kind of why I called."

"You mean I'm hired again?" I said.

"If you want to be."

"Why?"

She took a beer out of the cooler and opened it. "Here's to all the women in the world whose husbands keep them in the dark," she said, and took a swig.

"What happened?" I said.

"I walk to Humiston Park and back every morning around seven. It takes me about an hour, and C.J. usually does his workout while I'm gone. It's a tight schedule in my house, we're like a couple of stop-watches. So this morning I had the wrong sneakers on, and my feet hurt, and I decide to go back to the house and change. I hear C.J. talking in his study, where his exercise machines are, with the door closed. There's no phone in there. I wondered if someone was in there with him, but it was just him talking, and there were pauses in the conversation, like he was listening to someone else."

"You said he doesn't use a cell, right?"

"Wait," she said. "I listened outside the door, hoping like hell that I wouldn't get caught. He was talking about money, accounts, things like that. I heard him say 'we're going to move it all, everything'. Those are the exact words. He was talking about getting faxes, something about Fed wires…I don't know if I have that right, but it was like a whole different person was talking. He doesn't do business at home, he just does his workouts, reads a lot, his beach walks and so on."

"Do you know who he was talking to?"

"I heard him tell someone he had to go, and I ran as quietly as I could to the laundry room, which is my domain, he never goes in there. Then I heard him go into our room and start his shower, which is another part of his routine. So I went into his study, and there was a cell phone on the desk—not a fancy one, just the basic kind. I turned it on and looked at the recent calls, and I wrote them down."

"Good work, Sherlock," I said.

"Yeah, but here's where I screwed up. I went back to the laundry room and waited for what seemed like forever for C.J. to leave the house, and he finally did. Then I decided to call a few of the numbers, because I'm stupid and impatient. At least I used the Tracfone you gave me, so they didn't know who was calling. The first number was a law office and I had an awkward conversation with a secretary and finally said 'wrong number'. The second call was an 809 area code, which I think is Puerto Rico, and someone answered in Spanish. I just hung up on that one. The last one was a long number with a '41' in it, which the Tracfone wouldn't connect me to. I Googled it and found out it was the country code for Switzerland. Here's the worst part; I called the number from our land line. The caller ID said 'B-A-P' and a guy picks up and says 'C.J.?', and I freak out and say nothing, so he asks if I can hear him, and I still say nothing, and so he says they got the fax and the wire is all set, confirmed on the other side for seventeen million. I say 'dollars?' and he says 'euros,' and then he freaks out when he realizes it's not C.J. He starts going crazy, and I hang up."

"Barbara, do you have any idea how much money you guys have? If you added it all up?"

"No. I manage the household money, but C.J. handles the investments and everything. I guess I just assume there's plenty of money, which is probably stupid and shows how spoiled I am."

The tide was coming in and a wave pushed the water to within a few feet of our toes. I would have loved to go in for a swim, but even in the gentle summer surf it would be a bad idea in my condition. Maybe, if I took enough OxyContin, I could be thirty-five again and could take Barbara in my arms and play in the breakers. She looked fantastic in her powder-blue tankini, and I noticed a tattoo at the bottom of her back that I'd missed before. It was a tiny crescent moon next to a full moon. It could have been two moles if you weren't looking closely.

"There's thirty million in various accounts on the Tampa side," I said. "Some of it is linked to D.B., some to Le and some to a business I don't know a lot about yet, but I assume he controls it. I have no idea how much is in your and C.J.'s name over here, but there must be something."

"You're kidding."

"I'm not," I said. "The problem is that it's so much money it doesn't make sense. Either C.J. had a bundle of money to start with, like an inheritance, or he makes a hell of a lot for a citrus dealer. Too much. That kind of money just smells bad."

Barbara took another swig of the beer. "How did you find this out?"

I didn't answer.

"Where did you go after I saw you at Cravings?"

"I went to Tampa again. I followed them around some. I ended up having a conversation with Le."

"What did you think?"

"She worried me a little."

"She was nice to me."

"I think she was conning you. Not to scare you, but I don't think she likes you."

She drained the rest of the beer.

"Where'd you get the tats?" I said.

"What?"

"The moons, on your back."

"Oh. Jacksonville," she said. "It was the name of a bar."

"Maybe I'll get one," I said. "We can play guess-what-the-tattoo-was when we're in the nursing home."

She smiled, but her thoughts were elsewhere. Finding out your husband has thirty million dollars that you were unaware of has to be something of a shock. I was having some trouble breathing; I just couldn't get enough air in, and what I could get in felt like fire.

Barbara gave me a concerned look. "Vince, you sound like a fish that washed up."

"I'm not doing so great."

"Come in the water," she said. "You need to cool off."

"I don't think so."

"I do," she said. "I promise you'll feel better." She took me by the arm and helped me lift myself off the chair and to my feet. We stepped into the surf, and I went sideways through the rollers while she dived into the first one and got her hair wet. The first waves hurt like hell, but once I got out beyond the break there was a sandbar where I could stand comfortably, with the water up to my shoulders. I bent my legs and bobbed up and down in the warm ocean. She was right—it was the first time I'd felt comfortable since the accident, not counting my semi-overdose at the Publix. Barbara swam up to me and put her arms around my neck.

"Does this hurt?" she asked.

"The opposite," I said.

She brought up her legs and wrapped them gently around my waist, under the water. "How about now?"

"Not yet," I said.

"I missed you," she said, and she leaned her face into mine and gave me a long, wet kiss.

*

I had been out in the sun for too long, and by the time I got home I was ready to roll into my bed even though the evening news hadn't started yet. I changed out of my bathing trunks and put on a favorite pair of red sweatpants and a T-shirt. No one on the planet looks good in red sweatpants, but in my present condition I didn't give a damn. My phone buzzed.

OK 2 cme ovr? It was Roberto.

Sure, where are you? I sent back.

Rdng my bke. B thr in 2 mnts.

I'm going to buy you some vowels, I texted.

Roberto opened the door and let himself in. He set his backpack down and went straight to the fridge for a Coke. He opened the can and drank deeply like he'd just crossed a desert with an empty canteen.

"Do your folks know you're here?"

"Yeah," he said. Apparently the war I'd anticipated was over before it had begun. I wondered why.

"Were you able to find out anything on Empex?"

"Yes, there were some things in the public records. They own some properties in Lake Wales: a citrus grove, a juice processing plant, a self-storage place and an office in the downtown part. But check this out." He took Glory's MacBook out of his bag and booted it up on the kitchen table. I watched his fingers fly over the keyboard as he navigated through programs until he got to a list of figures and accounts. "This is what I saw the other day, before you cut off their phone line. Except now it's different."

"What is different?"

"You remember I told you some of the money was in their name, but most of it was in the name of that company? Take a look."

I squinted at the screen. There was an entry that said "Empex Import/Export LLC," and to the right of it was a zero.

"That was almost thirty million dollars on Saturday," he said.

"Can you tell where it went?"

"No, I already tried, but that account is too heavily encrypted. I can get into the other accounts, and I didn't see any money coming in. I have the PIN for their joint account in case you need any cash; it still has over a million in it." He smiled.

I knew he was just trying to be funny, but it worried me. I put aside my curiosity about where the Empex money had gone and opened myself a Coke. It was time for a discussion with my young friend.

"Roberto," I started, "When I was fourteen, I was obsessed with a guy named Houdini. I had books about him, and he was like a magical guy, he could open any lock and escape from anything."

"Yeah, I know about him."

"I tried to be like him," I said, "And I taught myself to pick locks. There was a locksmith in my hometown who showed me some tricks, and I got very good at it. My dad was out a lot and my mom went to bed early, and I began sneaking out of the house at night. I broke into people's homes. I don't remember how it got started exactly, but I couldn't stop myself."

"Did you take stuff?"

"Yes. I only took cash, and not a lot, but I was the kid in school who always had money and could treat the others to movies and so on."

"Did you ever get caught?" he said.

"Yes. Twice. The second time was the day after my eighteenth birthday, and so I wasn't a juvenile anymore. The judge gave me a break and said if I went to college after high school he would throw it out and purge my record. I lasted a year and dropped out to become a cop."

"You still do it though, right? You let yourself into people's houses?"

"Yes, and it's still illegal. I rationalize it by thinking that it's a part of my work, but it's a fine line, and if I got caught, it wouldn't be a fine line at all. It would be a felony."

"Kind of like hacking," he said. He knew where I was going.

"Exactly," I said. We didn't say anything for a while.

"Vince," he said, and then he was very quiet. He couldn't look at me. I thought he was going to cry. "There's something I have to show you. I talked to my parents about it, and they said I should show it to you. By the way, they're not mad at you, they really like you, even my mom. They told me to come over here."

"OK," I said.

He closed the program that was open on Glory's computer and opened up the Internet browser. He navigated to AOL, which is what Glory always used for her home page and email. He signed in, using a different name from what her account name had been; this one was *hulahoop9864*. September 8th, 1964, was her birthdate, but I had no idea where the "hulahoop" part came from.

He opened the email program. There were emails from various senders, some obviously spam, and then he re-grouped the messages to "from" instead of "date received," and I saw a whole page of messages from someone named *Pacobell6969*. He scrolled down, and there were several pages of them from the same sender. They were arranged chronologically, beginning about three years ago. The last one was received at two in the afternoon on the day Glory died.

"Roberto, what is this?"

"It's a lot of emails from a guy, to her," he said. His voice was quivering. "There are some others under "sent" that go from her to him, but not a lot. She pretty much stopped answering his emails after a year. I'm sorry, Vince. I'm really sorry." He started sobbing.

"When did you find this?" I said, but he couldn't talk, and I let him be. I suddenly realized that this was what had prompted him to ask me about his friend a few days ago, shortly after I'd given him the Mac. It had probably eaten the poor kid up. I wondered what I was going to find in the emails, but I knew from Roberto's reaction that whatever was there would be bad. I felt dizzy, like I was sitting on the edge of a precipice, and someone was about to push me off.

I could wait; Roberto needed me right now. I put my arms around him and held him until he stopped sobbing. It took a while, and I felt terrible for him, but he had finally gotten it off his chest.

"You did the right thing, Roberto," I said. "I know that wasn't easy."

"I have to go home now," he said. "I'll leave the computer. I don't want it anymore."

"You want a ride? We can put the top down, and the bike can go in the back seat."

"No thanks," he said, "I need the exercise." He was getting his composure back. He left and I was alone, with a thirteen-inch window into a part of my wife's life that probably should have died with her.

*

I went through the emails chronologically. It was all sickeningly familiar—I had read this story so many times before. Sometimes I could take on a husband-and-wife case and lay it bare after five minutes on their computer. People who were fooling around were often remarkably lax about hiding it, and my theory was that they wanted to get caught, for whatever reason. It was a shitty way to end a marriage, though there wasn't any good way that I'd ever heard about.

Glory wasn't the angel, and the guy wasn't the devil. The emails told a tale of mutual passion, and I guessed from the dates of the earliest ones that their first encounter happened when I was on a case that took me down to the Keys for two weeks. Ironically, the case had been about an errant husband, and it ended in a divorce settlement in the many millions. So while I was out catching one bad guy, another bad guy caught my wife.

Reading their exchanges was an entirely different feeling from reading the emails of people I didn't know. There was nothing in them that was directly negative about me, no specific complaints, but my failures as a husband and a lover were implied. *I've never, ever felt like that before,* she wrote, early on. I should have stopped reading right there, but she hadn't stopped writing, and I wished more than ever that she would just walk into my kitchen, alive, and I could throw myself at her feet and apologize for being so inadequate. I read every single one of her emails and most of his, although I hated every word he wrote. The guy was such a slimebag—he went on and on about how hot she was, how wonderful, how beautiful—and I gagged. I wished I'd said some of those things to Glory, but I'm not that type. I thought I'd shown my love for her in other ways, but any fool knows that a woman wants to hear it out loud sometimes, and a man does too.

It appeared that they had been lovers for about six months, and then she changed her mind. There was no explanation in the emails; she just kept putting him off. It drove him crazy, and although his messages were polite there was an undercurrent of hurt and anger. I didn't blame him; he'd lost hold of an amazing woman, just as I had. From then on, right up until she died, the emails were one-sided. He tried everything he could to get her interest, and on the rare occasions that she wrote back she was distant.

There wasn't a single giveaway as to who the guy was. Probably some dildo at her gym—that's where she spent a lot of time, and you could shower up afterward and hide your traces. I'd never suspected a thing. I felt like Barbara this afternoon at the beach when she'd raised her beer to toast all the women whose husbands left them in the dark—that equation could certainly work both ways.

I had the computer open on my lap while the television news blared in the background. A tropical storm was over the Virgin Islands and had turned toward Florida. It was supposed to gain hurricane strength overnight and could make landfall in two days. The program cut to a Cialis ad and showed a greying couple snuggling on the couch, giving each other knowing looks. I flung the laptop across the room at the TV. It bounced off the screen, leaving a scratch in the glass as the couple kissed and the disclaimers started.

My chest pain was intensifying, and I drew rapid, shallow breaths, not able to get enough oxygen. It was time for two more of the pills, and I considered washing a handful of them down with a beer—or several. The numbness and guilt I'd felt while reading the emails were morphing into a black cloud of anger. This changed everything. Glory was somebody's dirty little secret. I was a cuckold and a loser, and all those candles I'd lit at her shrine for the last year were for the wrong saint. Nothing meant anything anymore, and if anyone tried to tell me I'd get over it—that this too shall pass—I would throw them in a dumpster and slam the lid on their fucking face.

*

I drove across the 17th Street Bridge with the convertible top down. There were only a few cars on the bridge so I didn't bother anyone when I pulled over at the highest point and tossed Glory's shiny little Mac over the rail, seventy feet down into the Indian River. It had done enough damage, and it belonged at the bottom of the channel where the barnacles could claim it. I got back in the BMW and drove the rest of the way to the barrier island and straight across A-1-A to South Beach. The wind was coming up, and I could hear the surf from the parking lot; it was louder than it had been in the afternoon, and I figured the storm in the islands was already having an effect. The drugs had kicked in and my chest had stopped hurting, but everything else about me was in agony.

This is where Glory and I had sat and read our books in the sun's heat, and I'd never told her how beautiful she looked and how amazing she was. Someone had stolen her from me, someone had jimmied the lock and entered the most intimate part of my life and had gotten away with the goods. I had the rest of the OxyContin pills in my pocket and a bottle of vodka on the passenger seat. I could just down it all and walk into the warm Atlantic and be shark bait. It sounded like a good idea—a lot better than going back to a dark house and a cold bed. It went against my grain, but after enough of the pills and the vodka there wouldn't be any grain to go against. My cell phone rang.

"Vince, where are you? I tried your house." It was Barbara.

"I'm at the beach."

"I need to see you, right now. I'm scared."

"I'll be in your driveway in five minutes," I said and started the BMW. I could get there in three if I hurried.

*

Barbara was watching out the window and she rushed outside and got into the BMW as soon as I pulled in to her driveway.

"Where's C.J.?" I said.

"He went out an hour ago, he didn't say where. We had one hell of a conversation after you and I left the beach."

"Is that what scared you?"

"No," she said. "It was the Lexus. It passed by the house and slowed down, twice. C.J. was gone, and I panicked."

"The red Lexus? You mean C.J.'s?"

"Yes."

I realized I'd forgotten completely about tracking the cars. My own laptop was at home, with my gun and everything else I owned except for a bottle of vodka and some painkillers.

"Maybe you should stay somewhere else," I said.

"No, I'm OK. I'm calming down some, now that you're here. If we could just wait until he gets back, I'll go in and I'll be fine."

"What if it was C.J. in the Lexus?"

"Not possible. I think you're right; it's the boy, not C.J. Besides, we really had it out, and he told me a lot of things I never knew before."

"Like what?"

"It started when I asked him about the money. I confessed that I'd overheard him. I also told him I'd seen the phone numbers, and I'd called the one in Switzerland. He didn't react at all…I think he already knew. And then he kind of broke down."

"How so?"

"He told me he was obsessed about money. He didn't feel safe unless he had plenty of it. He said it had gotten out of control, but the upshot was that we'd never have to worry about money for the rest of our lives."

"Keep going."

"I asked him where he got it, and if he'd inherited it. He said no, he couldn't tell me, it was too dangerous, but he hadn't inherited anything. He said his mother and father were dead and left him nothing. It's the only time I've ever heard him say a word about them. He said they hated him while they were alive. His father was a colonel in the Army, and had insisted he go to Vietnam instead of college. He got into some kind of battle in the jungle, and he ended up deserting from the Army and was smuggled out through Cambodia, to Canada. They knew he was alive, and his father tried to hunt him down, and he's been hiding ever since."

"Holy shit."

"Yeah," she said. "It explains a lot."

"Did you ask him about his so-called brother, and the other wife?"

"Yes," she said, "but it was like his tongue was cut out. He looked like he wanted to talk about it, but he couldn't. I never saw so much pain in his eyes. He finally got in his van and took off."

"How long ago?"

"About an hour. I was looking out the window, worrying about him, when I saw the Lexus pass. Then it passed again, and that's when I called you."

The garage door opened in front of us and headlights illuminated the driveway. It was C.J., coming home in the van.

"Go in with him," I said. "Do you have your phone on you?"

"Yes, in my pocket."

"Keep it with you and call me if anything strange is going on. I won't be far away." She got out of the car, and I drove out of the driveway and down their road to a spot under a moss-draped oak where I could park and see the house. I wished I had my gun, and I remembered I had the Lupo in the trunk. I brought it inside the car and lay it across my lap. I also wished I had my toothbrush and a good novel, as I was planning on spending the night right there in the BMW. Once again Barbara Butler had crashed my pity-party, and I was quietly grateful. At the same time, I was still seething with anger over the emails, and if a red Lexus crossed my path, I was thinking I might just pepper it with buckshot and ask questions afterward.

TUESDAY

I WAS ABLE TO STAY awake until dawn by listening to the radio and keeping the car windows open. I wondered whether I was also keeping the neighborhood awake, but nobody sleeps with the windows open anymore; everyone has the air conditioning running. They are missing out—the sound of palm fronds rustling in the night breeze is a powerful soporific, and I had to fight hard against my drug-enhanced drowsiness to keep a proper lookout on the Butler house. Nobody came or went, and no red Lexuses passed by. At six AM I decided to go home and get some rest.

Before I went to bed, I opened my laptop to see where the Lexus was. Once again, there was no signal from it. Either I'd misdiagnosed the problem and it wasn't the batteries after all, or someone had discovered the unit. The next chance I had I would pick up a brand new box and hard-wire it in.

I took another dose of the drug; just one pill rather than two this time. Sitting in the car all night had taken its toll, but I didn't want to have any problems weaning myself from it and end up in rehab. As tired as I was it was impossible to drift off while my mind digested all the data I'd gathered from the previous day. According to Dr. Doug, C.J. had multiple personalities, neatly paired to two families. Then C.J. is on the phone moving money around, lots of it, and Barbara finds out and calls me and I'm hired again. Not only that, but she also semi-jumps my broken bones while we're swimming. That was definitely the high point of the day. Then Roberto comes over, and I find out about Glory. That was the low point.

And then Barbara, who has just re-employed me to find out about the money, can't wait and confronts C.J., and his secrets start spilling out. Meanwhile somebody is driving a luxury car back and forth in front of their house like a predatory animal. And my chest feels like a cement truck just rolled over it. I got up and took the second pill—I badly needed some sleep, and they say the food is great at the Betty Ford clinic anyway.

*

My phone rang just before ten, and I emerged from a dream where I was underwater, swimming among a cloud of fish, looking for a computer at the bottom of the sea. I must have been holding my breath; because, as soon as the phone woke me, I gasped for air. The caller ID said "Butler,C.".

"Mr. Tanzi?"

"Yes?" I said.

"This is Charles Butler. C.J. Butler."

"How can I help you, Mr. Butler?"

"I'm looking for my wife," he said. "I was hoping you knew where she was."

"When did you last see her?" I said.

"She went for her walk, to the park. I shouldn't have let her. You know what happened last night."

"What time did she leave?"

"Seven," he said. "Three hours ago. She is usually back by eight. But she's impulsive sometimes."

"I know," I said. "Do you want me to come over?"

"Maybe. Let's give it another hour. She might just be shopping. I tried her mobile, but it went to voicemail."

"Call me as soon as she's back, OK?"

"I will. And if you hear from her, please do the same," he said.

I was worried. And if C.J. was worried enough to call me, I was even more worried. He'd called her cell, but he probably didn't know about the Tracfone, so I dialed it. It rang several times, and then I heard some noise, but no one was talking. It was white noise, like a fan, or a waterfall. And then I heard Barbara's voice, not directly into the phone, but from a distance.

Where are you taking me?

Shut up. A different voice. Then, nothing.

Is this Lake Wales? Barbara again. The white noise was the sound of a car. She was on the road somewhere, and I suddenly had a sick feeling in the pit of my stomach.

Lady, if you don't shut the fuck up I will use this thing, the other person said. She must have answered the Tracfone and left it on so that I could hear them talking. She was trying to tell me where they were.

What is that? What's in your hand? the other voice said. I recognized the crackling falsetto of an angry teenager—Philip. The conversation stopped, and I heard a clattering noise. After that, there was the occasional sound of a passing car.

Barbara's Tracfone was now lying on the side of the road, somewhere around Lake Wales.

*

I called C.J. and told him to come directly to my house—that would be the fastest. I said to hustle, we were going to Lake Wales, and I was going to have some questions for him and didn't want any bullshit answers. I packed the BMW while I waited. I had the Glock, two loaded spare clips with an extra box of ammo, and the Lupo with a box of shells. I put it all on the back seat where I could get at it quickly if I needed to. C.J. was in my driveway in ten minutes.

The BMW isn't as fast as the SHO was, but it's nimble when you want to pass people, and I was in a hurry. C.J. sat white-faced in the passenger seat, partly from my driving and partly from what I'd told him about what I'd heard on the Tracfone. The road opened up after we passed I-95, and I got the car up to about eighty and kept it there while we talked.

"Where would he take her? It's Philip, right?"

He looked at me, but couldn't respond—like he'd had his tongue cut out, as Barbara had described it. It was as though he wanted to tell me, but he couldn't force the words out. They were jammed somewhere between his two personae, and I had to find out how to unlock them.

"Can you please slow down?" he said.

"No." I took the car up to ninety.

"C.J., you know where they're going, right?" I said, over the noise of the motor. "Philip and Barbara? Tell me where they're going." I took my eyes off the road and stared at him as the needle approached one hundred.

"For God's sake, slow down," he said.

"Not until you tell me."

"There's a juice plant," he said. "We own it. It hasn't operated for years—it's too old to pass the inspections now. It's in the middle of a grove we own."

"Where?"

"Behind the self-storage units. There's a dirt road. We own the whole area between there and the Lake Wales airport. We'll be there soon if you keep driving this fast."

*

The road behind the storage units led to a metal gate that was flanked by two sturdy concrete posts. A tank might be able to run it down, but not the little BMW. C.J. got out of the car, opened a keypad on one of the posts, and entered a sequence of numbers; the gate swung open. I counted three surveillance cameras pointed at us; one on top of a chain-link fence that enclosed the grove and two others high up in a palm tree. *Pretty high-tech for a juice plant that doesn't operate anymore*, I thought.

Once we got past the gate the road narrowed to little more than a path through the orange trees. A truck with pickers could pass through, but the traffic could only go one way. The trees were Valencias, the best for juicing, and they were bare of fruit except for some drop, rotting among the trunks. Harvest season for Valencias was past, and the grove was deserted, quiet and fragrant.

"Turn right," C.J. said. We came to an open gravel lot where two ancient fruit trucks were parked alongside a high stack of wooden pallets. Across from where we entered stood a corrugated metal building with a flat roof. It was connected to a smaller wing with a concrete loading platform and a new-looking overhead door. The main building was the size of a high school gym, and I guessed that it was at least fifty years old, though it had been kept up—no broken windows, no sign of the vandalism that plagued old structures. A water tower on metal stilts rose above it, with "Vereda Fruit Processing Co." stenciled on it in fading orange and black paint.

The red Lexus was parked next to the building. There was no one in it.

"Please stay in the car," C.J. said, and he got out of the BMW. He entered the building through a side door. I decided that I needed to see what was going on for myself, and I slipped the Glock into my belt holster and put an extra clip in my pants pocket. C.J. had left the entry door open, and I stopped when I reached it and looked inside. It was an open span, littered with wooden pallets, but with no machinery or equipment. The floor was a patchwork of poured concrete and bare ground. The place stank of cat pee, probably from years and years of fruit juice and rot, or perhaps some feral cats had taken shelter there. The smell was overwhelming. There were two rooms partitioned off against a wall, one of which had windows to the interior and looked like an office. The other walled-off room also had windows to the work floor, but they were blacked out, and the access door was heavily secured. If I'd been alone, I would have checked that one out first.

Philip and C.J. were at the opposite end from me, talking heatedly. I couldn't hear what they were saying at first, but it got louder and their voices echoed across the empty floor.

"Where is she?" C.J. said. It sounded like he'd already asked several times and was now losing his patience.

"Stay out of it," Philip said back to him. "It's none of your business."

"She is my wife," C.J. said.

"Mom is your wife!" Philip screamed back.

"Philip…" C.J. said. The boy saw me standing in the doorway, and went rigid. He pulled a gun from his pocket and pointed it at me, and then swung it around to point at C.J.

"Stay away from me!" he shouted, and I decided to leave my gun in its holster, thinking that if I drew it would make matters worse. Philip dropped his arm to his side and ran toward the other side of the building. He opened a door and bolted into the part of the structure where the bay door was. I tried to follow, but with my cracked ribs it was impossible to run, so I hobbled as fast as I could across the open floor. C.J. and I reached the space where the boy had gone, but it was empty—the bay door was open and the hot sunshine spilled in. There was no sign of Barbara anywhere, and I was praying that he hadn't killed her already.

Philip started the Lexus and sped into the grove leaving a trail of dust. C.J. and I got into the BMW, and I turned the key. There were a hundred ways he could have gone as the grove was a grid, with nothing but rows of trees with paths between them. He could be anywhere.

"Would he go back out the way we came in?" I asked C.J.

He shrugged. "It's the only road out." I looked in that direction, but there was no dust, and there should have been if he'd left that way.

"There's a fence all the way around the grove, right?"

"Yes," C.J. said.

"No other gates?"

"Just one on the airport side. They lock it. You can't go in there."

"Where?"

"That way. Down that row, turn right toward the runway."

I punched the BMW, and we bumped along though the trees. The harvesting rows weren't really roads, they were grass, and the low-slung car was not the ideal vehicle for a pursuit, but I got it up to forty until C.J. told me to turn, and we approached the fence that bordered the municipal airport. Two chain-link panels formed a gate that was topped with barbed wire and locked together with a heavy padlock. I could see the nose of the Lexus parked up ahead, hidden between the trees. Philip saw us coming and roared out of his hiding place. He crashed through the gate, ripping it up off the ground and squeezing the car under. The bottom of the fence panels wreaked havoc with the Lexus' fancy paint job, but Philip was far ahead now, and he accelerated hard as he reached the runway. I followed in the BMW, and the broken fence tore long stripes on the convertible's top as we passed underneath.

It was a drag race, and I was losing. Philip was way ahead. He hit his brakes and executed a perfect drift onto a taxiway, then turned onto the opposite runway in the direction of a concrete hangar and several parked planes. I cut the corner, bumping across the low grass and almost caught up. I was right behind him when he tried to make another hard turn toward the road that would take him out of the airport. He braked and tried another drift, but the screeching tires slid too far and the Lexus spun. It skidded across the runway and crashed into a parked Cessna, nearly breaking it in two. Philip got out of the car and ran. I stopped the BMW. C.J. opened his door and ran after him. I lifted myself out of the seat and hobbled over to the wreckage. The Lexus was intact, but the small plane was tilted up on one wingtip with half of the fuselage missing.

As I circled around the car, I heard a noise. I looked in the window. There was nothing inside except my old Baby Glock, which I scooped up and pocketed. I heard the sound again and realized where it was coming from—the trunk. I popped the release switch and hurried to the back of the car as the trunk lid opened, letting out a blast of superheated air. Barbara was inside—her mouth, hands, and feet bound tightly in silver-grey duct tape. She was curled into a fetal position, gasping in rapid, spasmodic breaths through her nose. Her skin was a florid pink, hot to the touch. I lifted her out, put her down on the scorching pavement and ripped the tape off of her mouth. I dashed back to the BMW to get a water bottle and splashed some on her face, then held it to her mouth so that she could drink. She emptied the bottle and her eyes opened, squinting in the harsh light. I found my penknife and cut away the rest of the tape, freeing her arms and legs.

She got to her feet, wobbling like a newborn calf, and put her arms around my neck and held tight. Behind her I could see C.J. and Philip—C.J. had tackled him, and they were on the ground at the end of the runway. Philip was sobbing, and C.J. was gripping him by the arm. I helped Barbara into the BMW and turned the air conditioning up to the maximum; she had a severe case of heat stroke and was lucky to be alive. We sat there, not talking, while C.J. walked Philip back across the tarmac. He put the boy in the passenger seat of the Lexus and came over to the BMW. I rolled down the window.

"She has heat stroke," I said. "We need to get her out of here."

"Can we keep this quiet?" C.J. said.

"Your kid just kidnapped someone, threatened me with a gun, and there's an airplane in pieces over there," I said, pointing. "How do you keep that quiet?"

"I'll deal with it," he said. "How much do I owe you?"

"You're not my client," I said.

"Ten thousand?"

"You're not my client," I repeated.

Barbara was coming back to life. "Go to Tampa," she said to C.J. "The boy needs you." She turned to me and said, "Drive," and I did.

*

I tried to talk Barbara into going directly to an emergency room, but she overruled me and gave me her now-familiar non-negotiable look. She had me stop at a CVS where she disappeared inside for fifteen minutes while I waited in the car, at her insistence. When she came out, she looked more like herself again. She had a gallon jug of water, a small bottle of Aleve, and a can of WD-40 which she had used to clean the duct tape marks off of her arms, legs and face while in the ladies room.

"I just saved myself about five hundred dollars in some stupid clinic," she said.

I was not happy that we weren't going straight to the doctor, but it seemed that the more that she was allowed to be in control, the quicker she got her color back.

"You going to be OK?"

"I guess so," she said. "It'll sink in later."

"Maybe I should stay with you for a couple days," I said.

She didn't say anything.

"Sorry," I said. "That wasn't a hit."

"I know," she said.

She told me what had happened. Philip caught up with her on her way back to the house after she'd taken her walk. He'd pulled a gun and made her get in the Lexus. She said they drove around Vero for almost an hour while he made calls on his cell, speaking in a foreign language, so she hadn't understood a word.

"He speaks Vietnamese with his mother," I said.

"OK," she said. "I was completely terrified for the first hour. And then he got on Route 60, and I forced myself to calm down and tried to figure out what I could do. I was thinking I'd just bolt at the next stoplight, but he had the gun on his lap the whole time, and I didn't dare. When you called me and the cell vibrated, I was able to get it out of my pocket and open it, but he saw it, and he threw it out the window."

"That was brilliant, and it worked," I said. "I heard enough to figure it out."

"He went crazy after that," she said. "He turned off the highway onto a side road, and I thought he was going to take me somewhere remote and shoot me. He made me get out of the car, and that's when he wrapped me up in the duct tape. Then he shoved me into the trunk and closed it, and we started moving again. It was pitch-dark in there, and I could barely breathe."

"You had heat stroke," I said. "You're lucky you survived. You need to go to a doctor—"

"I need to go to the Keys and lie on the beach," she said. "This is totally wrong. C.J. said he'd take care of everything."

"What were you doing out walking this morning?"

"I know; that was foolish. I'm just so tired of being cooped up and scared."

"Barbara, I'm going to call the cops. I've talked to his probation officer already, and they need to know about this. He's dangerous."

"I agree. C.J. will go crazy though."

"I don't know how to say this nicely, but C.J. may already be crazy. I went to see a shrink I know the other day, and we talked about it. He thinks it's something called Dissociative Identity Disorder, and it's a serious mental illness. His guess is that it started when he was very young, and it might have gotten worse in Vietnam."

She processed that while we drove, in silence.

"There's a hurricane coming," I said.

"I think I'm already in the middle of one," she said. "I'm going to close my eyes for a minute. I have a headache."

She leaned her head against the passenger window while I drove. I opened the glove box and pawed through my wife's old CDs, thinking that I'd play one, but it made me sad to look at them, and I wondered which songs she'd listened to with *Pacobell.* I still hadn't told Barbara about Glory's emails, but that had nothing to do with her.

*

Barbara slept all the way back to Vero, and I had to wake her up when we got to her driveway. C.J.'s van was parked there—he must have already arranged for it to be picked up from my house. She said she was exhausted and needed some time to herself. I said I'd come back later and would sleep on her couch. I didn't say so, but I didn't feel she was safe yet, despite C.J.'s intervention with Philip.

Two small things were stuck in my mind as I left Barbara, bothering me, like grains of sand that find their way into an oyster and sometimes produce a pearl, but usually just make the oyster itch like crazy. Number one was the juice plant. Why was it wired up for security when nothing was there? The first chance I got I would let myself in and check it out. I almost had enough time to do it now, but I'd driven enough for one day, and my chest hurt more than usual from lifting Barbara out of the trunk of the Lexus. And it might take me a while to get inside, because the locks I'd seen on the blacked-out room were the keypad type, and they were a pain. Also, I'd need to disable the security cameras on the way in, so I didn't end up performing a felony on YouTube.

The second thing that bothered me was what Barbara had said about Philip speaking Vietnamese on his phone. I doubted his mother was calling to ask him to pick up some buttermilk on the way home. Le was in on this—how much I didn't know, but she might be every bit as dangerous as the kid, if not more so. Now I was regretting leaving Barbara at her house. Le could be anywhere. As soon as I got home, I would call Frank Velutto and fill him in on the whole case. It was time. I needed backup, and I wanted somebody to be watching Le.

I hadn't had any lunch and was suddenly famished. I drove to Casey's, a café in the middle of Central Beach with superb burgers that you could eat at a patio table in the open air. It was late in the afternoon, and the lunch crowd of bankers and shoppers was long gone, so I had a table to myself. I don't like to talk on my cell phone in public, but there was nobody around and I owed someone a phone call—Shirley Magan, Philip's JPO in Tampa.

"Magan," she said when she answered. Some people definitely watch too many cop shows.

"Ms. Magan, it's Vince Tanzi. We spoke last week about Philip Johannsen."

"I remember," she said.

"I told you I'd call you if anything came up. Something did. He abducted a client of mine, at gunpoint. She's OK; I found them, and it's over. He went back to Tampa with his father."

"Did you witness it?"

"Not the actual abduction, but I'm the one who got her out of the trunk of his car, and I witnessed him pointing a gun at me."

"I'll need you to come in," she said. "Where are you?"

"Vero," I said. "I can't get over there today, and there's a storm heading up the coast."

"You're the one who is the former police officer, right?"

"Yeah," I said. "Retired. I'm a P.I. now."

"That's good enough for me. I'm going to pick him up and put him in the Hillsborough Juvenile facility. Don't say anything, I don't want him running."

"OK," I said.

"Mr. Tanzi?"

"Yes?"

"Thank you," she said. "I'll call you after the storm passes through; I'm going to need you over here for a statement. Is there anything else I should know?"

"Yeah," I said. "He doesn't have the gun anymore." I didn't bother to explain where it had come from in the first place.

"Good," she said, and we hung up.

I tried Frank at the office, and they said he was already gone for the day. I dialed his cell, and it went to voicemail. I thought about leaving a message, but didn't. I'd just try him later.

*

I wasn't ready to go home yet, so I dawdled around Central Beach. I ended up at Humiston Park; Barbara's destination on her daily walk. A group of young mothers in loose dresses and big sunglasses chatted while their children played on swings and climbed on something that looked like a huge plastic fish. The kids were barefoot, and they laughed and chased each other while their moms socialized.

I found a shady bench and watched the kids play. The wind had picked up, and I could hear the breakers, now definitely getting louder in advance of the storm. One of these days a Category Five hurricane would come and take out the whole barrier island. It wasn't much more than an overgrown sandbar—with several billion dollars' worth of structures on it. Coastal Florida seems so civilized until the one-hundred-forty-mile-an-hour winds come along and fling manhole covers around like poker chips.

I was beginning to get used to my chest pain and my drug regimen. It didn't hurt any less, but it would eventually get better, and I was lucky to be alive. My ribs would heal faster than my heart, which was having a hard time over Glory's infidelity. For now I needed to compartmentalize the emotions—I had work to do. Later on I would see how I felt. I figured I would get over it in thirty years or so. We Catholics may be all about sin and forgiveness, but we Italians are all about holding a grudge.

There was a ring around the sun. They say that it's caused by ice crystals in cirrus clouds, although the notion of ice anywhere seems implausible in the August heat. They also say it's a sign that a storm is coming. I had hurricane shutters on the house, and I figured that the wind would be reminding me to lock them down tonight.

*

Frank Velutto's tan Mercedes was in my driveway when I got home. I parked the BMW next to it and got out. He wasn't in the car, and there was no one in the neighborhood except the couple across the street, outside making storm preparations. They ignored me; I was the neighborhood pariah after my jail stretch, even though the case had been thrown out. It was almost seven o'clock, and I wanted to shower and shave before I went over to Barbara's, plus I needed to pack a bag if I was going to sleep over.

The door to my house was unlocked and the alarm turned off. I surprised Frank in the kitchen; he jumped when I said his name.

"Vinny, sorry, I let myself in," he said.

"Where'd you get the key?"

"Carole had one, remember?" he said. He had not only let himself in, he'd poured himself a scotch, and a generous one at that.

"And the alarm?" I asked.

"Yeah, we had that too," he said. "Don't you remember?"

Actually, I remembered that I had changed the code when I'd gotten out of jail back in the spring, and I certainly hadn't told Frank. Only Roberto and I knew what the sequence was. But Frank was a cop, and cops knew all the guys at the alarm company. They could just switch it off if he said so.

"Frank, what are you doing here?"

"Um…I came to ask you something, Vin." He looked wasted, like he'd already had plenty to drink.

"So ask."

"You remember that computer you got Glory? The thin one?"

"Yes."

"Well, this is kind of awkward, but I was wondering if you wanted to sell it. I was thinking of getting one for Carole, and I didn't know how to ask you."

"I thought you and Carole were separated."

"Yeah, well, I'm trying to fix that."

"So, Frank, you break into my house and make yourself a drink and now you want to buy Glory's computer?"

"Hey, I didn't break in. I had a key, OK?" He backed out of the kitchen, and we migrated toward the living room. "I'm sorry about taking your booze. I didn't think you would care and…I'm fucking messed up, man."

"I see that," I said.

"So where's the computer?" he said. I looked around the room. I could see several drawers that were open that weren't open when I'd left the house in the morning. Frank had gone through the place already.

"It's not here," I said. "Don't you remember? Your forensics guys went through the place, and they didn't find it."

"Yeah, I remember," he said. In fact, according to the report Frank had been the first cop on the scene. He'd excused himself from the case because we were friends, but he'd directed the initial part of the investigation.

"So, you still got it?" he said.

"I tossed it in the river," I said.

Frank's face went dark. I knew that look. It was the same as my dad's, right before his fury would explode. "You're fucking with me, right Vinny?"

"No," I said. "It's in the river."

"Then who's sending me the fucking emails? From Glory's account? Who's telling me she's not dead, and she's coming to get me? You want to answer me that?"

"I don't know what you're talking about, Frank."

"Last week. I fucking jumped out of my skin. 'I'M NOT DEAD BUT YOU'RE GOING TO BE.' You scared the shit out of me until I figured it out. I felt like coming over and burning your fucking house down."

Roberto. Holy shit. Frank was the guy…*Pacobell6969*. Roberto had flushed the grouse.

"Somebody else sent that email. Not me." I felt oddly calm. Frank was getting more and more agitated. "I'm going to get myself a drink," I said.

I got a bottle of bourbon from the cabinet and poured a highball glass half-full. At the same time I took my phone out of my pocket and touched an app that worked as a recording machine. I put the phone down on the cabinet, next to the bourbon bottle. I had a feeling that I would want this conversation on tape.

"So you're Pacobell."

"Christ," he said, and he slumped into a chair. "Who else knows?"

"I'm not going to tell you that," I said.

He pulled out his gun, a Glock 26 just like mine. He aimed it at my chest. "Who else knows, Vin," he said, his voice now measured and calm. "Who sent the email?"

"Put it away, Frank. I already got drawn on today, and I'm not in the mood."

"I'll do it, Vin. I already tried once."

I thought about that, and another tumbler clicked into place. "At the Ford dealership?"

"Yeah."

"OK Frank, a fourteen-year-old kid knows. You going to shoot him too? Because we found out you were fucking my wife?"

He put the gun down and hung his head. "You don't get it, do you," he said. "But you will. You're too fucking smart."

I looked at his gun, the Baby Glock. It was the same caliber as mine, a nine millimeter. The final tumbler clicked, and the bolt slid open.

"So tell me how it happened," I said.

He looked at the rug and began to talk, in a hollow monotone. "She wouldn't talk to me. I would drive up to her on the street and she wouldn't even look at me. For six months she was crazy about me and then she just turned it off."

I didn't say anything.

"You and I went out for a drink. I'd emailed her five times that day—I was going crazy. I just wanted to see her. I had a pocketful of crushed-up Ambien, and I put it in your drink when you went to take a whiz. I wanted to get you good and fucked up, and I didn't care if it killed you, either. And then you went home and passed out, and I let myself in. I had a key, and I used to know the fucking alarm code, she gave it to me. We used to do it right here on the couch, when you were out of town."

He took a big swig of his scotch. His words were hitting me like little poison darts, and the venom was racing through my blood.

"She's in the living room, she's reading a book and she's had some wine, and I'm a little drunk too. She's way pissed off that I came to the house and she's yelling and I start yelling and she's afraid you're going to wake up. I grab her, I'm trying to kiss her and she knees me hard in the balls and I fall on the floor and I can't fucking draw a breath. She's screaming at me and I pull out my piece and I shoot her once in the stomach. She's on the floor and then you come out and fall down the stairs head first and you look like you're dead. You still have your gun on your belt so I take it out and put it in your hand, then put another one into Glory, in the chest."

"Two bullets, two guns." My words sounded far away, like someone else had said them.

"I loved your wife, Vinny. I couldn't help myself. I killed her and I ruined your life and I ruined mine."

I felt my own gun, in the holster at the small of my back. It would be easy to just put a slug in him. Everything was on tape. I never wanted to kill somebody more in my life. Frank was now crying, which made me hate him even more.

"I never meant to hurt her," he said. He put his drink down. "I miss her every day." He stood up and walked over to the half-bath in the entry hall and closed the door.

I took a long drink from the bourbon glass. It was the first hard liquor I'd had in a while, and it burned on the way down. Hearing Frank Velutto say that he missed Glory was the last poisoned arrow that I could take. I reached behind my back and unsnapped the Glock.

There was a loud bang from the half-bath. I opened the door. Frank was seated on the john, slumped forward, with the back of his head blown away. His gun was on the floor. Glory had painted the walls a deep crimson, and Frank's blood was exactly the same color, just wetter. He beat me to it.

*

My first call was to the Sheriff's office. I got through to the duty officer, Bobby Bove, who had been around for as long as I had and knew his job. I gave him the basics, and he said there were two deputies out near the house, but he'd get someone to cover and would come over first, and I thanked him. I needed someone with some experience to survey the damage before some rookie hothead got there and jumped to the wrong conclusion.

I called Barbara next, but the phone rang and went to her message machine. It wouldn't have surprised me if she had just passed out; sooner or later the shock of what she'd been through would sink in. I left a message telling her that I wouldn't be over and to stay inside, and to call the police if anything was wrong.

I went upstairs and flushed the rest of the pain pills down the toilet. I didn't want to complicate things any more than they already were. Everything else I left untouched, and I waited outside on the front lawn for Bobby. The wind was coming up hard now, and the palm trees were swaying like drunks coming home from a bar.

Bobby arrived within minutes. I told him where Frank was, and he asked for my gun, which I handed over to him. He dropped it into a plastic bag. I also told him where my cell phone was, next to the bourbon bottle. I asked him to be careful with it; it had a recording that would explain what had happened. Shortly afterward the street turned into a carnival of flashing blue lights, and I was led to one of the gathering squad cars and locked in the back. A few stray neighbors collected at the end of the driveway, wondering who I'd killed now.

*

The interrogation room at the county office was familiar to me, from both sides of the table. Besides Bobby there was a new assistant D.A. who I hadn't met before named Bill Thornton. He was African American, half-a-foot taller than me, and he didn't look pleased to have been roused from his bed. They made me listen to the tape several times and explain the sequence of events in my own words. They were respectful, but they were in shock too. When cops lose one of their own, even if it's not exactly in the line of duty, the rest of them are just that much closer to their own mortality. No one congratulated me on solving Glory's murder. By three in the morning it was clear that they had a suicide, not a homicide, and Bobby Bove drove me home. He took me into the house while I collected my things, since it was still taped off for the forensics team to return to in the morning. I thanked him, got into the BMW, and drove to the Spring Hill Suites, where I took a room and lay on the bed in my clothes, thinking about my dead wife and her dead lover while the glass in the windows began to shiver from the fury of the oncoming wind.

WEDNESDAY

THE RAIN AND THE UN-medicated pain in my ribs woke me, otherwise I might have slept until noon. I turned on the TV and every channel was talking about the storm which was off the coast around Jupiter and was headed north. The forecasters said it was poking along at a slow pace, but was still a Category Two, and wherever it made landfall would get walloped.

There were four messages on my cell phone, three from newspapers and one from Barbara. Someone at the Sheriff's office must have leaked what happened, but I had no interest in talking to the press. I called Barbara, and she answered on the first ring.

"Where are you?" she said. Her voice sounded anxious.

"At the Spring Hill Suites." It hurt to talk. I was wishing I hadn't flushed my stash and was already making plans to see Sonny, my pharmacist.

"Vince, what's going on? I'm in my car, going to the high school. They evacuated the whole island."

"Come here, I have a room. I have a few things to explain."

"There was something on the news..." she said.

"Yeah," I said. "I'll tell you when you get here."

I got a quick shower and changed into a fresh set of clothes. I didn't have anything for the rain, but I still planned to venture out, even if I'd get soaked. I had to stop at Sonny's, and from there I was going to drive back to Lake Wales, to the juice plant. The way hurricanes worked it might not even be raining there.

Barbara showed up at my door looking like she'd gone swimming in her clothes. It wasn't cold, but she was shivering just the same. She shucked off her jacket and sat on the side of the bed, peeling off her tan shorts.

"I'm going to use your shower," she said.

"OK," I said, and I turned my head away, suddenly modest. I pretended to look at the TV.

I called Sonny while she bathed, and he said he'd get me a refill, I could come over any time. Barbara was out of the shower, toweling off with the door slightly ajar, the steamy air escaping from the bath into the room. I pretended not to watch as she wrapped her hair in a towel and wrapped another one around her torso.

"There's a robe in the closet," I said.

"Too late," she said. "You've already had your peep show." I blushed.

She sat next to me on the bed. "So. What happened?" she said.

"A cop named Frank Velutto shot himself in my house," I said. "Last night when I came home."

"They didn't say that he shot himself on the news. They just said he was killed by gunfire."

"I didn't shoot him," I said. "But I thought about it. I found out some things about my marriage that I didn't know."

"So he's the guy."

"What guy?"

"The guy who had an affair with your wife," she said.

"How do you know about that?" I'd never said anything to Barbara about the emails. "Was that on the news?"

"No. I didn't tell you this, Vince, but Glory and I were kind of…friends. She took a Pilates class from me, at the club. We got to know each other, and sometimes we'd have lunch after class. She asked me, a couple of years ago, if I'd ever had an affair. I said no, but that opened the floodgates. She didn't tell me who it was, but she gave me all the details and said that she was desperate to end it. She loved you a lot, you know."

"Not enough to be faithful," I said.

"Being faithful has nothing to do with how much you love somebody," she snapped, "so don't give me that crap."

"I'm—"

"You're just as guilty as anyone else. You slept with me, and I'm married. Don't confuse love and desire, they're two different things."

"Jesus, I didn't…"

Barbara held out her hand to silence me. "I know you loved your wife, and I know she loved you back. You were lucky." She got up and stormed back into the bathroom, shutting the door behind her.

I crossed the room and opened the bathroom door. She was sitting on the john, naked except for the towel around her hair. "Barbara—"

"Get out of here!" she said. I closed the door and went back to the bed. There were too many emotions swirling around in my head, and my ribs ached. The news blared from the TV while the rain beat against the window, trying to drown it out. The latest storm projection now had Vero Beach right in the crosshairs.

I took the easy way out and left her a brief note, then closed the door quietly behind me and went down the hall and out the front of the hotel into the cascading rain. I was soaked down to my underwear before I got halfway to the BMW.

*

Sonny came to the door with shaving cream covering part of his scalp. The pit bulls were inside, sound asleep on a velour-covered couch.

"You're just in time, man. Do the back, OK? I always cut the shit out of myself." He held out a disposable razor.

"You trust me not to lop off an ear?"

"Dark side of the moon, man. I can't see back there."

We went into his kitchen, and I finished shaving his head. "You're going through that shit way too fast," he said. "You a junkie already."

"I had to flush it," I said. "The cops were coming."

"Yeah, I saw you on TV. They used your old mug shot. You're a badass motherfucker. I shouldn't even be talking to you."

"I didn't shoot the guy," I said.

"I heard all about it from my sister," he said. "That's fucked up."

He toweled off his head and handed me another packet. "Don't flush these," he said. "If it gets in the water supply, we all going to be walking around like zombies."

*

I stopped at my house to pick up supplies for Lake Wales. The doors were still taped, but the garage was not, and everything I needed was there. Lock picking is an art that involves patience and finesse, but there are times when stronger methods are the only way. I anticipated a serious challenge at the juice plant, judging from the hardware I'd seen on the door of the blacked-out room. I packed a ten-pound sledge, a stud finder, a hacksaw, a rechargeable reciprocating saw, and a small chainsaw with a fourteen-inch bar. These were not my finesse tools, but they worked when other things didn't.

The rain thinned out by the time I passed the interstate highway and by Twenty Mile Bend it stopped, although I could see large swaths of the storm on all sides of me. I had taken two of the OxyContins, but that didn't take away the sting of Barbara's words. She was right, of course; I had no business getting all sanctimonious about the purity of my marriage. I knew that Glory had loved me, and I knew I loved her. Any woman could have fallen prey to Frank Velutto's movie-star looks and his hot pursuit. She'd tried to get away from him, but it was a death trap. Frank was thought of as something of a skirt-chaser. Although I'd never actually known of an affair he'd had, people just assume that the more handsome ones among us are out there scoring. He was probably not accustomed to being turned down by anybody, and when Glory had shut him off, he went crazy. Sex just might be the most destructive drug of them all.

My phone rang, and the caller ID said "Velutto." For a moment I panicked, but I realized it couldn't be. Frank was in the morgue with a tag on his toe. I'd watched them load his corpse into the ambulance. I answered.

"Who is this?"

"Vince, it's Carole. I heard about what happened."

"I'm sorry, Carole."

"Don't be," she said. "They told me he shot himself, it wasn't you. Although you would have had every right."

"You knew?"

"Yes, and I am calling to say I am so sorry, Vinny. So goddamn sorry."

"Glory told you?"

"No, I found the emails. I confronted him, and he lied and lied until I finally beat it out of him. It was after Glory died, and I just...assumed that you'd killed her, like everybody else did. I assumed you'd found her emails, and that was what made you do it. Bobby Bove told me the whole story. I was so wrong, Vinny. I feel terrible."

"Thanks Carole...I appreciate that. I'm kind of confused right now though..."

"I'm sorry, I just had to get it off my chest."

"No problem. I'll call you when things settle down, and we can talk," I said, and we hung up. The sound of Frank Velutto's gun going off in my bathroom was beginning to echo through Florida.

*

The storm had closed in again and large droplets began to drum on the torn cloth top of my car as I entered the road behind the self-storage units. The metal gate was open, and I drove right through. If anyone was in there, they'd see me on the closed circuit TV, but as I pulled into the parking area it was clear that I was the only person on the property. I got my duffel from the trunk and jogged to the building, entering by the same door I had on the day before. The rain had now stopped, but it was so overcast outside that I had to switch on the interior lights to see my work. I surveyed the locks, and knew I would be there for a while if I tried to pick them. The cylinder in the doorknob was probably fifty years old and wouldn't be a problem, but above it was a brand-new Samsung Digital Deadbolt that required an RFID card. You could also key in the code by guessing, but that could take a year, and you'd still have to be lucky. I went back out to the BMW for my more persuasive tools.

The first thing I tried was the blacked-out window. I smashed out a section with the sledge only to find it was backed by a steel plate that was bolted from the inside and felt solid. I might have been able to hammer it out, but I didn't have the strength in my damaged condition.

I switched on the stud finder and located a section of the wall that was free from any plumbing or electrical conduit. The wall studs were set sixteen inches apart, so it would be a slight squeeze, but I decided I would be able to get through, even with my cracked ribs. I started the reciprocating saw, and it tore through the sheetrock on the exterior, but the inside wall was lined with thick plywood, and it was slow going. I broke a blade and had to replace it, but eventually I had a hole that was big enough to climb through, and I hadn't sawn through any pipes or electrocuted myself, which was a minor victory. I pushed myself through the opening, head first, and ended up on the cool, concrete floor of the closed-off room, in total darkness except for the blue flicker of three small TV monitors. The cat-pee odor that permeated the rest of the building was especially intense here. I got out my penlight, found a wall switch, and the room was suddenly bathed in fluorescent light.

It was a lab. Not the crude, homemade kind I'd seen in motel rooms and garages when I was a cop; this one was state-of-the-art, and the art was the manufacture of methamphetamine. Storage bins and chemical vats lined the walls, and at the far end of the room there was a boiler for the distillation. I counted six fire extinguishers; a prudent precaution—many of the chemicals used to make meth were highly flammable, and the more primitive labs had a nasty habit of blowing up. At a hundred bucks a gram, a meth lab of this size and sophistication could bring in millions. Millions that could be laundered through a cash business—like vending machines—and then sent offshore to a discreet bank to be custodied under the name of some dummy corporation—like Empex Import/Export LLC. So C.J. Butler the citrus broker was also a meth broker, and he was obviously a very big one. My three AM paranoid delusion from the week before had turned out to be real.

At the other end of the lab was a gray metal desk with a computer and the video surveillance screens. This was apparently C.J.'s real office, not the one on East Stuart Avenue where I'd first seen him. I booted up the computer, but there was no way to log on, and I didn't want to call Roberto; I'd imposed on him enough. I noticed an external hard drive attached to the computer by a USB cord, and I unplugged it and slipped it into my pocket. The TV screens immediately began to beep, and for a moment I thought I'd tripped an alarm, but when I looked at the screens, I saw movement. A truck was passing through the front gate and was coming up the drive. It was a small, white panel truck; a Ford Transit. I shut the lights off and hurried back through my entrance hole. I quickly gathered my tools and tossed them in my duffel. I made it outside and flung the duffel into the passenger seat, then started the car and drove off into the grove in the same direction that Philip had, on the previous day. I parked behind a stand of fruit trees and got out of the car to see who was coming.

The panel truck parked across the lot from the building, and two men got out. They walked toward the building carrying brown paper shopping bags in their arms. I had a suspicion that they weren't delivering groceries.

Fifteen minutes later they were gone. I didn't dare go back inside—all my instincts were telling me that the Vereda Fruit Processing Co. was about to be history. I was more than a hundred yards away, but when the building finally blew, the force of the explosion knocked me over and fragments of metal and concrete whizzed by my head. When the dust cleared, there was nothing remaining except for the loading dock platform and the twisted metal stilts of the tower; everything else was scattered around the yard in pieces. A few timbers smoldered where the lab had been. The building had been obliterated, and no forensic team on the planet would be able to tell whether it had been a meth lab or a day care center. I brushed the dust off of my shirt and patted my hip pocket—I still had the portable hard drive. I hoped that whatever was on it would be enough to put C.J. Butler away for a long time.

*

The gates were still open on the way out, and I hit the accelerator when I got onto the pavement of Highway 60. I wanted to put a fast couple of miles between me and the grove before somebody reported that a bomb had gone off and the police arrived—I'd had enough press coverage for one morning.

I stopped in the Wal-Mart parking lot and dialed Doc Edwards, the cop in Tampa who had visited me in the hospital and had given me his card. It was time to call in the cavalry.

"Edwards," he said, gruffly. Another one who watched too much *CSI*.

"Tanzi," I said.

"The P.I. from the hospital?"

"Yeah."

"What do you have?"

"Who covers Lake Wales for the DEA?"

"That would be the guys here," he said. "They have a pretty busy office in Tampa."

"Somebody just blew up a meth lab." I gave him the location, and told him it was owned by Empex Import/Export LLC which was connected to D.B. Johannsen and probably his wife. I also told him they wouldn't find much of the building left, but I had a portable hard drive that might be helpful.

"How did you come by that?"

"Craigslist," I said.

"I trust you got your computer back."

"I did."

"I'd like to get that hard drive."

"I'll leave it at the Lake Wales P.D. I have to get back to Vero."

"The hurricane is hitting there right about now," he said.

"I know. That's why I have to go back," I said, and hung up.

*

By the time I passed under the interstate there were cops everywhere, attempting to keep people off the road and away from the storm's fury. I had the local news on in the BMW, and the hurricane was in the process of making a direct hit on Wabasso, a little community along the river a few miles north of Vero. The wind was tearing everything apart, and I had to drive around downed trees and power lines to get to the Spring Hill Suites. I parked the car and opened the door into the wind, and then almost couldn't close it, it was blowing so hard. I was knocked over twice in the parking lot on my way into the hotel. The automatic entry didn't open, and I realized the power was out. I pushed open a side entrance and finally got inside, out of the pounding rain.

"We're full," a clerk said.

"I'm already checked in," I said. "Do you have a generator?"

"We're starting it right now. There's only enough for the overhead lights, the outlets won't work."

"How about the water?"

"We'll have it as long as the mains are running," he said. That was good, because I was headed directly for the shower; I was dirty, chilled and soaked to the bone.

The ceiling lights were working again by the time I got to my room. Barbara was gone. I hoped I hadn't sent her out into the storm with my stupid remarks. I took out my phone to call her, but there was no service, and I realized the local cell towers were probably storm casualties. I picked up the hotel phone, which worked, and I dialed, but her phone didn't answer, and it dawned on me that if my cell didn't work, hers wouldn't either. I stripped off my clothes and entered the bath.

Taking a hot shower in the middle of a Category Two hurricane was as decadent a pleasure as I'd ever enjoyed. The whole area around me was under a fierce meteorological attack, and meanwhile I was soaping my thighs and fogging up the mirror, oblivious to the destruction, in my marble-clad stall. I stopped short of croaking out the Barry White medley that I usually sang in the shower. People out there were getting their whole lives trashed. If there was a God, She would be adding this incident to my permanent file.

The bathroom door opened, and I could see Barbara through the cloud of steam. She was dressed in a snug-fitting workout suit. I heaved a sigh of relief.

"Where were you?" she yelled over the din of the shower.

"Out getting dirty," I yelled back.

"I'll bring you a robe," she said. I turned off the shower and toweled off. Barbara came back in and handed me a terry cloth bathrobe. She watched while I put it on.

"You owed me a peep show," she said. She was smiling. I guessed I was being forgiven.

"Barbara, I'm sorry for what I said."

"About what?"

"About being faithful. It was hypocritical."

"That's not what pissed me off," she said.

"What?"

"Don't ever walk into the bathroom when I'm on the john," she said. "That's a deal killer, OK?"

"Jeez, sorry."

"I mean it. Don't ever do that again." I nodded. Stephen Hawking was right—men might someday untangle the mysteries of the universe, but they will never understand women.

Barbara went back into the bedroom, and I followed a few minutes after when I had dried off and combed my hair. She was sitting on a modern-looking green sofa that was in the workspace section of the suite. I sat down next to her.

"I went to Lake Wales," I said. "I almost couldn't get back into Vero, it was blowing and raining so hard."

"I've been watching it from the weight room. It's a huge storm. I wonder if my house will still be there."

"We can go out later," I said. "Barbara, I found out what that juice plant really is. It's a meth lab. A drug factory. They were making methamphetamine there."

"Oh god," she said. "Did C.J. know about it?"

"He owns the property. I think it's where most of his money came from. I also think Le was involved; I saw one of their delivery vans there this morning."

"Are you going to tell the cops?"

"I already did," I said. "Someone blew the place up, while I was there. The DEA people will investigate it, and it's going to be bad for C.J."

She looked away from me, then rose from the couch and looked out the window at the raging storm. "I don't care anymore," she said. "I don't care what happens to C.J."

I didn't say anything.

"What do we do now?" she said.

"We can't go anywhere," I said. "It's crazy out there."

"So we're stuck here together," she said. "OK."

"There are two beds," I said. "We don't—"

"I know," she said. "I'm not—"

"Not that—" I began.

"Vince," she said, "I really like you. But it's not going to work."

"Don't tell me I'm getting fired again."

"No, that's not what I'm talking about. I'm just…damaged goods, OK? You're telling me my husband is a drug dealer, and I've been washing his underwear for twenty years."

"I'm sorry."

"Don't be. I asked you to find these things out. But you and I have to…"

"You don't have to say anything, Barbara," I said. "I understand. I'm not exactly on solid ground myself."

"I'm exhausted," she said.

"Me too," I said. "You take the bed by the window."

She got under her covers and was silent within minutes, while I lay awake listening to the wind. She was right, neither of us had any business being intimate, it was a bad idea. I kept trying to convince myself of that, but I felt like I'd just broken another rib, the one right below my heart.

*

I woke up at seven PM, according to my phone. I'd had a four hour nap. The storm had passed and it was now quiet outside, with weak sunlight peering in through the corners of the blinds. Barbara appeared to still be sleeping, but she turned under the covers and faced me from the other bed.

"You snore," she said.

"That was the hurricane."

"You snore louder than the hurricane," she said. She slipped out of the covers and walked into the john. I was careful not to follow. I got up and dressed in dry clothes. I was sitting in an armchair wiping the moisture out of my holster when she reappeared, dressed only in her bra and panties. If she was really trying to end our relationship, she was doing a lousy job of it. She found her bag and removed a makeup kit, then went back into the bathroom, while I sat with my confusion.

I tried my cell phone and found out that I was getting reception. The first thing I checked was my email, and I had a few dozen of them from reporters and curious acquaintances. No doubt I would be getting some more calls like Carole Velutto's where the people who had shunned me would now want me back into their lives. Personally, I didn't give a damn. If I was going to start being invited to parties again, I would decline; I seldom went to any of them even when Glory was alive. The only two people I cared about at the present moment were my young friend Roberto, and the woman who shared my room, but not my bed.

I checked in with Roberto while I waited for Barbara to dress. He was fine; he said there were a lot of trees down in the neighborhood, and the power was off. He said he'd biked past my house, and it looked OK. I told him about Frank Velutto, as gently as I could. I didn't want him to feel guilty about the fact that he had emailed him from Glory's account and now he was dead. I lied a little and said that Frank's suicide had nothing to do with it, and that it would come out that it was Frank who had shot Glory and Roberto had helped me find that out, and that I would always be grateful to him for that knowledge. I added that I thought the worst was over with the case he'd been helping me on, and that C.J. Butler was going to be out of commission soon. We agreed to get together when I got back to the house and we'd catch up then.

Barbara came out of the bath, dressed and looking refreshed. "Let's go look around," she said.

"They won't want anyone on the roads except emergency vehicles," I said. "Too many lines and trees down."

"I just want to see if my house is in the ocean," she said.

We took the Barber Bridge over to the island and surveyed the devastation. There was a roadblock on the mainland side, but Barbara insisted they let us through, and they did. Workers with chainsaws were clearing away stricken trees from the roadways, and there were rows and rows of expensive homes that were missing part or all of their roofs. The barrier island had been in one hell of a fight and had lost on a decision, but not a knockout, as it was still there.

We crossed A-1-A and continued over to Ocean Drive where the beach shops, hotels, and brokerage houses were. Piles of sand lay across the road, and you could hear the surf pounding away in the storm's aftermath. The Driftwood Hotel was still standing. It had seen worse. The Riomar area where Barbara lived was relatively untouched. The neighborhood was older, so the trees had stood longer and were hurricane-tested. Roof tiles and shingles were scattered everywhere, and people's insurance rates would be soon hitting the stratosphere as they did after every major hurricane when the insurance companies scrambled to recover their losses.

A big live oak had come down across her front yard, and I parked the BMW next to the uprooted trunk. One of its branches had smashed open a front window, and the tree had also taken out the power lines on the way down. C.J.'s van was safe in the garage. Barbara entered and surveyed the interior in semi-darkness. I walked around the outside and didn't see any other damage to the building except for some loose shutters. It could have been much worse.

She came out and met me in front of the house. "It's actually OK inside."

"You need to cover that window," I said. "I can help, if you've got a sheet of plywood."

"I'll get one later," she said. "Vince, I think I'm going to stay here."

"That's not safe," I said. "And there's no power."

"I'll be all right. I have candles and everything. I need to be on my own right now."

"Then I'm staying with you," I said.

"No," she said. "Not this time."

"Look," I said. "If you're going to be like this, then I can't do anything for you. I can't protect you anymore."

"That's your decision."

"This is fucking crazy," I said.

"I need a ride back to the hotel to get my car," she said.

She got into the BMW, and I drove her. Neither of us said a single word.

*

I was in no hurry to go home to my dark house. Instead, I drove to South Beach to watch the crashing surf. The storm tide brought the water all the way up to the dunes, across what was normally a wide stretch of open sand. The waves were still ten feet high, and a couple of kids were out on surfboards, getting the rides of their lives. I hoped they were good swimmers, because if they lost their boards the rip tide would take them halfway to the Azores.

If I was angry at Barbara, I was completely pissed off at myself. How had I let myself get so close to her? I wasn't a goddamn kid anymore—I ought to know better. She was a client, and I had let my guard down and allowed things to go way too far between us. I told myself I wouldn't let it happen again, but it felt like a hollow promise.

One of the surfers caught a perfect curl and tucked himself under the break—a giant blue canopy barreling just over his head. At exactly the right moment he shot out and flew up and over the top of the wave, temporarily joining a line of pelicans that were coasting over the breakers looking for food. Things were returning to normal after the hurricane, and although the wind and surf had altered the contours of the beach, the rollers still came in, the fish still swam, the sun rose in the morning, and the fat tourists from Ohio nourished their sunburns and yelled at their kids. Life would go on.

THURSDAY

THE STORM HAD SWEPT THE air clean of humidity, and so I left the windows open at the hotel. Since I'd already paid for the room, I decided to stay and enjoy the hot water and TV for one more night. Somehow, going home felt like giving up.

I didn't stir until five in the morning. I got up and showered and shaved, and then I sat on one of the sofas and looked at the empty bed where Barbara had napped the afternoon before. A good night's rest should have left me feeling better about things, but I felt worse, and I reached for my little packet of joy from Sonny. He was right, the stuff was seductive as hell and I really had to watch out or I'd be out picking up trash along the interstate in an orange jumpsuit and leg irons.

I went out to the parking lot and got my laptop. I hadn't checked any of my snooping programs in a while, and I was curious if there were any recordings from the Johannsen house from after C.J. and Philip had driven the Lexus back home. According to Shirley Magan, Philip would have been picked up by now, remanded to the Hillsborough Juvenile facility. I should probably make yet another trip to Tampa, as she'd asked me to give her a statement. Maybe I could just do it over the phone; it was time to get back to my own house and check it out. There'd be some clean-up to do, for sure.

The first conversation was between the three of them, sometime on Tuesday afternoon when C.J. and Philip got home. Le was there waiting, and she was in an ugly mood. She alternated her shouting between Vietnamese, directed at Philip, and some foul-mouthed English, aimed at C.J., who was now D.B. There was some stomping off and door slamming, but nothing from the exchange gave me any more knowledge than I already had, except that the tiny woman had a big bad temper.

The next recording was at eight o'clock the same evening. The television was on in the background. The doorbell rang, and I heard C.J. answer it. It was hard to distinguish the words because the conversation was held at the front door threshold and the nearest microphone was in the kitchen, but I got the gist. It was the cops, looking for Philip. C.J. told them he wasn't in; he was away with his mother on a trip. They pressed him, but he wouldn't give them anything more than that. The cops must have known they were being stonewalled, because they didn't waste any more time. When that happened to me in the old days we'd get a warrant and come back, and half the time we'd find who we wanted in the bathroom or under a bed. But after they left there was nothing else on the tape except the TV. A few minutes later I heard C.J. talking, from the bug in his man-cave. He was on the phone.

Where are you? Then silence.

Then he said, *Don't come back. The police were here, looking for Philip. I think they wanted to take him. You'd better stay somewhere else.*

There was another long silence as C.J. listened. *It's under control, Le. No, she's not the problem. Leave her alone. The problem is the guy she's with. I can handle him.*

There was some more back-and-forth, but nothing important was said and they hung up.

So I was C.J.'s problem, and I could be handled. He'd already tried to pay me off at the Lake Wales airport, and I thought I'd made it clear that I wouldn't be bought. So if he was going to handle me, I'd better watch my back. The reassuring part was that Barbara was no longer the focus, I was.

The next recording was from Wednesday morning, while I was driving to Lake Wales to break into the juice plant. C.J. was on the phone, and I heard another one-sided conversation. He was talking to Le again. He told her he was going to "close the operation," and he needed some of her men to take care of it. He wrote down a phone number and repeated it back to her, and I wrote it down also; Doc Edwards would surely like that. My little bugs were paying off.

After that there were no more recordings, except for the television coming on every so often. I could still get a live feed, so I switched it on. C.J. was up and moving around the house, with the morning news blaring.

I left the room and wandered down to where the hotel served a continental breakfast. There was not much there because of the storm, but some heroic employee had managed to get a big pot of fresh coffee going. I got a cup, balanced some day-old pastries on a paper plate, and returned to the room. I decided I'd try Doc Edwards; maybe he was an early riser.

"Edwards."

"Vince Tanzi," I said. "I have something you're going to like."

"Give," he said.

"The phone number that our meth-lab-owner friend called, to get someone to burn the place down." I gave it to him.

"The DEA is all over this," he said. "They already had a file on the vending company. Every one of their drivers has a record, and they were sniffing around for months, but it was a tightly-run operation."

"Did you find anything on the hard drive?" I asked.

"Did we ever. Money trails, dealers, production records, a friggin' gold mine. I don't know how we're going to explain how we got it. An anonymous concerned citizen turned it in, or something like that. We showed it to the judge last night, and we're going into the Johannsen house and the vending office in a few minutes with the warrants. You caught me in my car; I'm on the way to their house."

"He's there, and he's awake," I said. "The wife and kid are gone."

"How the hell do you know that?"

"Do me a favor," I said. I told him where the bugs were. He said he'd collect them, and would hold them for me. Anything from my tapes would be inadmissible anyway, and it might also land me in jail.

"How'd you make out in the storm?" he said.

"Don't know yet," I said.

"You're in the Tampa papers today," he said. "You sure get a lot of press. A cop shot himself in your house? What was that all about?"

"Some other time, Edwards," I said. "Good luck with the bust. Let me know when you get him, OK?"

*

I checked out of the hotel and thought about swinging by Barbara's, but with the DEA and the Tampa cops swooping down on the Johannsens, I figured that for once I could relax. If she wanted to be alone, then I would respect that. I didn't like it, but perhaps I had better start getting used to it.

My neighborhood was a mess. The development was not a fancy one, and the builders must have skimped on the roofing because there were tiles all over the ground and the blue tarps were coming out to cover the holes. My roof was pockmarked with patches of exposed plywood where tiles had been. I had some tarps in the garage, but I didn't think I could deal with an extension ladder, with my ribs the way they were. I would have to call someone, get in line and wait.

The inside of the house was untouched, and the power was on. I brought my gear in from the car, including the two Glocks, which needed a good cleaning and oiling after all the exposure to the rain. I turned on the TV. The local news was all about Wabasso, and Gifford, the community just west of it. The eye of the storm had passed right through there, and there were boats tossed up on the land and a number of houses that were simply not there anymore. They didn't have any figures on how many people had been hurt, but it was bad. I felt even guiltier for riding it out in a snug hotel room. A few lost roofing tiles on my house seemed like a minor inconvenience next to the devastation I was seeing on the TV. I hoped Sonny was all right.

Roberto arrived on his bike. "No school," he said, and went to the fridge. "You're out of Coke."

"There's a ginger ale in there," I said. "It's probably older than you are."

"Cool."

"How's school this year?"

"Boring," he said. "Catch me up."

I told him about the trip to the juice plant and what C.J. had been up to. I said the cops were on it and would collar him soon. He was impressed that I'd scored the hard drive. We didn't talk about Frank Velutto, and I made a mental note to not let him go into the downstairs bathroom before I'd cleaned it up. I had no idea if the cops had or hadn't, and it might still be a bloody mess.

"What if I decided to do what you do?" he asked. "Be an investigator. Do you think I'd be good at it?"

"I think you'd be good at anything you want to try," I said. "But you don't want to be a P.I. Most of it is waiting around, and you deal with a lot of stupid people who have made big mistakes."

"I could be a cop."

"That's worse," I said. "It's a lot of sitting around too, and a lot more dangerous."

"Is that why you quit?"

"No," I said. "I loved being a cop."

"Then why?"

"Hang on," I said. I went into the half-bath. It had been wiped clean and smelled of sanitizer. There was a piece of sheetrock missing from the wall where the slug had gone in; the forensics guys must have removed it, otherwise it looked like nothing had happened there. I stood at the john and thought about Frank, and Glory. I reflected on my life, the mistakes I'd made and the few successes. Roberto was just about to begin his life as an adult, and he took everything I said as gospel. I enjoyed that, it felt good to be a hero in someone's eyes. But at the same time I wasn't going to bullshit him: I cared about him too much. I zipped up and returned to the kitchen.

"The truth is that I left the Sheriff's because I was asked to," I said. "You know how I can get past any lock. I never stopped doing that. Guys would lock their keys in their cars and it was "call Vince". I was also the go-to guy when we needed to get into somewhere that we weren't supposed to. Nobody talked about it because cops can't do that; you can't bust into someone's property without a warrant. But there were times when we really needed something badly, so I made it happen."

"And you got caught?" he said.

"No, I never got caught. I was good at what I did. But one time I went into a house over in Fellsmere where a bad guy lived. I found a gun that was a murder weapon. We suspected that he'd killed three people with it, and we had a tip that it was in the house, but we couldn't get a warrant. So I broke in and took it, and we made up a story. Then the whole thing unraveled in court. The D.A. was beside himself, because they couldn't try the guy again and he went free."

"Oh," he said. "Not good."

"Real bad," I said. "I still see the guy on the streets. He should be in jail. I had twenty-five years on the force, and the Sheriff told me they would allow me to retire, but if I didn't, I'd be canned."

"Do you wish you were still there?"

"Sometimes. I miss some of the people I worked with. But this is better. Not good enough for you though. You can make a lot more money doing computer things."

Roberto drank his ginger ale while I opened my mail. There was an express envelope from the insurance company with a check. It was for nearly the full amount that I'd paid for the SHO. That was the good news; the bad news was that my premium would quadruple if I bought another one.

"Hey," I said. "You ever think about going to St. Eds?"

"Snob school," he said. "Besides, it's like twenty-five thousand a year."

"They have financial aid," I said. "And I have some extra money. I could swing it." I definitely didn't need another man-toy; the BMW would more than meet my needs.

"Yeah," he said, "but my parents—"

"Roberto, I don't have any kids to spoil. And you're too smart to be lost in the crowd at the high school. The St. Edwards kids aren't snobs; they're smart kids like you with the same needs. I'll deal with your parents."

"Maybe you shouldn't bring over any flowers this time."

I laughed. "I'll talk to your mom and dad. Then we can go over and check it out. All the hot girls go there, you know." Roberto blushed. Girls might not be on his radar yet, but if they weren't, they would be soon enough.

My phone rang; it was Doc Edwards. "You were wrong, he's gone."

"Did you find my listening things?"

"Yeah, I got 'em. I wish I could get away with that kind of shit," he said.

"Trust me, you can't," I said. "But I heard him in the house, right before you must have arrived. He must have bolted."

"There's a banged-up Lexus in the garage, no other cars."

"Is the boat there?"

"Boat?" he said.

"A big sport fisherman on the back dock."

"No boat," he said. "Damn. We didn't think of that." C.J. must have seen them coming and slipped out. Cops with warrants aren't always too subtle.

"There isn't anything in the way of evidence in the house, not even a checkbook. The place is bizarre. Did you see the plastic slip-covers?"

"Yes, but remember, I was never inside the house," I said.

"Yeah, it's creepy. Any idea where he'd be?"

"Not if he left on his boat," I said. "But he's got a house over here. And another wife."

"You're shitting me."

"She was my client. Somebody took some shots at her. I was hired to find out who."

"Did you find out?"

"I think so," I said. "At this point I think it's either the son or the other wife, the one over there in Tampa. Or both of them."

"Any idea where they are?" he asked.

"No," I said. "Are you guys looking for them yet?"

"We are now," he said. "Keep in touch, OK?"

"You too," I said. I didn't like what I was hearing. I was worried all over again, especially for Barbara. I asked Roberto to excuse me while I called her, but her cell didn't answer. I left her a voicemail, and told Roberto I had to go.

*

There was a power company crew at the Butler house sawing up the big oak. Barbara didn't answer the door, but her car was in the driveway. I thought about getting my kit out, but the front door had been left unlocked, so I let myself in and looked around. Her cell phone was on the kitchen counter, charging, as the electricity was already back on. The house was empty, but I found a phone book on the table, opened to "Building Supplies" in the yellow pages. I checked the garage, and the van was gone. Barbara had gone out somewhere; now I was doubly worried. I remembered—I still had a tracker on C.J.'s van. I ran back to my car and opened the laptop.

The blue dot was pulsing, but not moving. According to the tracker she was out of town by the Indian River Mall, across 20th Street. There was a Home Depot near there. I took the bridge back to the mainland and hurried west, keeping the laptop open in case she moved.

Fifteen minutes later I was turning into the Home Depot lot when I saw the minivan coming in the other direction with a sheet of plywood tied to the roof rack. I honked loudly, but Barbara didn't notice. I would have to turn into the lot and do a fast U-turn. Just before I made the turn I saw another car leaving, a few cars behind Barbara. It was a white Ford Transit van.

I swung the BMW around in an arc as fast as I could, but they were already well ahead and out of sight. I watched the blue dot flash on the tracker as Barbara turned back onto 20th Street toward town. The traffic was thick and narrowed to one lane at points where clean-up crews tackled the downed trees and debris. A flagman stopped me in front of the First Christian Church, and I watched the blue dot get even farther ahead. I needed to catch up.

They were now in the old part of downtown Vero, going east. They could be heading back to her house, and I hoped the tree men were still on the site; that might give her some protection. The blinking dot slowed before the intersection with Indian River Drive, and the van turned left by the Publix. The dot stopped moving. I had a feeling I knew where she was—the bakery cafe—the same place she'd come out of when she'd taken a shot in the purse. I was ten blocks behind, and I swerved around cars like a crazy person to get to the lot. I almost hit a pedestrian and some people honked at me, but I had to get there fast, so I pushed the BMW to the limit. I screeched to a stop in the lot a minute later. Barbara's van was parked out front, and the Transit van was at the opposite end. I could see "Le's Vending" stenciled on the door, and there was someone in the driver's seat—Philip. Was he waiting for Barbara to come outside? No—the passenger-side door was open. Someone had gotten out in too much of a hurry to close it, and I knew who that was.

I patted my back for the Glock and remembered—I had brought both of the handguns into my house when I'd arrived from the hotel. Goddamn it. I usually have a sense about when I should be carrying, and this was definitely one of those times. I had the Lupo in the trunk, but that would scare the shit out of everybody in the place. So what, I decided, and I grabbed it and slid two shells into the chambers as I ran for the front door of the cafe.

The tables were busy with people sipping coffee and peering into their computers. The first ones to see the shotgun were two women waiting in line at the register, and their high shrieks sliced through the crowd noise. The whole restaurant turned to look, and the patrons ducked for cover under their tables, leaving a forest of open laptops above them. Barbara and Le were nowhere in sight, and it was now silent except for the hissing of the espresso machine. A white-faced clerk looked at me from behind the pastry counter and tentatively raised both hands above her head.

"Asian woman?" I yelled. "Just came in?"

"Bathroom," she stammered.

I ran to the far corner where the bathrooms were, clutching the shotgun. The ladies room door was locked from the inside. I could hear Le's shrill voice inside, screaming.

"Open the door!" I yelled.

"She has a gun!" I heard Barbara yell, from inside.

I took a fork from one of the tables, bent the tines and jammed it into the lock, but it was way too thick. I knew exactly what tools I needed, but they were in the trunk of my BMW, and there wasn't any time. The door was solid; there would be no kicking it in. I ran back to the counter. "Bathroom key!" I yelled. "There's a woman in there with a gun. I'm an ex-cop."

The clerk got a key out of the register, and I snatched it from her trembling hand. I ran back and swung open the door as Le aimed a .22 Derringer and shot Barbara, who collapsed on the hard tile floor. Le swung the gun around as I raised the Lupo, and we fired. Her slug hit me in the shoulder and knocked me back. My shot hit her torso and left a hole so big you could almost see through it. Le's small body crumpled backward against a metal trash can and slid down onto the cold tile. I felt someone come up behind me; it was Philip, and when he saw his mother, he screamed and ran to hold her, then turned and ran for the door, his hands covered in her blood. I took a tentative step toward Barbara, but my legs gave out from under me, and the last thing I remember was the smell of gunpowder and freshly-baked croissants.

FRIDAY

D.B. TOLD me to just stay in sight of the coast and enjoy the view, but I wasn't enjoying anything. The attorney had said the police were looking for me, and I didn't know what they knew or didn't know. We were passing the tip of Sanibel Island, heading for the bridge under the causeway to Punta Rassa. I'd never operated the boat, but D.B. said not to worry, I would know what to do. Philip was below decks in the air conditioning, playing video games. He hadn't come up since we'd left Tampa Bay. He had been crying on and off ever since he'd driven home yesterday and I decided to leave him alone with his grief. I had no time for such things.

I was going to clean up everything and leave no tracks. The lab was gone. The vending business could be sold—the lawyers could handle that. It would go to a competitor, albeit at half the price that it would if Le was alive. Le's people, the drivers and couriers, could be paid to be quiet. The only one who worried me was Barbara's person, and I would have to deal with him.

D.B. pointed out the shore birds and threw pieces of bread off the stern at two pelicans that were following us. If he was feeling anything about his wife, he didn't show it. This was like a pleasure cruise for him. He showed me the charts that pointed the way into the Caloosahatchee River to Fort Myers and the canal that led to Lake Okeechobee, and then out the St. Lucie Canal to Stuart on the east coast. We could cross Florida in a day.

We refueled at a marina in Cape Coral. D.B. was right; I had no problem maneuvering the boat alongside the dock where we tied up. He sat behind me in one of the white vinyl fighting chairs that he used when he fished. "I have to leave now," he said.

"I know," I said.

The boat could hold two hundred and fifty gallons of fuel, and I paid in cash. I opened the cabin door to check on Philip, but he didn't even look up, he was so absorbed in his game.

When I got back above, D.B. was gone.

*

The only good thing about being shot is that they don't immediately make you fill out any insurance forms. They have to fix you up first, because it completely screws up the system if you croak in the middle of the paperwork. I'd been in the emergency room and then the O.R. for an entire afternoon and evening, and no one had waved a single signature page in my face. I figured they'd make up for it later, and I was right. My morning-shift nurse, Clara, had to help me hold a pen to sign, since my shoulder was bandaged and I couldn't move my arm.

"This is fucking ridiculous," I said, and I regretted the profanity when she flinched. Most nurses are pretty battle-hardened, but she'd said this was her second month out of nursing school, and she hadn't yet had to deal with many grouchy old men like me.

"You can just make an X," she said. She looked about sixteen, angel-faced and on the cherubic side.

Clara checked all my machines and pronounced me alive. She refilled my water glass, and I took a left-handed sip. They must have had something good in the IV bag, because I couldn't feel any pain and I was groggy as hell. Clara left and a doctor came in, a woman who I remembered, sort of, from the surgical table.

"I'm Dr. Campion," she said. "I operated on you last night."

"Did you take care of Barbara Butler also?"

"No, that was Dr. Humphrey."

"Is she out of surgery? The nurses won't tell me a goddamn thing."

"She's in critical care. We can't really say much, because we're still waiting for her family."

"That doesn't sound good."

"She'll recover," she said. "But it was close."

"Who do you mean by family?"

"We couldn't reach her husband," the doctor said. "Her sister is on the way from Jacksonville."

"Is there a cop in there?"

"You mean security?"

"No, I mean is there a cop assigned to her? I need to talk to them," I said.

"You need to rest. It was a small caliber bullet, but it made a mess of your shoulder," she said. "And you have a concussion."

"I need to talk to the cops, right now," I said. "It's important."

"You can't, I'm sorry. Doctor's orders."

"Pass me the phone," I said, pissed off now.

"You really need to rest, Mr. Tanzi," she said, "There's—"

I shushed her and sat up in the bed. The blood rushed to my head, and I was woozy as I swung my legs off the side of the bed and reached for a telephone on a side table. I called the Sheriff's while Dr. Campion loudly protested. I got Myra, at the dispatch desk.

"It's Vince."

"Man, you got a nose for trouble," she said.

"Myra, can you get a deputy down to the hospital, like right now? There's a patient here who is at risk. Her name is Barbara Butler, and she's in critical care."

"She the lady who got shot? You OK, Vince? I heard you both got shot."

"I'm fine. She's not. Is Bobby Bove around?"

"I'll put you through."

I got to Bobby and told him the situation. C.J. and the boy could still be at large, and that could be trouble for Barbara—and for me. I asked him to call Doc Edwards in Tampa and fill him in. The sooner the two of them were located, the sooner I'd be able to rest, like the doctor wanted. She had overheard me giving the details to Bobby Bove.

"I'm sorry," she said. "I should have listened to you. I'm a little out of my depth."

"Don't worry about it," I said. "Just do me a favor and don't let anyone in to see her until the cops get here. Especially not anyone who says he's her husband, OK?"

"OK. By the way, your blood work showed a pretty high level of opiates when you came in," she said. "What's that all about?"

I explained that it was the second time I'd been shot in a week. And I'd totaled my car and broken two ribs. Aside from that, I was fine. She frowned, and left. I'd worn myself out talking. I leaned back on the bed and went back to sleep.

*

At lunch a new nurse woke me and delivered the tray. She was accompanied by Bobby Bove and Bill Thornton, the assistant D.A. who had debriefed me the night that Frank Velutto shot himself.

"Did you get someone to cover the woman?" I asked.

"Not yet," Thornton said. "Let's talk about it."

"What's the matter with you guys?" I said. Whatever drug they were feeding me it wasn't doing anything for my temper. "Get a deputy up there, now. Then we talk."

Thornton scowled, but Bobby Bove took his radio off his belt and spoke into it. "Done," he said, turning back to me. "Now tell Bill what you told me."

I filled him in, starting at the beginning. Bobby said he'd talked to Doc Edwards and his contact at the DEA, and they had an all-points bulletin out for C.J. and Philip. I wondered if they were on his boat, halfway to Cuba.

Bill Thornton was a cool customer, the kind of guy who never smiled. If he had a sense of humor he didn't show it when he was working. "So, what are you leaving out?" he asked.

I wasn't going to say anything about Roberto; he didn't need to be involved. Nor did I mention that I'd broken into the Johannsen house and bugged it. My tracks were covered, thanks to Doc Edwards. I didn't say anything about the money, C.J.'s dirty millions, because that might also lead back to Roberto's hacking capabilities. I had also left out the fact that I'd fallen ass-over-tin-cups in love with my client.

"That's everything," I said.

"So how did it go down in the ladies' room?" Thornton said. "Who shot whom?"

"Le shot Barbara when I opened the door. Then she aimed at me, and we shot each other at the same time."

"A .22 isn't much of a match for a sawed-off, is it?" Thornton said.

"What do you mean by that? She was shooting to kill, and I shot back."

"Maybe you can tell me why the EMTs found a bag of OxyContin in your pocket?"

"Yes, I can explain," I said.

"I just find it a little strange that a cop kills himself in your house and two days later you gun somebody down in a bathroom."

"Hey, Thornton," I said, my blood pressure making the machines go ballistic, "are you fucking listening? Have you talked to the DEA? That woman was running the biggest meth lab in Florida. She fucking shot my client, and shot me, and I shot her back, OK?"

"Hey, cool down, Vince," Bobby interjected.

"No, you guys get the fuck out of here before I shoot you too," I said. "Assholes."

They rose and Thornton said, "We'll come back later."

"Assholes," I said, as they shut the door.

*

I slept again until four in the afternoon when another nurse checked my vitals and helped me to the bathroom. Le's bullet had hit my right shoulder, and my cracked ribs were on the left side, so it hurt to move either arm regardless of the painkillers they were feeding me. The nurse left me to pee alone, and then helped me back to the bed.

"You should be out of here tomorrow," she said.

"Really?"

"The insurance companies won't pay for more than a day if they can help it," she said.

"Can you do me a favor?" I said. "Can you take me out for a wheelchair ride? I want to visit another patient."

"You should stay in bed," she said.

"Please?"

"My shift ends at seven," she said. "I'll take you then."

*

A bored-looking deputy sat in the lounge of the Critical Care Unit. He showed no interest when we wheeled past. If this guy was watching out for Barbara's safety, I might as well not have bothered.

The shades were drawn in her room, but I could see her in the bed, hooked up to a console of machines. A woman sat in a visitor's chair thumbing through a fashion magazine. She didn't acknowledge me. She wore a pink T-shirt that was a size too small, and a tangle of blue and green tattoos extended out of her sleeves and up her neck like jungle vines. The bottom of each earlobe was stretched around a wooden insert the size of a napkin holder and the top was perforated with rows of little silver rings, like a spiral notebook. I could still see the resemblance, despite all the paraphernalia.

"You must be Barbara's sister."

"I'm Vicki," she said. "Y'all are not supposed to be here."

"I'm Vince," I said.

"I guessed that," she said. "She doesn't want to see you."

"Is she all right?"

"She's going to live, if that's what you mean. The bullet went into her lung, but missed her heart. And now you have to git."

"What do you mean that she doesn't want to see me?"

"She's married, for starters," she said. "And you were supposed to be her bodyguard, right?"

"Yes."

"Well, look at her," she said. "Don't bother sending no bill." She dismissed me with a wave of her hand and went back to her magazine.

"Vicki—"

"You git or I'm calling that deputy outside."

I signaled for my nurse to wheel me out. Barbara had apparently been awarded the charm in her family, not her sister. On the other hand, the woman was correct. I had been hired to protect Barbara, and there she was in a hospital bed with a hole in her chest.

*

I lay awake listening to the beeps and pulses of the monitoring equipment in my room, too groggy to watch television. I replayed the events of the last week and realized I'd failed. So what if I'd uncovered a drug operation. Le's death had come too late. I still didn't know where C.J. and his son were. In the morning I would check on that, assuming that I was good for anything. There was too much going on and too much blood had been splattered on the walls, and I just wanted to shut it all out and lie on a warm beach with Barbara until we both healed. According to her sister, that wasn't going to happen. And Bill Thornton might just put me back in jail. I wished for the dark release of sleep, but it didn't come.

SATURDAY

GUSTAVO AND ROBERTO HELPED ME into my house and onto the couch. Lilian was already there, making a soup in the kitchen; the hearty Cuban kind that would stink up the house for days. Gustavo said they were going to adopt me for a while, and I should just relax and accept it.

I dutifully ate some of the soup and listened to Lilian's instruction about what to eat to speed my recovery. She said she'd be bringing over meals with special ingredients passed down through the generations that were sure to help me, and I should stay off the drugs. The hospital had given me Tylenol with codeine. I'd taken some a few hours ago, but it was having little effect. If the pain was going to keep up at its current level it would require something stronger. Maybe Sonny made deliveries.

When they left I called Doc Edwards on his cell. I had to use the speaker on my phone, as I couldn't hold it up to my ear.

"Any sign of them yet?" I asked.

"We're not looking for them anymore," he said. "They called it off."

"What do you mean?"

"The hard drive you gave us had a nasty little feature that wiped out all the data. The techs got around it the first time, but when they were trying to copy it, it got wiped. We fucked up. No data, no collar."

"You don't have anything else?"

"The juice processing plant had some trace chemicals around, but it could have been anything—household cleaners, brake fluid, whatever. The people at the vending company won't talk. We leaned pretty hard on some of them, but I suspect they're being paid off."

"Did you try looking in the computers at the vending company?"

"Yes," he said. "Nothing. Believe me, we look bad on this one. The guy has a lawyer, and he's all over us. The judge is ripshit."

"What if I testify?"

"Sorry, but I don't see it," he said. "He's free, for now. Is that going to cause trouble for you?"

"I don't know yet," I said.

"What kind of mess are you in, Tanzi? I got a call from a deputy named Bove. He told me about the bakery shoot-out. I stood up for you, but maybe I shouldn't have."

"Thanks," I said. "Nothing I can't handle."

I called the hospital to check on Barbara. They had moved her out of the CCU and into a patient room, which was good. I got Vicki.

"She can't talk to you," she said.

"I just want to know if she's OK."

"Listen, mister. She don't want to talk to you, you got that?" she said. She hung up the phone. I was getting stonewalled, or maybe she was telling the truth and Barbara had had enough of me, permanently. Either way, it was clear that I did not have an ally in her sister.

*

Sonny pulled into my driveway in a dark green Subaru Outback. I could see him looking up and down the street after he got out of his car. He obviously didn't like doing this. I came out of the house into the heat and met him in the driveway.

"Nice ride," I said, smiling. "I see from your bumper sticker that you support Maine Public Radio; that's very commendable."

"I don't support nothin' except my ex-wife," he said. "I got the car from a friend who runs a funeral parlor."

"You could be a Subaru kind of guy," I said.

"Cheap transportation, man. Those old people move down here from up North, they suck on their oxygen tanks and die. Motherfucker only has six thousand miles on it."

"Plus you're saving the planet."

"Let's go inside, man. It's hot, and we got business."

I let him in, and we stood in the cool of the kitchen.

"Nice place," he said. "You look even more like shit than last time."

"You must have flunked out of charm school," I said.

"I ain't gonna lecture you."

"Don't," I said. "It's been a truly rotten week."

"That's what all the pill-heads say. They always have some reason that they got to have some more."

I shook my head. He was wrong. I was in real pain.

He reached into his pocket and took out a small envelope. "I got you fifty more. After that, you're on your own."

"What do I owe you?"

They go for forty bucks each on the street. That's two grand. You can give me five hundred, but that's it, man. I ain't getting you any more of this shit."

I took the money from my stash and paid him. "Don't worry so much, Sonny," I said. "I got it under control."

"That's what the pill-heads say too, man."

*

I tried Barbara's cell, and it went to voicemail. I tried the hospital room again, but Vicki answered and I hung up. I got off the couch and turned on the TV, but it was all bullshit. If it had been two weeks ago, before I'd met Barbara, I would have already been well into a thirty-pack by now, and things would be just an acceptable blur. The pills did as good a job as the beers did, in fact, even better. I popped two of them and then took a third, just for the hell of it. After a few minutes somebody could have hit me in the face with a two-by-four, and I wouldn't have felt it. Lilian came back at dinnertime, but I couldn't be bothered to get off the couch, and I asked her to leave it in the kitchen and thanked her, slurring my words.

The pain came roaring back at midnight, and I got out two more of my little yellow pills. I didn't bother to eat Lilian's food, which was still on the kitchen counter. I called Barbara's cell again and left another rambling message. Sooner or later she would answer. Until then I didn't want to feel any pain, I was sick to death of pain.

WEDNESDAY

SONNY'S ENVELOPE LAY ON AN end table next to my couch, where I had taken up residence. The packet was nearly empty—I'd hit the stash hard since the weekend. Take two pills, call Barbara, go to voicemail—repeat every eight hours. In between I'd slept badly, showered ineffectively, and eaten sporadically. However, I had done a very good job of feeling sorry for myself.

Lilian had just dropped off my lunch when the phone rang. It was Bobby Bove.

"They're not going to charge you," he said. "But you ought to be nicer to Thornton."

"I'll make sure to send him a big bouquet of roses," I said. "Fuckhead."

"He's the one that made the case for you, once he understood it was you that found the meth lab. He lost his younger brother to an overdose."

"He's still an asshole," I said.

"Yeah, and you can be one too sometimes," he said.

"Sorry, Bobby," I said. "That was out of line. I'm in a shitty mood."

"By the way, that guy's in Vero," he said.

"What guy?"

"The one everybody was looking for, and then they called it off. Charles Butler. Some deputy spotted him and then found out they weren't looking for him anymore."

"Where was he?"

"He's tied up at the Vero Beach Yacht Club," he said. "Him and a kid. The deputy said they're living on a boat. It's called the *Numb Nuts* or something like that."

"*Nickels and Dimes.*"

"Yeah, that's it."

C.J. was back in Vero, with Philip. I tried Barbara's cell one more time, but it went to voicemail. I called the hospital, but they said she was no longer a patient. I tried the house, and it just rang with no answer or voicemail, but Barbara had to be there. I wondered if I could drive. There was only one way to find out.

*

Getting out of the BMW took a superhuman effort, even with a fresh couple of pills in me. I'd driven it to Barbara's without incident, but steering with my left arm wasn't easy and the rigid sport suspension made it hurt every time I ran over a palmetto leaf. What I really needed was an ambulance, with a svelte blonde nurse to dab the perspiration off my forehead.

Vicki answered the door. "She ain't here."

"This is important," I said, and I pushed past her. Barbara was in the living room, sitting in a recliner with a tray across her lap. The TV was on in the background, and she switched it off with a remote. Vicki chased after me.

"She can't talk to you now," Vicki said. "She's—"

"It's OK, hun," Barbara said. "Leave us, please. Sit down, Vince." She motioned to me toward a chair as Vicki left the room, huffing on the way out. "She's a little over-protective."

"I can see that," I said.

"So were you ever going to call me again?"

"I must have called you a hundred times," I said. "Check your voicemails."

"Vicki won't let me use the phone."

"Seriously?"

"When she's here it's like I'm a prisoner in my own house. You should see the crap she's making me eat. Have you ever had a fish oil smoothie?"

"Are you feeling OK?"

"It's a little hard to breathe," she said. "It's getting better. I run out of energy pretty quickly."

"Barbara—C.J. is in Vero."

"I know," she said. "He's been here twice. The first time he took the van, and some of his things. He was here this morning, too. We had a talk."

"What did you talk about?"

"Nothing, really." She looked away.

"Nothing?" I said. "Really?"

"Just some things about the house, how I was, and so on."

"What? Why are you not telling me?" I said. "Let's back up. Le shot you, and I killed her. She's dead. You were almost dead. His drug business is blown into tiny pieces in Lake Wales, which is about the only good thing to happen because he'll stop killing a bunch of teenagers. The cops were chasing him all over Florida. And you're telling me he dropped by for some chitchat. Excuse me, but that's bullshit."

"There are some things I can't talk about, that's all."

"Why?"

"I don't want to get into it, Vince."

Vicki popped her head in the door. "Are you upsetting her? You'd better go on home, mister."

"Back off," I said, too loud.

"I'm calling the cops," she said, and she disappeared.

"Barbara, I don't get it. You hire me, and then you fire me. Then you hire me again because you find out C.J. has a boatload of money. And I find out where it's coming from. And now you won't even talk to me."

"I didn't get your phone messages," she said. "I—"

"Bullshit," I said. "I was a cop for twenty five years, remember? I can tell when people are lying to me."

Vicki walked into the room. "The police are on the way," she said.

"It doesn't matter," I said. "I'm done." I slammed the door hard on the way out. I don't like it when clients lie to me—it's a waste of my time. Worse than that was that I had thought that Barbara trusted me, and it hurt that she didn't. I eased myself back into the BMW, which felt like a leather-clad torture rack. What I should do is go home, take another two pills, and get some rest.

No. What I should do, I decided, is drive over to the yacht club and get in C.J.'s face, whether I was in pain or not. Barbara was lying to me, and I needed to find out why.

*

A young woman sat at the reception desk of the club, texting on her phone when I walked in. She looked up, and I could see by her reaction that I looked a little scary. I had tried to calm down, but my confrontation with Barbara had really made me angry. "Which slip is Mr. Butler's boat in?" I said.

"I'm sorry but we can't—" she began.

"Fuck it, I'll find him." I brushed past her, out the back door to the boat slips.

The Vero Beach Yacht Club is a small marina in the shadow of the Barber Bridge. There are only about fifty boats tied up, and I immediately recognized the *Nickels and Dimes;* it was in the last slip of a dock that extended directly behind the clubhouse building. There was someone aboard, too. As I got closer I recognized C.J. and he recognized me. I let myself aboard the big Riviera, clutching the rail with my good hand as I swung my legs onto the deck.

"Mr. Tanzi," he said. "You should be resting."

"How does it feel to be down to one wife, Butler?"

"There's no need to be rude," he said. I showed myself around the boat while we talked. It was practically new, or at least it had been kept in pristine shape as it showed none of the fading and wear that the Florida sun does to boats. After a few years down here the gel coat gets dried up and crackly like the shell of a sea turtle.

"So where's the Empex money?" I said. "Offshore?"

"We can come to an arrangement," he said. "Even if you're above that sort of thing, there's Barbara to think about."

"She's your wife, not mine."

"Come on," he said. "We both know better than that."

I wasn't going to admit I'd slept with her, but he'd scored a point. I peered down into the cabin. It was all polished teak and sleek upholstery, as spotless and comfortable as the interior of a Bentley. There was a head with a shower, a spacious galley and dining table and two double berths. A charcoal gray Lenovo laptop was open on the dining table. I eased myself down the steps and looked at the screen. It was displaying a spreadsheet. "Whose is this?" I said.

C.J. came from behind me and snapped the computer shut. "That's Philip's," he said. "And now it's time for you to get off my boat."

"Where's Philip?"

"He left to run an errand," he said. He took me by the elbow on my good arm and tried to hustle me back up the steps. I was in no condition to put up a fight, and I let him lead me to the deck.

"I remember a kid about Philip's age when I was a deputy," I said. "He'd lost all his teeth and his face was covered with zits. He was a good student and he had a future, until he got fucked up on meth. We busted him three times, and he OD'ed the day after he got out, the third time. I went to his funeral."

"Leave now or I'll call the police."

"That's what your sister-in-law said fifteen minutes ago."

"If you haven't figured it out, Barbara's playing you," he said. "You're not her first boyfriend. And you're not very bright for someone in your business."

I didn't have an answer for that, but it didn't matter. I had just opened one last lock, one that I hadn't even noticed before, and I was about to step through a whole new door.

*

Roberto was home from school when I reached him on his cell. "Hey," I said.

"Hey," he replied.

"Do you remember when you found that program on the Johannsen's computer? The one that got you into some kind of server?"

"Yeah," he said. "It wasn't necessarily a server, it was just a link to another computer."

"We were thinking that it might be a computer in Le's office, right?"

"Right."

"Could it be a laptop?"

"Sure," he said. "It didn't have to be anything with a lot of power. The programs don't use a lot of space."

"So if it's a laptop, could you get into it?"

"Probably, as long as the computer in the Johannsen house is on," he said. "I'll try." I waited while he typed. I could hear the clicking of his keyboard through the phone.

"Nope," he said. "It's not booted up."

"Stay by your computer," I said. "I'll call you in a couple hours."

*

I now knew every landmark between Vero Beach and Tampa like it was my daily commute. The sun was in my eyes for much of the trip and every muscle and bone in my body ached, but it felt good. I'd stopped at the house and packed my gear. I had also dumped the last few OxyContin pills into my toilet and flushed them away. It was time to focus, and I was starting to scare myself. Sonny was right, I was turning into a pill-head, and that needed to stop.

I was closing in on this case, and as usual, it was about money. Most of the seven billion of us on the planet don't have any more than a food bowl and a mat to sleep on at night, but the people who do have some money can't ever seem to get enough.

Barbara never went to college and never found a career, but she had latched onto a cash machine. And C.J.'s mental instability had turned him into a greedy, paranoid opportunist who could rationalize owning a meth lab because it generated huge profits, whatever the danger or the social cost. If something unpleasant went on in C.J.'s life he could always assign it to his "brother". How convenient.

But something had changed, and C.J. was now moving his money around. My guess was that it started a month ago, and Le had found out about it and decided that Barbara was the threat. The money was moving in Barbara's direction. That was why she'd started shooting. She may have known about Barbara all along and accepted it, but she sure wasn't going to accept getting the short end of the financial stick.

It could have been Philip doing the shooting, but I guessed it was Le, although the boy may have been along for the ride. He was definitely under her sway. He'd probably kidnapped Barbara to deliver her to his mother.

Then Barbara had confronted C.J. and he somehow got her on his side, at least enough to where she was happy to fire me before I found out anything more. Then she overheard C.J. moving the money, and she decided to hire me again, just to hedge her bets. And then she puts up a wall.

It was reckless of C.J. to say she was playing me, but I'd pissed him off, and he wanted to hurt me. He must have thought that he was going to get away with all of this.

Not if I could help it.

*

Hawkeye was out watering his lawn in the evening heat. I parked the BMW in the Johannsen's driveway, got out my tools, and walked up to the front door. I could see the alarm panel through a window and could tell by the red LED light that the cops had left it unarmed. Hawkeye wandered over while I worked on the front door lock, which was putting up a struggle.

"They got a spare key in one of those magnetic boxes," he said. "Over there under the electric meter. The kid uses it when he forgets."

I smiled. "Thanks," I said. He waited at the door while I collected the key.

"You're not a bank security guy, are you?" he said.

"Nope," I said.

"Sure hope I'm doing the right thing."

"You are. They're drug dealers," I said.

"Lot of that here. Lots of kids on dope. I'll stick with my martinis."

I opened the lock with the key and entered the dark house. Hawkeye went back to his lawn as I switched on a light and went to the computer. I booted it up and called Roberto.

"It's back on," I said.

"Stay on the phone," he said. I kept the cell phone to my ear while I walked around the house. It was a mess; the DEA guys and the cops had taken it apart. The plastic slipcovers for the upholstery were piled in a heap in a corner—someone must have checked out every seat cushion. They had wanted to bust these people real bad, but they didn't have a damn thing.

"I'm in," Roberto said, and I returned to the computer. I watched the cursor move as he manipulated it, remotely. He opened a program and a spreadsheet appeared on the screen. At the top of it was a heading that said "EMPEX".

"Print it, OK?" I said.

"OK. There's a contact book and emails too."

"Print anything you can," I said. "Can you tell if it's a laptop?"

"It's Windows-based," he said. "It should say what kind it is right here." I watched as he navigated to "System". In large blue letters it said LENOVO. "Yeah, it's a laptop," he said.

"So you're looking at that computer right now, right?"

"Yes."

"Can't you tell where it is?"

"Dude," he said. "Ask me something hard."

"OK. Let's see. How about—what do women want?"

"If I knew that I wouldn't be at home on the computer," he said, and I laughed until my ribs hurt. Maybe he wasn't the blushing ingénue that I had thought. I watched the screen while he navigated.

"According to this, the laptop is in Vero Beach, Florida."

"Fantastic," I said. "I happen to be headed that way."

*

It was dark as I passed through Lake Wales. The night was warm, and I stopped in a convenience store parking lot to put the BMW's convertible top down. I needed the rushing air to keep me awake and distract me from the pain in my shoulder and ribs. I was also feeling the effect of the withdrawal from the drug. It wasn't a cold sweat, shaky hands kind of thing—more like the feeling you get when the flu is coming on. I'd only been taking the oxycodone for a little more than a week, but I had gained a new respect for how addictive it was. No wonder it had crept in and taken over the lives of so many ordinary people who were not who you'd think of as the druggie-type.

By the time I got back to Vero, it would be very late and Bobby Bove would be in bed. I wanted him to be the point man on this one; I trusted Bobby even though he and Thornton had pissed me off at the hospital. I assumed the warrant was still good, the cops had just decided to lie low for now because the evidence had evaporated. Warrants usually stayed open for ten days, and that would allow Bobby and his friends to board the boat, get the laptop, and collar C.J. and his son if they were still around. I stopped in Yeehaw Junction for gas and checked my own laptop, as I still had a tracker on C.J.'s van. The van was in the parking lot at the Vero Beach Yacht Club. I decided I would spend the night there too, and would call Bobby in the morning. I didn't want anyone slipping away in the dark; I was too close to getting the goods on C.J., and I wanted to put him away just as much as the DEA did, if not more. We would see if I was not very bright, as he had said, or if I was one step ahead of him.

*

I parked at the other end of the yacht club lot from C.J.'s van. I had a view between the buildings of some of the boats, although most of them were obscured. The docks were brightly lit, but the parking lot was nice and dark, and I kept the convertible top down, drinking in the night while I surfed on the laptop to keep myself awake.

Actually, I wasn't paying much attention to the computer screen. I was thinking about Barbara. She was shutting me out for some reason, and that hurt more than my ribs. I didn't understand why. If she was playing me, like C.J. said, I didn't get the angle. I couldn't believe that she was on his side; I had heard her say she didn't care about him anymore, and those words had sounded authentic. If she would see me again, I would confront her. Even if she didn't want to see me again, I would confront her—I had to know where we stood. I thought about Frank Velutto getting shut off by Glory, and I almost had some sympathy, but not really. The songs say that love can make you crazy, and they're right, but that doesn't mean you shoot somebody.

The stars were out in force, and I closed the laptop and leaned back on the leather headrest. I missed my wife. I thought I'd hold a grudge for the rest of my life, but I was wrong. I needed to forgive her if I was going to be able to move on. I said so, out loud to the night, and the stars winked back in acknowledgement.

THURSDAY

I HEARD A CAR START in the parking lot just before dawn. It was the van, and it left out of the far entrance, away from where I was parked. I hadn't seen anyone walk up to it, but I had been drowsy and distracted in my thoughts. I turned on the tracking software and watched the blue dot going down A-1-A. If they had taken off with the computer, I was screwed.

I decided that I could track them later if I needed to—this was a chance to check out the boat, and if the laptop was still there, I would take it. I walked around the side of the building and through a gate that led to the docks. C.J.'s boat was in the same slip at the end, partially lit by a big halogen lamp on a high pole on the next dock over. I walked out to the boat and listened. There was no noise, and the interior lights were out. I climbed aboard and carefully turned the handle on the latch that opened the door to the cabin below. I waited for my eyes to get used to the darkness. The light from the dock cast my shadow on the galley table, and I shifted to the side and saw that the laptop was still on it, where I'd seen it the day before. I crouched down and entered through the door, and then crossed the cabin floor as quietly as I could and reached over to grab it.

Something crushed down hard on the back of my neck, and the darkness became complete.

*

When I regained consciousness, Philip was trussing me up in sticky gray duct tape like a spider's breakfast. He'd wound my arms tight to my chest and was now wrapping my thighs together, along with my ankles. I would have struggled, but his father was sitting on an upholstered dining seat, pointing a vintage Colt Commander at my face. I recognized the gun—it was the one I'd discovered under the toilet in his fake office.

"Tell me what you know," he said.

"Apparently not much," I said. My voice sounded as cracked as my skull.

"What do the police know? Tell me, and I'll let you go."

Bullshit. I had gotten in his way, and I was going to be fish food.

"Do you mind if I ask you a question?" I said.

"Ask," he said.

"Who is Avery Bellar?" I said. "And why are you holding his gun?"

He frowned. "How do you know that name?"

"I might be a little smarter than you thought," I said. "OK, let's trade. You answer my question; I answer yours. I'll start. I found the passport and that gun in your office, along with some money and a map. Now it's your turn. So who are you?"

"I'm a Canadian citizen," he said. "Naturalized."

"Was that before or after you deserted in Vietnam?"

He frowned again. "After. I was born in the U.S. I grew up on army bases. When I got out of Vietnam, I went to Canada and got an identity there."

"Tell me the whole story. Then I'll tell you what the cops have," I said.

"I could just beat it out of you," he said.

"You're not the type," I said.

"Philip, go above," he said, and the boy left us.

He exhaled. "I was in a recon platoon looking for NVAs in a little hamlet. Tan Tieng. One of those tiny places in the jungle where they'd cleared out some fields—enough to graze a buffalo and grow some crops. We were on the perimeter, eight of us, when we took fire. The first one to get shot was the lieutenant, and he was dead. There was a sergeant who took the radio and called in an air strike, but in the meantime we were getting creamed and had no cover. Two more guys got hit, and they died immediately; it was sniper fire and they were lining us up."

He stopped and gazed at a point beyond me. Somehow I had opened the floodgates, which was good. If I was going to survive this, I had to get him to trust me.

"Go on," I said.

"No one alive knows this story," he said.

"I'm a good listener," I said. As if I had a choice, wrapped up like a burrito on the floor.

"We had to do something, and so we rushed the hut where the firing was coming from. They got two more of us on the way in, but we threw in some frags and the hut exploded and the firing stopped. There were only two of them, and they were Viet Cong, not NVAs, but they'd killed five of our eight. Everyone else there were villagers—women and children, any of their men would be in the jungle. So it was me and two others, and the other guys started going hut-to-hut, shooting. Women, little kids, everybody. I screamed at them to stop, and they just laughed. I got out my gun and shot them both."

"Jesus Christ."

"Only two of the villagers survived, a young girl and her grandmother. I took them into the jungle because I knew the air strike was coming; a few minutes later two F-4 Phantoms came in and obliterated the place. It was gone."

"The girl was Le?" I said.

"Yes."

"So," I said, "Which one are you really? The fruit broker, or the guy I played golf with?"

"I've told you enough," he said. "It's my turn to ask you a question."

"OK, but just tell me who I'm talking to. Is it you, or is it your brother?"

His eyes lowered, and he appeared to be looking at the gun. "My brother is dead. He died in the war. He was one of the two soldiers I shot in Tan Tieng."

"Your real brother?"

"Avery. He was a sadistic son of a bitch. He tortured me when we were kids, but my father never did anything about it. Avery was the one who could do no wrong."

There was nothing I could say to that. If I made it out of here, I would piece it together later, and Dr. Doug Leyburn would have a field day. The duct tape was wound too tightly around my chest, and my breathing became labored.

"Undo this and we'll talk more," I said. I've negotiated in situations like this before; you have to be forceful, but not threatening. It's a delicate art.

"Not a chance," he said. "What do the police know, specifically?"

"They have physical evidence from your lab," I lied. "They have all the Empex business records from a portable hard drive that was there, with all your bank records, and they've frozen all the assets. You're under twenty-four-hour surveillance. If you don't let me go, you'll just make it worse."

"You're lying," he said. "They would have picked me up if they had anything like that." He went up above, and I heard him make a call on his cell. He came back below.

"And the money is right where it's supposed to be," he said. "We're going for a ride. You've become a liability." So much for my negotiating skills. I'd just negotiated a pair of cement socks and a swimming lesson.

C.J. went back above and closed the door, and it was dark in the cabin except for the weak dawn that was beginning to filter in. The diesel engines roared into life. The boat rocked as they cast off from the slip, and I could feel us pick up speed as they steered into the Indian River. The sunlight was coming in through the starboard windows, so I knew we were going north, toward the Sebastian Inlet. The inlet itself was a tricky little waterway, and the currents were strong, but a big boat like the Riviera could cut through it with no problem, and then we would be out in the Atlantic. Once you were a few miles off the coast you could knot someone up with an anchor and they would never be found.

Someone like me.

*

I wiggled as much as possible, but all I could manage was to thrash around like a fish on the floor of the cabin. My arms were taped up to my sides, mummy-style, and although the tape could possibly be torn open, I had no leverage and no sharp edges to use. I could bend my legs at the knees, but I could not get to my feet. We had been under way for at least ten minutes, and it was only a few miles up the river to Sebastian. I had to come up with something, and I didn't have much time.

The door to the head was open, and it banged back and forth against the cabin wall as the boat rocked. One of them had forgotten to shut it. I wiggled across the floor until my feet were next to it. It took several tries, but I trapped it between my ankles and held it still. The effort made my chest roar with pain, made worse by the tightly-wound duct tape that made breathing almost impossible. I inched closer to the door until my knees were bent, still holding it between my feet, with the lowest bands of tape now touching against the squared-off edge of the door. With enough force I might be able to rip the tape. I pushed my legs against the door edge, hard, again and again, and the corners cut into the skin on both ankles until they bled. I kept ramming the tape against the door edge, not thinking about the pain;

the tape was beginning to give. It was crude, but it was working. I rammed hard, over and over, until I felt the pressure on my ankles loosen as the tape began to rip. The more I rammed, the more it ripped, until I was all the way through and my ankles were freed.

I bent over into a fetal position and tried to get up. With one calf forward and one back I was able to get some lift, but I fell backward twice until I realized I had to have something behind me for support. I wiggled over against the galley stove and tried my scissor-lift again. This time it worked, although my injuries were now screaming. I was standing—with my thighs and torso still bound, but I was mobile.

The cabin door was secured by a small brass latch. I grabbed the handle with my teeth and twisted it down. It opened, and I pushed the door forward with my head. If C.J. and Philip were at the helm, I would be looking at their feet, but they were up above and out of sight on the flying bridge, and I had the area to myself. I climbed the steps to the helm and squinted in the full sunlight. We were cruising at eighteen knots according to the instruments on the console—fast enough to waterski. I could see small sandbars off the port side, and the shore of what looked like Sebastian in the distance, with its riverside restaurants and Tiki bars. We were well out in the channel, hundreds of yards from either bank of the river, and if I tried to jump, I would never make it to shore.

The boat was turning in a slow arc toward the inlet, and I realized that at this speed we would be out into the open Atlantic within minutes. If I waited until we reached the churning water of the inlet entrance, I'd be nearer to the shore but the currents would drown me. If I was going to do something, I had to do it now.

I hobbled down to the cockpit deck and threw myself over the rail like a discarded amberjack. I bounced in the wake, and then it was quiet as I went underwater and heard the boat speed away. I dolphin-kicked my way up to the surface and took a huge, gasping breath. The boat continued toward the inlet, leaving me out in the open river, a long swim from dry land. I floated on my back and kicked, every movement of my legs transmitting an electric current pain to my torso and shoulder, but I was free and they hadn't seen me flop overboard. The river was calm and the sun was rising over the barrier island, already strong. The sound of C.J.'s boat diminished to a distant hum, and it was quiet except for the squawking coughs of pelicans nesting on the shore.

A sport fishing boat came into view, heading for the inlet, and I kicked the water wildly, hoping to attract their attention. My thrashing earned me a mouthful of briny water and I gagged and wondered if today was the day I would die.

I saw the boat change course and head toward me. They slowed, and one of the people aboard jumped into the water with a life ring and swam me over to a platform at the stern of the boat. I couldn't move, and another of the men took out a fish knife and unbound the duct tape from me, and I could finally breathe freely again. I lay on the platform and took in as much air as I could, unable to speak. Across the varnished mahogany transom was the name of the boat in large gold letters, just above my head: *GLORY HALLELUJAH*. I squinted up at the puffy morning clouds. Someone was watching over me.

The white-haired man who had cut away the tape shook his head. "I thought you was some kind of dying fish," he said.

"If you hadn't come along, I would have been," I said.

*

The fishermen dropped me off back at the Vero Beach Yacht Club on the condition that I would call an ambulance as soon as was on dry land. I climbed off the boat onto the dock and thanked them for saving my life.

"Catch and release," the white-haired guy said. "You didn't look like good eatin' anyway."

I had already called Bobby Bove from the boat, with one of their cell phones. My phone was in the BMW, and I dialed Bobby again as soon as I got in.

"We got them," he said. "The Coast Guard had a boat right near the inlet."

"Did they find the computer?"

"Yes. Are you OK?"

"I guess so," I said. "I have a lump on the back of my head the size of a tangerine."

"Do you want me to send someone?"

"No, I'm just going to go home and get in bed," I said. I was too tired to call for the ambulance. "Let me know what they find on the laptop."

"Will do."

*

I was sticking to the leather seats of the BMW, so I stopped at a drug store on the way home and bought a roll of paper towels and a can of WD-40: Barbara's cure. I sat in the parking lot of the store and dabbed myself with it, but the tape residue was firmly attached to the hair on my arms and legs, and I decided I didn't need a can, I needed a bathtub full of the stuff. I gave up and drove to my house.

I was tempted to clean up and then pay a call on Barbara. If she was playing me, I wondered how she'd react when I told her that C.J. was going to jail, and if she'd been counting on his money for her meal ticket that ticket had just been punched. It could wait. I was exhausted, and I hadn't had any sleep except for the involuntary kind that Philip had provided me when he'd cracked me on the head.

*

I didn't stir until the afternoon light had faded and the peepers came out. There's an old irrigation canal behind my development that's a breeding ground for mosquitos, but it's also good for frogs, and if I leave the windows open I get serenaded. I lay there on my bed, listening and surveying the damage to my body: a slug in the shoulder; a nick on the scalp; assorted bumps, bruises, and cracked ribs from the car crash; a bonk on the head when Le shot me and I hit the floor; and one more bonk from Philip. It was all I could do not to call Sonny and beg for more pills. Everything hurt like hell, and my impromptu swim in the river hadn't made it any better. I needed a week on the beach somewhere where the phone wouldn't ring, where I wouldn't have to chase anybody, where I wouldn't get shot, and where the only decision I'd have to make would be what factor of sunscreen to apply.

On the other hand I was still alive, and I felt more alive than I had in a year. I'd outwitted a bad guy and taken some of his toxins off the streets. I hadn't exactly protected my client, but she wasn't dead either. I'd found out who killed my wife, and it wasn't me. In the process I'd lost Frank Velutto, who was once my friend. I'd almost lost myself to the siren song of pain pills, but I'd crept back from the edge. And I'd let my guard down with a woman whose motives I was now questioning. The phone rang.

"It's Bobby again," he said. "We got two DEA guys here, a state cop, our mutual friend Mr. Thornton the D.A., your friend Edwards from Tampa, and a lady JPO from Tampa who's picking up the kid."

"Did Thornton like the roses?"

He chuckled. "We're playing "who's got jurisdiction". Everybody wants their mug in the paper next to your fish."

"Good luck with that. What did you find on the computer?"

"According to the Tampa guys, it was everything they had already seen on the hard drive before it got wiped, plus much more specific bank account stuff. That's what I'm calling about. Your girlfriend is in trouble."

"She's not my girlfriend," I said.

"Then how do you know who I'm talking about?"

I paused. "Let's not get into it right now, OK?"

"OK. But they found a lot of money in her name. Like a shitload of money."

"She doesn't know about it," I said. I wasn't sure that was true.

"OK," he said. "But we're going to pick her up for questioning tomorrow. You may want to talk to her first. Just a heads up."

"Thanks Bobby."

"Don't thank me yet," he said. "We're picking you up too."

*

I put down the receiver, then lifted it back up and called Barbara. She picked up on the first ring.

"I've been meaning to call you," she said.

"What happened to your guard dog?"

"I sent her back to Jacksonville last night after you left."

"I need to come over," I said. "The news is not good."

"Oh. Are you going to get angry at me again?"

"I'm not angry at you."

"You sound angry," she said.

"It's just something we have to discuss."

"What happened, Vince?"

"I'll tell you when I get there," I said.

*

She was in her recliner with a magazine on her lap. She looked pretty, even with no makeup and in her bathrobe. I had come right from the house and needed a shave and a fresh shirt, but I hadn't bothered. I wasn't trying to impress her anymore, and I was cranky from the lack of pain drugs. I got straight to the point of my visit.

"Your husband is in jail. He and his son took me for a ride in their boat this morning. They wrapped me in duct tape and were going to throw me overboard, but I got away. The Coast Guard picked them up, and there was a computer in the boat with the business records."

"From the vending business?"

"No. From the meth business. With detailed bank records."

"So they'll get him?"

"Yes," I said, "With any luck. It's the evidence they needed."

"Oh," she said.

"There is apparently a lot of money in your name."

"I know," she said.

"You know?"

"I owe you an explanation, don't I?"

"Yes." I sat on the couch across from her. "Explain."

"Oh God," she said, "It starts a long way back. When C.J. was a citrus broker he used to give me money every week, and I'd put it in the bank. I built up quite a lot over the years, over a hundred thousand dollars." She took a sip from a mug. "You want some tea? Vicki left it for me. It's kind of disgusting."

"Keep talking," I said.

"About ten years ago he went under. There was a freeze in the groves, and I didn't know it, but C.J. was into futures trading and he lost everything. He'd also invested for a lot of the growers, his clients, and they all lost money, and they turned on him. We were broke except for what I'd saved, and he didn't have any clients left."

"Then what?"

"Then he comes home from his trip—the Wednesday through Friday thing—and he says he has a new business partner. I ask him what the business is, and he won't tell me. But the money starts rolling in, and I decide…I don't really need to know. We just kept pretending he was a citrus broker." She took another sip. "This tastes like herbal wallpaper paste."

"Stop trying to talk me into it," I said.

"So I'm still handling the household bills, but about a year after C.J. starts the new business he says he's moving everything offshore, and we meet with a guy in West Palm Beach from a bank. It's in Switzerland, it's called "B-A-P" for short. After that I've never even seen a statement."

"The one you overheard C.J. talking to? The one we talked about at the Tracking Station beach?"

"Yes. I wasn't telling you everything."

"Why?"

"I thought he was moving money to Le. I thought he was getting ready to dump me and live over there with her and the boy."

"Didn't you have any control over the money?"

"Not after it went overseas. I have a half million or so here, but according to what you said there was a lot more that I didn't know about. I needed you to find out what was going on. I got scared when that guy said he was moving seventeen million euros, and that's when I hired you back."

"So you were after the money," I said. "You weren't really worried about getting shot at."

"No—I was scared all right, but when we rode home from Lake Wales that day, C.J. swore he could handle that. He can fix things. He fixed my whole life. But now I realize he just wanted you out of the picture. I should have known better."

"There's no money, by the way," I said. "I mean there was, but they'll confiscate it. They can also take your house, your car, everything."

"I don't care about the money anymore," she said. "When you told me about the meth lab, I wanted to crawl off and die."

"If I remember correctly, you shacked up with me in a hotel instead. Same difference?"

She chuckled and wheezed at the same time. "Please don't make me laugh, Vince; it really hurts."

"I'll try to be only mildly amusing."

"Thanks," she said.

We both went quiet and sat there in her living room while Barbara sipped her tea and I thought about how much she'd held back from me. I'd been played, all right.

"There's more, isn't there?" I said.

"Yes," she said. "There's more."

I stayed quiet.

"When I got out of the hospital, C.J. came to see me. He told me he was leaving, and he wanted me to come with him. He said he loved me. He'd put all the money in my name, not Le's. He was going to get me a new passport, and we were going out of the country with the boy. He's very persuasive when he wants to be."

"So what did you say?"

"I said I would."

"OK." I was looking at the wall.

"Your feelings are hurt, aren't they?"

"No," I said.

"Now you're the one who's lying."

I didn't respond, but she was right. "Why? I don't get it. Why does he have such a hold on you?"

She looked away.

"Barbara, please. Cards on the table."

"You're going to judge me," she said.

"I won't," I said.

"C.J. met me in a strip club," she said. "A titty bar, in Jacksonville where I grew up. It was called the Two Moons Club. And I wasn't in the audience, I was the one with the titties."

"So?"

"It gets worse."

"Go on," I said.

"I did tricks on the side. I was pretty wild back then. And it was good money. You don't know me, but I grew up trailer trash."

"Barbara…I knew a lot of women in the game. There were good ones and bad ones."

"When I told you about Le being a prostitute in Vietnam you seemed so…"

"I said something crass, right? I didn't mean to."

"C.J. took me away from that. It wasn't easy—there were people who controlled me. That tattoo you saw wasn't a tattoo; it was more like a brand. We were like cattle. He basically bought me."

"And ever since that, you've lived your life according to his rules," I said.

"Worse than that. He owned me. It was probably the same for the other wife. Even Vicki got caught—he was always sending her money, to help her out, and she got hooked on it. To be honest, so did I. She and I didn't grow up with much."

"So that's it? He owns you, and you're leaving the country with him?"

"I—"

"You disappoint the hell out of me, you know that?"

"Vince—"

"C.J. said you were playing me and he was—"

"Vince Tanzi, would you shut the fuck up for two seconds?" she yelled. "Christ."

I shut up, but I was simmering.

"He came over here this morning at four AM. He let himself in and woke me up. He wanted me to pack a bag and go to his boat. He said we were going to South Florida, to get me a passport."

"But you didn't go with him," I said. "That was right before they took me up the river."

She paused to take another sip of the tea. "I told him to go fuck himself," she said. "I sent Vicki home last night and started thinking clearly. I owe him nothing. If people find out about my past and they can't handle it, that's their problem. And I knew the money would disappear one way or another. I don't want it, and I heard what you'd said about him killing teenagers. Honestly, I'll be glad to be broke. I'm going to go out and get a job and start all over again. Or maybe I'll finally go to nursing school."

"You might have a job making license plates," I said.

"What do you mean?"

"The police want to see you tomorrow. They want to see me too. We're going to need a lawyer to be there."

"I haven't broken any laws," she said.

"I haven't either," I said, "But it's not always that simple."

She thought about that for a while. "Now I'm worried," she said.

"Don't be," I said. "I know some good lawyers. We can negotiate."

"Oh God," she said. "You must be so angry at me."

"No, I'm not," I said. "I was, but I feel better now that I at least know the truth."

"Do you want a drink?"

"I gave it up," I said.

"Food?"

"Not hungry."

"I can't do sex. I hurt too much," she said.

"Me too," I said.

"Then let's watch some TV."

"Sounds good," I said, but it wasn't. It was some reality show, and I wondered what they had to pay the people to humiliate themselves like that. Probably not very much.

We sat next to each other on the couch, and she noticed the sticky tape residue still all over my arms and legs. She got up and came back with two mugs of the herbal tea and her can of WD-40. She rubbed off the residue as we sipped the tea.

"This stuff is a powerful aphrodisiac, you know," she said.

"The tea or the WD-40?"

She laughed. "Remember, you're supposed to be only mildly funny."

"I'm trying," I said.

"You're shocked about what I told you, aren't you?"

"Sorry, but no," I said. "I'm relieved. I couldn't figure out what C.J. had on you."

"You'll never trust me again," she said, as she dabbed the solution on my arms. I thought about that, and decided that she was probably right. Somehow, it didn't matter.

"Don't worry about it," I said.

"Hey," she said.

"Yes?"

"Do you think your lawyer can negotiate me keeping the boat?"

"I have no idea," I said.

"I've always wanted to go down to the Keys in a boat," she said.

"What about nursing school?"

"It doesn't start until January," she said. "I was looking at the schedule on the computer when you called."

Her hands felt good on my skin. Better than anything I'd felt for a long time, including the seductive caress of the painkillers. I might not ever trust Barbara again, but I didn't want to be without her.

"So…do you know how to drive a boat?" she said.

"Not really," I said. "But I could learn."

Acknowledgements

I would like to thank early readers Connie Harvey, Isabel Dennis, Suzanne Semmes, Mike Humphrey, Roy Cutler, Willard Siebert, John Caputo and Sara Dennis. Special thanks to Deb Heimann and Joni Cole; wise editors and great friends.

This book is dedicated to Chod Edwards, late of the Indian River Sheriff's Department, and to my father, who believed in me, and laughed at my jokes.

About the Author

C.I. Dennis lives in Vermont and New Hampshire with his family and a whole lot of dogs.

Also by C.I. Dennis:

Tanzi's Ice
Tanzi's Game
Tanzi's Luck

As Zig Davidson:

Unglued

Cover artwork and concept by Alexander Dennis
Additional cover design and production by Morgan Kinney Designs
Author photo by Peter Lange
Formatting by ebooklaunch.com

www.cidennis.com

33673803R00113

Made in the USA
Middletown, DE
22 July 2016